T0247603

Pretty Dead Things

Pretty Dead Things

A Novel

LILIAN WEST

NEW YORK

Published in the United States by Crooked Lane Books, an imprint of The Quick Brown Fox & Company LLC.

Crooked Lane Books and its logo are trademarks of The Quick Brown Fox & Company LLC.

Library of Congress Catalog-in-Publication data available upon request.

ISBN (hardcover): 979-8-89242-002-0
ISBN (ebook): 979-8-89242-003-7

Cover design by Lucy Rose

Printed in the United States.

www.crookedlanebooks.com

Crooked Lane Books
34 West 27th St., 10th Floor
New York, NY 10001

First Edition: December 2024

10 9 8 7 6 5 4 3 2 1

For my parents.
Thank you for never allowing me
to settle for less than an extraordinary life.
That ring found us.

Clarity

Diamond clarity refers to the absence of inclusions and blemishes.

—Gemological Institute of America

clarity

clar·i·ty | \ kler-ə-tē

: the quality or state of being clear: LUCIDITY

—Merriam-Webster

Hickory Falls

June 14, 1953

Diamonds are such silly little things.

When cut just right, a diamond can capture a rainbow inside, an entire Crayola-box universe hiding within its angles. Some girls get absolutely giddy about their diamond rings and wave them in the air, tempting the sun's rays to unleash their prism of light for others to envy. The woman nervously spinning the band around her finger right now wasn't one of them.

A plain gold band from the dime store would have been fine. A little green tarnish never hurt anyone. And yet she loved this ring for what it meant today and going forward. *Love. Stability. Happy endings.*

She drew the lace curtain back with one hand and peeked outside, careful not to let him see her. Although she didn't believe in bad luck, she wasn't willing to tempt it. Not today.

The morning's rain had been heavy enough to wash away a layer of dust left behind by gravel-road travelers, but light enough to spare the grass-hidden puddles or an unpleasant squish when she walked. The gray clouds in the sky had sailed on, leaving giant white puffs in their place. In one, she could make out the shape of a cat ready to pounce. In another, she saw a face, the eyes shifting out of place as the cloud lazily floated wherever the wind wished it to go.

The daffodils were in full bloom, and the crispness of their yellow, the green grass, and the blue of the small lake in the back-yard made the scene look like a paint-by-numbers portrait. The white wooden folding chairs, four on each side of a narrow grass strip leading up to the oak tree, were the only foreign things in this snapshot of nature.

She saw him glance in her direction and quickly dropped the curtain to hide out of view, peeking between the folds to make sure she hadn't been seen.

Looking in the mirror one last time, she smoothed her dress, out of nervousness rather than need, and patted a few loose hairs back in place with the palm of her hand. The contrast between her light green eyes and dark hair always got her noticed, but the navy dress seemed to highlight her unique coloring even more. Most first-time brides wore white, but she wasn't like other women. She never had been. Traditions meant nothing to her; they were simply memories created by others who followed society's lead. She chose to listen to her inner voice and live authentically. So, no, unless a white dress had called to her as "the one," a navy dress and a bouquet of pink peonies would have to do.

The few hairs that had come loose from her side braid did not want to be tamed, so she decided to let them fly, knowing per-fectly well that the wind from the water would loosen others soon enough. Grabbing the bouquet of pink peonies from the vase on the side table, she shook them gently to dry their stems, drinking in their sweet smell.

Before daffodils and a giant oak tree, they would begin their new lives together in the shadow of the tiny cabin on the edge of the lake. The objectors would have to lie silent today. Those who did not understand were not welcome here. That left very few, but she was fine with that. They had love, and she had to believe that, despite everything, love was going to be enough. It had to be. The gossip and rumors that had plagued their time together were not allowed up the gravel driveway that led to the red cabin door. The whispers had no power. Not today.

Chapter One

Baubles. Cora loved the word. It was one that sounded too cute to be real.

Baubles. The more she said it, the less real it sounded.

Cora topped her coffee off with a generous amount of cream and sat down at her kitchen table to explore the glass jar of colorful buttons, costume jewelry brooches, and gemlike trinkets that she had carried home like a treasure from the estate sale that morning. She had paid five dollars for the jar, prepared to go as high as twenty if forced to engage in a bidding war, but no other attendee seemed even remotely interested.

Cora had jumped up and down when she won, earning her a few judgmental glances from the men and women inspecting a table full of tarnished silver and gold-gilded frames. She now sat before the treasure of colorful plastic gemstones and metal that had turned into a kaleidoscope from the early afternoon sun that soaked her bauble treasure.

She'd found the estate sale while searching for a local tailor to see to a sizable hole that had appeared in her favorite sweater. The roads here all looked the same, and she found herself in a continuous loop through the small town until a final wrong turn led her to a gravel road. Cora found that to be one of the many odd things about Hickory Falls; a person could be driving on pavement one minute and merge onto gravel the next, without sign or warning. Because she had nowhere to be that day, she drove leisurely while looking for a place to turn around. The bright yellow estate sale sign had been a rather welcome surprise.

Now she sat, looking at her purchase with the glee of a child about to stick their hand into a prize box.

Cora had always been drawn to color, a fact that anyone would guess by looking around her apartment. Although the landlord had given her permission to paint, within reason, she had gone with an all-white pallet for the walls, choosing instead to incorporate bursts of color with flea-market artwork, pillows, and piles of books that served as both reading material and end tables. Her home was an eclectic yet chic happy place, and her new collection of baubles fit right in.

Cora had entertained the idea of leaving the treasures in the jar and using it as a bookend on one of the built-ins that surrounded the old brick fireplace, but her curiosity got the best of her. She might very well pour the trinkets back into their glass home after inspection, but for now she was looking forward to dumping the contents onto her kitchen table and exploring her morning's find.

Cora flipped the jar over onto the tabletop and tried to stop a handful of marbles and buttons that rolled toward the edge, a few tiger-eye marbles a bit too quick for her as they fell to the floor and continued to roll across the room. She watched one disappear under the stove and a few more bounce off the baseboard before coming to a slow stop along the kitchen's tile grout. Cora glanced in their direction and made a mental note to pick them up, but knew deep down that she would only remember when she stepped on one later.

With one hand cradling her coffee cup, she raked through the pile of remaining baubles on the table with her fingertips, careful to spread the delicate contents into a thin layer for easier viewing.

The first thing that Cora noticed was a jade brooch. It was oval and small in size, the smooth green of the center adorned by a chunky gold border that, although aged, had not discolored the way that cheap metal does. The pin was secure along its back, and the piece was exactly the type of thing that Cora had hoped to find when she'd first spotted the goodies that morning.

She set the brooch aside, already thinking of how beautiful the green would look against the crisp white blouse that she had purchased the week before. The blouse was too plain on its own, and the brooch too beautiful to be displayed on anything but a blank canvas. This, Cora decided, was an indisputable fate in fashion—a sweet serendipity that only shopaholics would appreciate.

Buttons comprised the majority of the collection before her. Large, medium, and small. Round buttons, square buttons, and a few ornate buttons that fell somewhere in between. Among the standard colors of the rainbow, there were tortoise shell, silver, and a bright purple set with sequined edges. The number of marbles came in a close second, a few so large and beautiful that Cora couldn't imagine they were ever intended for children's play.

Because she had no expectations, Cora really couldn't be disappointed. Among the finds was a group of safety pins locked together through a rubber band, a few pennies, one bobby pin, and a thimble that she set aside in case she decided to take up sewing someday. It was like a potpourri of mismatched and miscellaneous items kept in one location.

As she swept her hands across the table to gather the trinkets for a return to their home, the sun made contact with a little something that sent a ray of light across the room. Cora smoothed out the pile again, careful to stop the marbles from making another escape, and found what had demanded the sun's attention.

It was a ring, incredibly small in size. Cora slipped it onto her pinky finger and got up to get a better view from the window. There was a single diamond, slightly raised and framed by the most delicate of detailed edging. The band looked silver, but had been worn and weathered, dirt shadowing some of its details. The dirt was like cement in some places and crumbled in others, a sweet earthy smell released into the air when Cora rubbed it between her fingers. She moved the ring under the light to get a better view inside the band and rubbed off the grime with a finger, to reveal engraved letters: *V & N*.

Or was it *Y & M*?

The letters had been worn smooth from contact and age, the tail of a letter here or a feathered arch there lost to the ages forever.

Cora returned to the table and continued searching for anything missed, now even more careful not to damage the remaining contents. That's when she saw it, dangling from the edge of one of the safety pins. Another ring, this one a band in matching silver and slightly wider than the diamond ring. Inspecting the inside, Cora noticed that it, too, had an engraving.

Alv w hay

She went back to the window, turning the band to and from the light to catch a glimpse of letters lost. There it was: *Always*.

Cora slipped the band on top of the diamond ring on her pinky. She felt different now; her fun little estate sale purchase that had been full of color and unknowns had handed her an incredibly old engagement ring and wedding band that did not belong here. The glass jar of baubles was supposed to be as silly as the word itself. It wasn't supposed to make Cora feel unsettled and sad for a woman she had never met. But there she sat, feeling both. She turned the rings around her finger and couldn't help but ache at the thought of how they had found themselves in such a place, so disrespected and uncared for. Somebody might be missing these heirlooms, their story one that some unsuspecting family member had yet to hear or even know about.

Cora wondered about *V & N*, or *Y & M*, two people who once shared something that she felt guilty being part of. Based on how old the rings looked, Cora could only assume that there was a time long, long ago when a gentleman got down on one knee and asked his love to join him on an adventure. She knew nothing about the woman who had worn this ring other than that at one point she had been loved.

Cora could have left it at that, a story that she could tell her friends and ponder possibilities over wine, with talk about a more romantic time. She could have put the rings back where she found them, surrounded by the colorful baubles that welcomed light into the room. She could have, but Cora knew she wouldn't.

These were not buttons to fill a jar or brooches to hide a lost button on her winter coat. These beautiful little things were like lightning glass in a sandbox. They had been waiting for someone to find them.

Sitting at her kitchen table that day, Cora could not have known that mysteries and secrets in small towns come in all shapes and sizes, and sometimes lie hidden in the bottom of a bauble jar, just waiting for someone to breathe life into them again.

Chapter Two

"Wait. You're not serious, are you?" Elliott took another gulp from his Corona Light and swished the lime around the bottle like he always did after taking a drink. "Cora, why would you even go through the effort? These rings are obviously old and worth nothing."

Cora was prepared for his reaction and now regretted telling him at all, his practical side something she both loved and braced herself for in their relationship. She had let herself get transfixed by the rings that day. It was a little disappointing that Elliott didn't share her excitement at such an unexpected find.

"It doesn't have anything to do with money. Clearly, they're worth very little. But their sentimental value might be priceless."

Cora locked eyes with Elliott, and they both laughed at the same time. "Is there a Hallmark card for that?" Elliott joked, taking one last gulp and tossing the bottle overhand into the trash bin across the room. "Swoosh. Three-pointer."

"Impressive shot," Cora said without even pretending to mean it. She twisted the diamond ring and band around her pinky finger, in wonder at its contrast between her own engagement ring one finger over. Elliott had done well picking it out. At almost two carats, the solitaire was classic in design, yet breathtaking in the "Four C's"—cut, clarity, color and carat weight.

"Compromise on one, and do the others really matter?" they had been warned by one particular jewelry store owner who tried to sell them a nearly flawless three-carat ring when he heard the title *doctor* preceding Elliott's name.

"I just don't think it's worth the trouble," Elliott said, pulling his loosened tie over his head and rubbing his neck muscles. Staring down into people's mouths all day was bound to result in muscle tension. Cora shuddered when she heard him pop his neck and then adjust his jaw before doing the same on the other side.

"That's so gross. Also, not good for you."

"It's the only thing that makes my neck feel better," Elliott responded, grinning. He found great joy in popping, cracking, or readjusting joints and muscles in front of her just to get a reaction. It was one of those gross habits that signaled a certain level of comfort and intimacy in a relationship. He wasn't really a fan of her tendency to pluck her eyebrows while watching *Saturday Night Live* in bed either, so they were both gross-habit offenders. "I had a lot of extractions today, and I hate pulling teeth on kids. When those roots are still in there, they can be a pain to get out."

Give Elliott an inch and he'd go a mile talking about work-related things that she really didn't find interesting, so she redirected his attention back to the topic at hand.

"I'm going to do a little digging and see what I find," Cora said. "Aren't you even a little bit interested as to *why* an engagement ring and wedding band would be tossed into a jar of marbles and buttons?"

Elliott had his head in the refrigerator, pushing past the bottled water to reach the last Corona Light. He had the top popped off before turning around. "No. Not interested at all."

"Figures."

"Maybe we should finish some of *our* wedding planning if you have so much time on your hands." Elliott said it with a wink, knowing Cora got a little agitated with the topic. Talk of planning the event always overwhelmed her.

"Well, it would be easier to plan if we actually lived together and saw each other every day," she said, pretending to inspect the ring closely in order to avoid eye contact.

"What can I say? My parents are old-fashioned souls, and living together was not going to fly. Since they're paying for the wedding, let's just play nice with Lydia and Dr. Wade, shall we?"

Cora always laughed when he referred to his parents by their first names, "Dr. Wade" being the name the younger patients used when referring to the older of the family dentists. Dr. Wade and Dr. Elliott had been in practice together for a few months now, and despite a difference in temperaments, the situation was working out quite well. Elliott's clientele tended to be on the younger side, whereas his father had been fixing the teeth of Hickory Falls's most senior residents since they'd first realized that dentures weren't always inevitable. The most common disagreement between the men tended to relate to the background music played in the office, the staff almost always silently siding with Elliott.

"Hey, if you find it fun digging around for answers to a likely impossible riddle, be my guest," Elliott said, bending his neck slowly from side to side and cracking his jaw again. Cora winced, annoyed that as their comfort level grew as a couple, so did Elliott's tendency to share his gross habits and conversation topics that would have been totally off limits when they were still "just dating."

This point had been driven home recently when he'd told her about a particularly bad tooth abscess while going to the bathroom with the door open, waiting momentarily to take care of business before continuing his story about puss and a gum-line infection. Then, just as casually as if they had been talking about the weather, he'd asked about dinner ideas as he washed his hands.

"Just be forewarned that there is absolutely nothing exciting that ever happens in this town, so if you're looking for a great story, you're going to be disappointed." Elliott leafed through the drawer of take-out menus, which Cora was happy to see. The hamburger in her refrigerator had taken on a green tint, and there was nothing left in her cabinets except crackers and a few cans of soup. She had planned to go to the grocery store today, but diamond rings in the bottom of glass jars had taken precedence over sustenance.

Elliott pulled his dress shirt from a tucked position and yawned in an image that Cora had grown accustomed to after his long days. Gone were evenings spent on the beach with a pitcher of margaritas and chips and salsa for dinner. Gone were street concerts on random Tuesdays and early morning jogs along the water as starfish and turtles clambered to make their way back to their salty home before beachgoers arrived. Their California college days were over, and reality had accompanied their arrival to Hickory Falls, a sleepy little Midwest town that embraced those looking for a charming escape during the summer.

Elliott had grown up here and was used to a way of life that focused its calendar around three local main events—July Fourth, when fireworks were shot from the banks of the Mississippi River;

the county fair every August, and the Christmas tree display in the town square, which always ended up being a rivalry between sponsoring car dealerships who all wanted to be remembered as the best celebrator of baby Jesus. Elliott affectionately referred to the town as quiet and lost in time, but Cora wondered if that wasn't a better description for what happened to those who became one with the Hickory Falls landscape. She loved Elliott and would follow him anywhere, but she had felt her inner light dim since moving there a few months ago. She needed to find a way to stop herself from becoming part of the quiet or the lost; Cora needed a story to lose herself in, and wondered if these sweet little lost rings would provide one.

"You just never know," she said, dropping the rings into a small red velvet satchel that she had found in her nightstand. "Maybe these rings hold a secret that will break the bubble of this sleepy little town wide open."

Looking back, Cora wondered if she had tempted fate with those words or if they had been an unknowing invitation to the universe to blow wind onto an ember that refused to die. Either way, her discovery of the rings put something into motion that neither she nor Hickory Falls was quite ready for.

The new girl from California was about to introduce herself to a part of the small town that had been hiding in the shadows for decades.

Chapter Three

"Do you take sugar in your tea, hon?"

Cora had never been called *hon* so much in her life. She'd counted five times since arriving ten minutes ago. She had been called *hon* upon arrival, once on the front porch, two times in the hallway leading to the kitchen, and once more since sitting down. Based on the speech of the sweet little woman bustling around the kitchen, matching floral teacups with their saucers, she'd swear they were in the deep South instead of the Midwest. Cora wondered for the first time if Southern hospitality was more about personality than geography.

"Beverly, thank you so much for letting me stop by," Cora began. "I'm sure my call was a surprising one, but the auction company was kind enough to pass along your contact information." She twisted to get more comfortable on the chair, the brown cushioned plastic sticking to one of her legs and making a grotesque sucking noise as she peeled it away. The calendar might have said that summer was coming to an end, but she had been warned about its tendency to hang on tightly in the Midwest.

It was an afternoon for air conditioning, but Beverly clearly preferred the fresh air that came through the screen door, fresh air that was filled with the smell of lilacs and fresh manure composting in the sun. Cora caught a glimpse of a man walking through the backyard, carrying a metal pail in one hand and a lit cigar in the other. A few steps more, and the robust smell of tobacco mixed with lilacs and manure was a pungency that made Cora's eyes start to sting.

"Well, it was a surprise, but not an unpleasant one." Clearly used to the smells of the farm, Beverly balanced two cups on saucers as she took the few steps from the stove to the table. The pink daisy-patterned cups balanced precariously as she struggled to keep them in place.

Beverly was a tiny little thing with tightly curled gray hair that looked like it had been put in place overnight by rollers and brushed out for softness. She wore rather trendy capri jeans, with the cuffs rolled up, and a button-up lavender blouse with bell sleeves. Her skin was well wrinkled, yet dewy; her pink lip gloss and light mascara, signs that she still took great pride in her appearance, even if she was only staying home for the day. She smelled of a familiar floral scent, the kind that comes with lotion and perfume gift combinations popular at Christmas.

"I have to be honest: I'm actually quite curious as to what it is that you'd like to show me. You didn't mention on the call, and I went through my mother's things so carefully before the sale. I can't imagine there are any surprises." Beverly took her seat across from Cora and smiled sweetly, a hint of trepidation lying under the surface.

Cora took a sip of the tea, the handle so delicate that she had to take the cup in both hands to keep from spilling. She realized that her five-dollar purchase had been the result of a death, a loved one's possessions scattered about on card tables for voyeurs and casual shoppers to enjoy. She felt guilty at her bauble joy, yet relieved that she had ignored Elliott and taken the time to return the rings to their owner. This petite woman sitting across from her had to be in her mid-seventies. If her mother had recently passed away, the rings could be eighty or ninety years old and deserved to be returned. Cora suddenly regretted describing this excursion as an adventure to Elliott. It was actually more like a duty that she felt obligated to fulfill.

"I'm so sorry about your mother," Cora began. "I stumbled on the estate sale by accident last weekend when I took a wrong turn. I'm a bit new to the area and found myself on a country road out of town. It was so pretty that I just kept driving for a while. When I saw the estate sale signs at the end of the road, I couldn't resist stopping by. Your mother had some really beautiful things, a few pieces of furniture that I would have loved to have."

Cora was babbling. She did that when she was nervous and couldn't shake the butterflies that had been fluttering about in her stomach since she'd pulled into the driveway. If Beverly noticed, she didn't let on, sipping her tea like they were two old friends who did this regularly.

"Joseph, my husband, and I moved in a few years back, after Mom and Dad went into the nursing home. Truthfully, she was in better shape than him, but we couldn't bear the thought of one leaving the other behind." She touched a seam on the floral wallpaper that had separated from the adjacent piece and was peeling upward. "I grew up in this house. I remember when Mom put up this wallpaper. Even as a young girl, I thought it was the ugliest

17

floral wallpaper that I'd ever seen, but I can't even entertain the thought of taking it down." She returned her gaze to Cora and smiled, a warm invitation for her to continue.

"So, anyway," Cora went on, "I bought a beautiful glass jar full of trinkets at the estate sale. There were buttons, marbles, a thimble or two—you know, just random things."

"Oh my, why on earth?" Beverly asked, waving her hand as if to dismiss the idea as nonsense. "We found that on a shelf in the garage, collecting dust. I was going to toss that old thing, but the auctioneer told me that I'd be surprised what people bought. Well, I guess I am!" She laughed now, and Cora right along with her, two tea-drinking ladies giggling at the thought of a jar full of colorful baubles. "Are you here for a refund?" Beverly joked. "I don't blame you if you are!" Cora felt herself begin to relax.

Beverly's smile revealed the most perfect of white smiles, and Cora—the soon-to-be-dentist's wife—found herself wondering if they were real or of the denture variety. If real, she was impressed and made a mental note to floss more regularly.

"Well, actually, you might be happy that I bought it when you see what I found inside." Cora pulled the small velvet bag from her purse and dumped the rings onto her palm, moving her hand toward Beverly so she could see better. She was giddy about the reveal, eager to surprise Beverly with the reunion of the rings to their rightful owner. "I assume these are your mother's rings, and I'm so happy to return them to you." Cora waited for a reaction, a delightful gasp or sigh of relief that such a cherished heirloom hadn't been tossed out like a baby with the bathwater, but Beverly didn't say a word. She didn't even move closer to inspect the rings or hold them herself. In fact, she looked a bit puzzled, perhaps even offended, as she gave the rings a suspicious glance.

"Oh, hon, those aren't my mother's rings," Beverly said, her tone crisp. She pulled out the necklace that had been tucked inside her lavender blouse, and Cora saw a sizable diamond ring on the end of the gold chain. "*This* is my mother's ring. She gave it to me when she entered the nursing home, and I wear it every day. I don't know what you have there, but I've never seen those rings before in my entire life. If they were my mother's, I would know."

Cora felt the air in the kitchen shift slightly. There was now a chill that hadn't been there before and a crispness to the energy that only moments before had been as soft as the edges of sun-faded marigolds on ugly wallpaper.

"Oh, okay," Cora said, sliding the rings back into their bag. The butterflies were back. Beverly's abrupt tone shift was a shock to Cora's system. "I'm sorry, I just assumed . . . I mean, they were in your mother's things, so I think you should still take them."

The screen door suddenly opened and quickly slammed shut, the older man that Cora had seen earlier, now wiping his brow with a handkerchief like one would see in the movies. His gray T-shirt was soaked with sweat, and he stomped through the kitchen on his way to a glass full of lemonade that looked like it was waiting for him. A lingering cigar smell floated behind him with every step, but the manure seemed to have been left outside where it belonged.

"Joseph, this is Cara," Beverly said. Finding no reason to correct her, Cora simply smiled politely and watched as he finished the drink in three solid gulps. Beverly looked at Cora and rolled her eyes apologetically. "Maybe it's time to bring in someone else to look at the mower, what do you say?"

"Don't be ridiculous," he responded, obviously angry at the suggestion. "I've fixed it fifty times before, and I'll do it again. That piece of shit won't win."

Beverly looked embarrassed, but in the loving way that spouses do when they've been married for years and have given up trying to change each other. "Joe, Cara bought something at the sale last week and found a little ring inside. Probably just costume jewelry, so I told her to go ahead and keep it. The only thing of Mother's worth anything is the ring that *I'm* wearing."

The sweaty older man dropped the handkerchief but didn't notice, his breathing beginning to steady now that he had consumed about two cups of lemon sugar water and was out of the hot sun. He raised an eyebrow and stared at Beverly for a moment before placing the glass in the sink and excusing himself. If Cora didn't know better, she'd swear she saw a flicker of something in his eyes, but it was probably sweat or the reflection of florescent bulbs that hummed in the lights above them. This visit had been an interesting one, but not for the reasons Cora had imagined.

"He's a finicky old fart," Beverly said. "You'll have to excuse his lack of social graces. He's been going twelve rounds with that mower and won't admit defeat."

Cora smiled and watched through the screen door as Joseph returned to the mower, his walk one of contempt and determination. She was surprised to see him turn around suddenly and pause, staring back toward the house as if he knew she was watching. His fixed gaze in her direction was unsettling.

"Listen, I just don't feel right taking these rings. I mean, they could be worth something." Cora only wanted to accomplish her goal of returning the rings and leave. There was a grocery list waiting for her in the car and an apartment that hadn't been deep cleaned in weeks. "I'm pretty sure that diamond is real. Costume jewelry usually doesn't opt for the half-carat look." Her attempt at humor was apparently lost on Beverly, who had now turned her attention to a cat that had moseyed into the kitchen at some point without Cora even noticing. It was purring loudly and rubbing its back along Beverly's legs.

"Hi, sweet Simon," Beverly said rubbing the cat's arched back. "Hon, I'm seventy-six years old. My kids don't want anything like this. You were sweet enough to try to come by to talk to me about what you found. You can keep them. I'm not sure if cashing them in will get you to Europe or anything, but maybe a really nice dinner out somewhere." Beverly leaned down to pick up the cat and kiss it on the top of its head before cradling it like a baby in her arms. Cora wasn't a cat person, but there was something about seeing it lie there completely vulnerable, and purr lovingly that made her wish she had a pet at home waiting for her.

That's incredibly kind of you," Cora said. "Before I accept the offer to keep them, I just want to make sure nobody else in your family would like them. Do you have any siblings?"

As much as Cora did appreciate the offer for her to keep the ring, the size of the diamond and the way light seemed to shine directly through it suggested it was worth more than what Beverly might think. Cora would hate to take advantage of the woman, especially when the find had resulted from her mother's death.

Simon had fallen asleep in Beverly's arms, and she stopped rubbing behind his ears momentarily, the sudden stop of movement causing his eyes to flicker open before he closed them again. Cora thought she saw something in Beverly's own eyes just then, the same little flash of light that Cora had seen in Joseph's only moments before. Whatever it was had come and gone in a split second, however. Beverly now resumed massaging her cat's head, much to Simon's appreciation.

"You really don't have to do that, dear," Beverly said. "My sister won't want the rings either."

Cora took another sip of her tea, which had become lukewarm and bitter. She pulled her phone and its stylus from her purse, ready to jot down the name and number of the person whom she now realized was a sister who would need to be contacted.

"Ruth lives right down the road," Beverly said, giving Cora the phone number. "Just be forewarned: she's a talker. If you stop by, you should probably be prepared to devote the entire afternoon to the visit."

"Well noted," Cora said with a smile to try to erase the tension in the room. She returned the rings to her purse and discreetly glanced outside, relieved to see that the mower was once again Joseph's sole focus. "I'll get out of your way now. Thank you so much again for taking the time to chat." Cora stood to leave, her legs peeling from the brown plastic seat and now temporarily tattooed with the lines of the chair's design.

Beverly followed her into the hallway leading to the front door, the cat still sleeping soundly in her arms. The walls were filled with photographs, some new and some incredibly old. Black and white memories with gilded matting mixed in with more recent snapshots in craft store frames. Family photos with bad studio lighting filled the space, spiral perms and blue eye shadow dating the images. Cora could tell that it was a gallery wall that never changed—once a photo was hung, it remained there forever. Had the pictures been removed, a perfectly preserved spot on the wall would have remained where the striped wallpaper had been protected for decades from the sun. Dare to remove the framed family photos, and their ghosts would hang there defiantly.

A large photograph in an ornate oval frame was the center-piece of the wall, other pictures emanating from it like rays from the sun. It was a wedding picture of a beautiful couple, the bride an image of perfection in a long-sleeved gown made of lace that billowed out into a pool of taffeta that accentuated her tiny waist. Her hair was piled into ringlets on top of her head, a few curls allowed to fall in a way that was too perfect to be random. She smiled proudly for the camera, a woman very much aware of her beauty. Her dark-haired groom looked a bit more serious, a slight smile evident with a steely gaze that lacked the spark of her stare. His right arm was secured around her waist, with a discreet amount of space still left between them. His left arm was bent behind his back as if at attention.

"What a gorgeous photo," Cora said. "Are these your parents?"

"Yes, that's Mom and Dad. Beautiful couple, aren't they?" Beverly asked. "She was beautiful inside and out, and theirs was a love story for the ages. They simply adored each other. You wouldn't find a sweeter woman in the entire world. The sun rose and set with her in my father's eyes." With the arm that wasn't cradling a sleeping cat, Beverly touched the ring around her neck affectionately. Cora looked back at the photo and now saw that ring on the bride's finger of the hand curled around a bouquet. "Everyone adored my mother. I mean, obvious beauty aside, she was the sweetest person I've ever known."

"Thank you, again," Cora said, eager to make her way to the front door. This visit had gone nothing like what she'd imagined, and she couldn't shake the feeling of having violated the space once filled by Beverly's mother. Her intentions were good; she had pic-tured a quick explanation and the return of the rings. Perhaps an appreciative hug or thank-you from the woman who had mistakenly let them go for a few dollars at an estate sale.

She turned to say something else, something typical of goodbyes to almost strangers, but stopped when she saw that Beverly was still looking at the photo of her parents, now clutching the ring and lost in another world.

Cora glanced out the front door toward her car and spotted Joseph standing in the shadow of the shed. The focus of his attention, which she had expected to be on the rusted mower he was going twelve rounds with, was now fixed in her direction. His hands in his pockets and eyes squinting in the sun, Beverly's husband was watching the house as if in wait. For what? Her departure? No, this visit hadn't gone as planned at all.

Hickory Falls

~

May 15, 1943

Even on her best day, one would be hard-pressed to hear anyone refer to Evelyn Hathower as sweet. Determined, yes. Perhaps even beguiling in her womanly charms, but never sweet.

"I wanted dark pink roses, not red. *Dark pink.* Red is so common." She spoke the last words like they had an aftertaste, a contagious stench of all that was ordinary.

"Evelyn, they're gorgeous. They're simply *gorgeous.*" There was no appeasing her, but her mother had to try. Navigating the highs and lows of Evelyn's mood leading up to the wedding was like being stuck in a rowboat among waves on the deep sea. Those around her had just learned to hold tight and wait for calmer waters. "Honey, your hair is exquisite," Mary Beth said, trying to change the topic. "Absolutely *exquisite.*" They were a family that liked to repeat words for emphasis.

Evelyn's hair really was something to be seen. It had taken hours with the curling rod to get every ringlet exactly right, and even longer to pile them on top of her head and secure them into place. The few curls that Evelyn had wanted to fall around her face didn't look "natural enough," so the entire process had been started over two times that morning. Having reached a level of perfection to Evelyn's pleasing, the air in the room had become noticeably lighter until Evelyn had caught sight of a crease in the lace of her dress. After dealing with hair issues and dress issues, and an unfortunate misstep by Evelyn's aunt when the word *snug* was used in describing the dress, Mary Beth didn't think she had the energy to deal with anything else. She loved her daughter, truly, but Evelyn was more on the salty side, while her two sisters were sweet; salty works well in combination but can be a lot when digested alone.

"Honey, it's time." Mary Beth waited for her daughter to emerge from behind the changing screen, and clutched her chest as if the air might take flight from her lungs when she finally saw her. Evelyn was gorgeous. The custom lace gown fit her like a second skin on top but flared into a taffeta waterfall from her tiny waist. Her up-do accentuated the dress detailing along the nape of her neck, and her bright red lips added a touch of glamour to a look that was both fashion-forward and classic in its design. She was breathtaking, and judging by her smile on seeing the finished product in the mirror, Evelyn knew it.

Of course, this would be a day that she remembered forever, but she wanted everyone in attendance to remember it as well and hold it as the gold standard for wedding ceremonies going forward.

"Oh, it was lovely, but it wasn't as beautiful as Evelyn's dress."

"The cake was delicious, but do you remember the strawberry filling in the cake at Evelyn's wedding?"

"Her hair was pretty, but Evelyn had such perfect curls around her face."

She could only hope her wedding would be the talk of the town for years to come. At the very least, her wedding portrait would be preserved in the most elaborate frame she could find and hung on the walls of her home for all to admire. This event was so much more than a wedding. It was a moment cast in time for her future children and her children's children to gaze on and comment, "Look how beautiful she was. Look how happy they were."

"I'm ready," Evelyn said, twisting the large diamond ring so it was positioned perfectly on her finger, and rearranging a few roses in the bouquet that had dared to fall out of place. "I'm ready to get married."

In a room not far away, a groom stood alone in front of a full-length mirror and adjusted his tie for the fourth time. It was too tight. Despite having fit merely a few days before, the tie, suit coat, and shoes were now all at once too snug. He pulled the tie loose one more time and took a deep breath, laying the ends of the silk flat against his shirt and measuring the right length before beginning the process once again. The dark gray tie was not one that he would have chosen himself, but he had not been consulted on many things about the day. He wriggled his toes against the tightness of his leather shoes and flipped one end of the tie over the other—over, under, through—until a knot had formed. He pulled it to his neckline and adjusted it in the mirror. Any minute there would be a knock on the door to signal his need to make his way to the front of the church and await his bride.

There were three large windows in the room, the middle of which contained a stained-glass figure dressed in a gray shroud, a hood covering most of his face. His gaze was turned upward toward a yellow star, and the look on his face was one of fear and awe. No doubt a saint of some sort. Lewis couldn't have told someone who he was or what the image was trying to impress. Truth be told, he had never stepped foot in this church until their premarital meetings with the pastor. This church, and all of the decor and guests that awaited him, had been carefully chosen by his bride-to-be, each one ticking off an invisible box on her mental list of wedding day must-haves.

Lewis studied himself in the mirror and knew that everything would look perfect to those in attendance. Inside, however, he felt the tightness of the suit against his frame and the noose of silk closing in on his airway. His heart rate had quickened, and a few beads of sweat appeared along his hairline. He removed the hankie tucked in his coat pocket and, careful not to disturb its pristine folds, dabbed his forehead. He repeated the reassuring words that had been spinning through his mind these past few days— *All grooms are nervous; she's a great girl; you'll be incredibly happy*—and tried to ignore a rising heat that had started at the tips of his toes and was slowly making its way upward.

Outside, Lewis and Evelyn would be an image of perfection. Mental boxes would be ticked with every photo taken and champagne flutes would be raised in toasts to the happy couple. Inside, Lewis would be fighting against the seams of a suit coat suddenly too small and burrowing holes in the tops of his leather shoes that fit too tightly. Inside, Lewis would be slowly suffocating.

Chapter Four

Juliet's hair was red today, her long side-braid revealing a few inches that had been shaved underneath. Her hair had been blue the last time Cora saw her. Juliet changed her hair color the way most women do handbags or shoes. She couldn't care less about those, a dark green satchel that looked like it came from a military surplus store being the only bag she carried. Cora had also never seen her in anything other than sandals that displayed blue- or white-polished toenails.

Tonight, Juliet was wearing lime-green, open-toed wedges and a black jumpsuit that resembled a garbage bag but somehow made her look chic. Cora, in contrast, wore a faded UCLA sweatshirt and ripped jeans. Her sandy-blonde hair was kept off her forehead by a clip that she'd found in her bathroom drawer but didn't remember buying. She wore no makeup and had just come from the salon down the street, her eyebrows still red from their regular waxing.

"Show me," Juliet said, taking a sip of her double shot espresso from its miniature cup. "Let's see these things. Are you sure they're real?" Juliet's blue eyes were framed by dark eyeliner along the top lid, a perfectly executed wing flaring out on the outer edge of both eyes in a look that Cora admired but could never pull off. On the phone, Juliet had sounded excited to hear the latest update in what she now referred to as the Great Jewelry Heist, entirely unbothered by the fact that their situation was neither great nor a heist. "I'm telling you, we should track down those *Antique Roadshow* guys. Are they still traveling the country somewhere, destroying people's hopes and dreams? I'm pretty sure my parents have an old painting or two in the attic that would at least get us in the door." Her eyes twinkled at the thought of such an adventure.

Cora opened the tiny bag and slid the rings out onto the palm of her hand. Each time she did that, she felt a jolt of surprise they were still there, like their very existence had become as mystical as the story that had formed in her mind. Elliott had just laughed when she told him about her meeting with Beverly the day before. It was clear that his interest in the topic was waning, the conversation over dinner quickly turning to his latest complaints about dental insurance coverage and a four-year-old who had to practically be sedated to undergo a routine cleaning.

As a compromise, Cora had changed the topic to a serial killer podcast, a topic they both enjoyed because of a shared morbid interest in the dark recesses of the human mind. Elliott really didn't want to hear about her infatuation with the rings and she really didn't want to hear another story about laughing gas gone wrong, so it was serial killers for the win.

"Ooh la la," Juliet said, taking the diamond ring and holding it to the light. She turned it this way and that, causing the dim lighting of the coffee shop and street lamps outside to reflect off the diamond. "These are really beautiful, Cora. You just don't see things like this anymore. The detail is amazing. Obviously old.

Made back in a day where quality meant something." Cora found Juliet's observation funny given her pleather jumpsuit, but then again, maybe her jumpsuit represented couture quality these days, and Cora was clueless.

Juliet slipped the diamond on her pinky finger, as aware as Cora was that the finger that originally wore it was much smaller than their own. "Good grief, she had tiny fingers, whoever she was." Cora caught a few girls staring at them from one table over and found herself feeling overly protective, the way a mother does when someone is judging her child. She angled her back slightly to make it harder for prying eyes to see.

"Girl, I think you've done your due diligence here," Juliet said, handing the ring back to Cora. "You tried to give them back— you're good. Keep them. Conscience clear." She was so confident in her statement that Cora couldn't help but agree. Juliet was a year younger than Cora but seemed so much older in terms of self-assurance. In other ways, she appeared years younger, evidenced at the time by a mood ring, swimming somewhere between blue and dark green, that she wore on her middle finger. Juliet returned her attention to her espresso, the momentary excitement over Cora's ring find already fading.

The bell over the coffee shop door drew Cora's attention away, and she watched a young couple walk over to the glass display window and survey the croissant selection. Her move to Hickory Falls had been a difficult transition, but she did love these quiet, little, tucked-away shops and watching people stroll the streets as if time were never an issue.

She was also thankful for Juliet, one of the only friends she'd made since she arrived. They had met at the local university's art show, a rather disappointing display of half-ass drawings that

Cora could have done over breakfast. They were standing in front of a chalk drawing of a giant owl that resembled a crude alien depiction, and they'd laughed at the same time, a quiet source of amusement that they shared over sips of cheap white wine from plastic cups. Cora missed her life in California, not necessarily because she had an amazing social life there, but simply because it had always been an option. Here, she had to look a little harder for things to do, and she found the constant search exhausting.

After the art show, Cora and Juliet had met for coffee and the occasional lunch. Juliet's fledgling yoga studio demanding much of her time. Elliott was glad Cora was making friends, although she doubted Juliet's Raggedy Anne red hair would fit in at her future father-in-law's table at the next fundraiser gala. Dentists, it seemed, ranked rather low on the funky meter.

Cora had enjoyed getting to know Juliet these past few weeks, and their friendship blossomed more with every conversation. They were now to the point of texting about Netflix shows, but not yet comfortable enough for Cora to ask if Juliet's eyelashes were real or, for that matter, her boobs that defied gravity under the tight tank tops that seemed a staple of her wardrobe. Those conversations would come with time; for now, she was excited to talk about the rings and get Juliet's opinion about next steps.

"Yeah, I know it's crazy," Cora said, readjusting her hair clip with one hand while staring at the rings resting in the other. "Now that I know about the sister, though, I feel like I have to talk to her. If she tells me to keep them, I'll consider the ring case closed." Cora knew that all of this wasn't necessary. She had satisfied the acceptable social norms by trying to return the rings, and could have simply kept them, reassured by the fact that sentimental keepsakes typically don't find their way into button bowls. Whether fueled by boredom or the need for a challenge, Cora wasn't quite ready to put the rings into her jewelry box at home and forget about them.

Dropping the rings back into their velvet bag, she tied it shut and returned it to her purse. Cora noticed Juliet smiling and shaking her head in obvious amusement.

"What?" Cora didn't know her friend well enough to know if she was laughing with her or at her. "I want to take this a little further, okay? Maybe there's a story here worth an article in the town paper. Diamond rings don't just show up unclaimed every day. Maybe they have a story to tell of their own." Cora loved to write as well as paint, and the possibility of writing for the local paper part-time had lingered in her mind for a while. In a town where stories about rainfall levels and new playground equipment made front-page headlines, she couldn't help but think this little find might provide a story worth telling in a town that desperately needed some new content.

"I was born and raised in Hickory Falls," Juliet said, nodding to the life outside the window. "Not to be mean, but I have yet to meet anyone even remotely mysterious here. If it weren't for my grandmother, I would have left by now." She drained the espresso in one final swallow and returned the miniature cup to its miniature saucer. "By the way, you need to meet her. She owns the little art gallery on main street and would love you. She always tells me that creativity skips a generation and that I get mine from her. Very humble." Juliet waved to a tall man who had just walked into the shop, but it was the kind of wave someone makes when they hope the person doesn't actually come over and say hello.

"Seriously, let's figure out a time for you to meet her. She's so glad that I've found a unique friend."

"Unique? Is that a compliment?"

Juliet adjusted the military bag over one shoulder and tossed a five-dollar tip onto the table. "In Hickory Falls, definitely."

Chapter Five

∾

Cora parked in front of the sleek-looking townhouse and checked the address again. Yes, this was it. Beverly's description of her sister living "right down the road" had led Cora to believe she also lived somewhere in the country, but here she was, just off Main Street, in what could only be described as the modern part of town. In Hickory Falls, "right down the road" could apparently mean in a neighbor's cornfield or the center of town.

Cora stood in front of the row of townhouses, all identical in their large picture windows and pale wood siding, looking like slices of bread perfectly aligned into a single loaf. If Beverly's house "right down the road" was a postcard version of a farmhouse with a wrap-around porch, this little village of modern homes was a glossy brochure of maintenance-free living within walking distance to the shops and restaurants boasted about on the Hickory Falls website. Cora wondered if the sisters were as different as their homes, a thought that lingered with her as she made her way past a row of yellow day lilies to the bright red front door and rang its bell, a colorful glass wind chime alerting nature that it had a visitor on its doorstep.

Cora listened as an obnoxious chime broadcasted the fact that her every action was being filmed and monitored by someone inside. Instinctively, she smoothed down a few flyaway hairs that had broken free from her ponytail. She listened and waited. The wreath on the door was one of those branch sunburst craft items that fan out in all directions; in the middle was perched a fake little blue jays family that looked morbidly out of place against the bloodred background of the door.

Cora could hear shuffling inside and then something shattering, followed by a "Well, shit!" loud enough to carry through the wall. She heard more shuffling, then a bit of sweeping, and another curse word or two before the deadbolt was unfastened on the inside and the door finally opened.

"Good golly, Miss Molly!" the woman greeted her, out of breath and laughing at something Cora didn't understand. "What a greeting for you! I dropped my favorite green ashtray. I mean, I don't smoke, but I love that dark green glass, you know? I buy it whenever I can, and I used this one to store all of my match books, which probably sounds silly because I just said that I don't smoke, and I don't, but I light candles all the time." Ruth stood before Cora, out of breath and without an ounce of family resemblance in looks or mannerisms to her sister, Beverly.

"Oh goodness, come on in, but be wary of any glass that I've missed." She held the door open for Cora and waved her inside with a dish towel that she clutched firmly in one hand. Cora had barely taken a step inside when the sound of breaking glass under her shoe confirmed that plenty of the dark green glass ashtray remained.

"Oh, shoot," Ruth said, leaning down and using the towel to spread the shards of glass every which way. "Oh, shoot. I really did love that ashtray. Why couldn't it have been the ugly bowl that Bev bought me for Christmas last year?" At that she cackled, an infectious laugh that seemed to catch even her by surprise.

Cora couldn't believe this was sweet little Beverly's sister. The woman standing before her had spiked, bleached-blonde hair and red glasses that matched her lipstick perfectly. She wore a giant turquoise beaded necklace on top of a white blouse and cuffed jeans, the only noted thing that Cora could tell Ruth and her sister had in common other than their petite frames. If Beverly, with her curled hair and conservative dress was like a picturesque small-town grandmother, Ruth fit the bill for unpredictable aunt, the one who might not always be appropriate, but who was really fun to sit by at holiday gatherings.

"I'm going to guess you like the color red," Cora said.

Ruth looked confused until Cora pointed to the door and her glasses. "Oh, honey. I just buy what's on sale." Cora laughed and immediately relaxed as she followed her into an equally colorful living room, complete with exotic fish tank and leopard-print throw pillows. Yes, the differences between the sisters were truly startling and growing by the minute.

"Have a seat!" Ruth gestured toward a stand-alone chair that had been upholstered in an unfortunate salmon color with a seashell pattern. A glass bowl full of sand and shells on a nearby table suggested the beginning of an ocean theme, a momentary focus that had been interrupted at some point by safari chic from the clearance aisle. Ruth disappeared quickly into an adjoining room, continuing to chat even when she was out of sight.

"I am so excited you're here," she yelled, presumably from the kitchen. Cora wondered briefly if she had been mistaken for another expected visitor, doubtful that some stranger's appearance from her dead mother's estate sale would invoke anything resembling excitement. "Bev gave me the heads-up that you'd be calling, and I just can't wait to see these little trinkets that you've found. How exciting." She emerged a few minutes later with a tray full of tiny appetizer plates and two glasses.

"Gin and tonic—hope that's okay."

Cora smiled politely and took a glass, steadying herself for the drink that she really didn't want. It wasn't even eleven o'clock in the morning.

"Very kind of you, thank you." It was then that Cora noticed the appetizer plates were filled with Oreo cookies and string cheese.

"Sorry—this is the best that I could do on such short notice. I used to be quite an entertainer, but I've realized over the years that all people really want is chocolate and cheese." Although Ruth's laugh was a true cackle, it wasn't of the pitch that gave someone goose bumps. Her laugh was one of those contagious kinds that made a person want to join in on the fun, regardless of whether they thought the conversation was worth a laugh at all. In Beverly's kitchen, she had been offered tea and fresh-squeezed lemonade. In Ruth's living room, she was drinking gin and eating Oreos. She seriously couldn't make this stuff up.

Ruth stuck one end of a cheese strip in her mouth and nibbled on it like a piece of spaghetti. She pulled both of her legs up underneath her and sat cross-legged, like children are asked to do during circle time. Even then, she fidgeted and twitched like a toy top that had been wound too tightly. Then a steady knock startled Cora, but it took her a second to realize that it wasn't coming from the door. Ruth shot out of her chair and ran over to the shared wall between her home and her neighbor's, returning the knock three times—knock, knock, knock.

"This is how old people flirt," she said with a wink, returning to her chair. "John, my neighbor, is a cutie pie. He's a bit younger than me, but that doesn't bother me. We've started watching *Game of Thrones* together and figure it will keep us busy for years to come." Ruth resumed her cheese-eating posture, sipping her drink between nibbles. "I really don't understand what's going on, but everyone seems to really like the show, so there must be something worth watching. Lots of violence . . . and some pretty steamy scenes on bear skin rugs, if you know what I mean." She said the last part out of the side of her mouth with a giggle.

"Thank you so much for taking the time to chat," Cora said. "I know this is all a bit strange, but I couldn't resist reaching out to you after talking to Beverly. She was so gracious with her time as well."

Ruth smirked as she raised her glass, toasting in silence to something that only she understood in the moment. Cora wondered if she was overdoing it with her politeness or if it was her description of Beverly as *gracious* that earned the smirk.

"Beverly probably already told you about the rings. I appreciate her offer for me to keep them, but I really don't feel right doing that, at least not until I've shown them to all family members to make sure they're not something one of you'd like to have." She brought the velvet bag out of her purse and handed it to Ruth, who now looked wide-eyed at the possibility of what lay within. She slid the rings out and inspected them closely, neither her eyes nor lips tipping Cora off as to her familiarity or lack thereof with her find.

"Oh, honey, I have no idea," Ruth finally said. "I've never seen these rings before. When Bev told me about them, I was hoping it was a ring that Mom had gotten for an anniversary, but that was a sapphire." Looking a bit disappointed, Ruth slid the rings back into their bag and handed it to Cora. "You feel free to keep these. They have no sentimental value for me, and if Bev has never seen them, I doubt they were Mom's. She would know." Ruth's jubilance seemed to have faded with the realization. Cora felt bad that she had gotten Ruth's hopes up for a sapphire that Cora couldn't deliver.

Cora took a deep breath and felt the weight of the rings lift from her shoulders. She didn't want any more gin or sandwich cookies. She really only wanted to close this little chapter and move on. Juliet was right; she had done her due diligence and could now keep the rings in good conscience. There would be no mystery or emotional reunion. There wasn't a story to be told or fun article that she could pitch to the local paper. The rings were simply old rings in need of a home.

"Well, I'm so sorry that they weren't what you had hoped to find, but I appreciate you taking time to see me today. You and your sister have been so kind. Is it just the two of you? There's quite an age gap." The last words fell from Cora's lips before she realized how rude they could seem, her face now feeling flushed. She couldn't help but notice how much younger Ruth was than Beverly, but pointing something like that out in polite conversation was out of line, and she hadn't had enough of the gin and tonic to excuse it. "Oh my gosh, I'm so sorry," she said. "I didn't mean to . . ."

If Ruth was put out, she didn't show it, sipping her drink and settling back into her chair to signal that a story was coming—one that might need a minute or two.

"Oh, you're right on that. There's quite an age gap," Ruth began. "I turned fifty-eight this year so, let's see . . . that would make Bev seventy-five. No, wait—seventy-six. Yes, she'll turn seventy-six in a few months. We're eighteen years apart." Ruth took what started out as a small sip of her drink but ended with her gulping about half the glass.

"Oh, wow," Cora started, but Ruth cut her off.

"I mean, it wasn't like Mom and Dad planned to wait until one kid became an adult before they had another," Ruth said. The cackle was back, but this time with a hint of something. A nervousness perhaps, or hesitancy, that Cora hadn't sensed before. The casualness of the conversation had taken a turn, and Ruth appeared to be proceeding a bit more cautiously. The woman who had just openly shared her flirtation with the younger neighbor was now choosing her words carefully. Ruth paused the way that people do when they assess whether it's safe to proceed and then, with a big gulp from her glass, shrugged her shoulders and decided to carry on.

"They had me after they got back together," she said flatly.

"Back together?" Cora asked, trying to be as polite as possible, but now suddenly intrigued. The word choice seemed odd, like they'd eventually found each other after being lost for a while. "Oh, I see. They were *apart* at some point?" The follow-up question was an obvious one but still seemed an abrupt one to ask a virtual stranger. Cora didn't know whether to apologize or wait for an answer. The entire conversation seemed a strange one to have, but then again nothing about Ruth or this visit could be characterized as normal.

Ruth traced the rim of her glass with the tip of her finger, her long painted nails too perfect to be real. She stared at Cora for what felt like a full minute but was probably a quarter of that; fifteen seconds of silence is quite powerful when it fills a room.

"Oh, you know—things happen." Ruth shrugged slightly to signal how common the situation was, but a sadness in her eyes suggested otherwise. She stared at Cora, studying her the way a person does when trying to decide if someone can be trusted. The energy in the room had taken a shift.

Cora smiled, unsure if that was the correct response to such a weighty statement. A corner had been turned in their conversation, leopard-print pillows and the quiet purr of the fish tank now the backdrop for a topic that Cora wasn't sure she wanted to know more about. She was preparing to excuse herself, but Ruth started talking again, and the opportunity for escape was lost.

"You're a sweet little young thing, so you probably haven't been dealt too much crap in life quite yet, but let me tell you something: life is downright ugly and messy. Anyone who tells you otherwise hasn't lived much."

Cora swallowed hard. She had been dealt more than her share of mess and ugliness in life, but said nothing.

"I'm the baby of the family, so everything happened before I was even a twinkle in my mother's eye, but I've picked up on things over the years," Ruth continued. "It's not really something my family likes to talk about, for obvious reasons." She paused briefly, probably wondering if she should spill sordid family secrets to a complete stranger, but whether it was the gin or some statute of limitations that had passed on retelling the story, she quickly relaxed again and continued.

"My family wasn't exactly *normal*. Mom and Dad married in 1943 and had Bev a few years later, but Dad left Mom for another woman at some point. He and the new wife had a baby, but that didn't work out, and he remarried my mom years later. Then I came along." She summarized the events very concisely and with little emotion, her father's adultery simply another leaf of life events on the family tree.

Cora felt a bit dizzy by the disclosure. By small-town standards, it was rather salacious, especially years ago.

"So, it's not just you and Beverly," Cora said. "You have another half sister?"

"Yes. Hazel."

"Beverly didn't mention her."

"Oh, I'm sure she didn't," Ruth said. Cora waited for her to elaborate, but Ruth merely looked at her and smiled. A slight tremor in her hands was obvious before she clutched her glass with both to hide the shake. Cora didn't know if the shake had been there all along or if it had developed with the turn of the conversation.

"Well, could these rings belong to Hazel? Perhaps her mother if she's still alive?" Cora had a hard time calculating the second wife's potential age in her head but assumed she was around the same age as Beverly and Ruth's mother. If she was the *other woman*, perhaps even younger.

Ruth just sat there, any hint of her smile or carefree nature now gone. Her eyes blinked rapidly—too rapidly—as if trying to erase an unwelcome memory that had come into view. The pause was long and awkward, and when she would think back to this moment later in the day, Cora would remember the energy as a bit stifling.

"You're welcome to talk to Hazel," Ruth finally said, ignoring Cora's actual question and transforming back into the lighthearted and joyful soul who loved Oreos and flirting with her neighbor. "She's a very nice woman."

Cora thought it was an odd way to describe a sibling, so formal and distanced. Ruth grabbed an Oreo and twisted the two pieces apart, studying the creamy white inside for a few seconds before putting the cookie back together and sticking the entire thing into her mouth. She chewed in silence as Cora thought of a way to escape what had become an uncomfortable setting. The air had changed in the room; an initial eclectic mix of designs and patterns now appeared chaotic and frenzied, a carnival fun house without the mirrors. There was nothing fun about this anymore. The sudden shift in Ruth's personality put Cora on edge, and a disturbing thought emerged that maybe there was something else in her drink.

"I better get going," Cora said, taking care to put her—thankfully—virtually untouched drink on its designated coaster. Ruth still sat cross-legged on the chair but had now turned her gaze toward Cora.

"If you talk to Hazel, I'd keep that to yourself," Ruth said, tapping the glass with her plastic nails as she searched Cora's eyes for understanding. Seeing nothing but confusion staring back at her, Ruth sighed and steadied herself to say something that she wished she didn't have to say out loud.

"Like I said, life is messy, and not everyone likes to be reminded of the ugliness. If you talk to Hazel, keep that to yourself." She pointed at Cora before grabbing some string cheese and struggling with the wrapper. Cora must have looked as confused as she felt herself to be, because Ruth dropped the cheese and sighed again when she noticed.

"If you talk to Hazel, do *not* tell Beverly."

Chapter Six

Elliott waved the empty pepper shaker in the air to get the waiter's attention, but he had already moved on from the dining room, through the double doors, and into the kitchen.

"I can't eat this without pepper. I mean, that just can't happen."

"There are more jalapeños on your side than there is cheese, so I think you'll be okay." Cora picked off a chunk of jalapeño that had escaped onto her side and flipped it back to his side, completely aware that the smell of the gross little things had already seeped into her tomato and spinach half. "I think you're good on spice."

"You can never have too much spice." Elliott signaled to another waiter who had just emerged, and finally caught his attention, waving the shaker around in the air to signal his red-pepper-flake emergency. Convinced that help was on its way, he was again able to focus on Cora and the story she had begun to share.

"The whole thing is bizarre, right?" she asked between bites. "I mean, these women are nice. Maybe a little eccentric, especially Ruth, but sweet ladies. Here I am, simply trying to do the right thing, and I end up in someone's living room, watching her eat string cheese and tell me that her father left the family. Left, had a baby, came back, had another baby. It's all confusing."

Elliott took the shaker from the waiter, giving him a head nod in thanks, and then began to dump more pepper flakes on the pizza than Cora had ever seen anyone use. Parmesan, yes, but she really didn't know anyone else who even used the pepper flake shakers. Picking up a sufficiently spiced piece of pizza, Elliott paused before taking a bite, looking at Cora with a bit of bewilderment.

"So, wait a minute. Who are these women?"

Cora's shoulders slumped in exasperation. "Are you kidding me? Have you not been listening at all?"

"No, no, I have, but I don't think I really registered their names. The first one you visited was Beth?"

"Bev. Beverly."

"And this one was . . . ?"

"Ruth."

Despite his claim of starvation just moments before, Elliott put down the piece of pizza and wiped the grease off his hands with a napkin. His look had changed from confusion to concern.

"What's the last name?" He asked the question right when Cora had taken an enormous bite, a long string of cheese connecting the pizza in her hand to her chin. She laughed with her mouth full, but Elliott didn't join in. He waited for her to compose herself and took a sip of his beer while watching her chew.

"Well, I don't know their last names. Beverly's married, and I'm not sure of Ruth's situation."

"Not their married names." Elliott was growing impatient. "Their maiden name." He couldn't let the pizza wait any longer, and picked up the piece again, folding it in half like a jalapeño pepper-flake taco.

"How am I supposed to know that?"

"Was there a name associated with the estate sale?" he asked through the pizza bite. "This was their mother's stuff, wasn't it?"

"Oh yeah. Um . . . let me think." Cora could tell that Elliott wasn't playing games, so she tried to navigate her mental files as quickly as possible, a task made all the more difficult by two glasses of wine that she had already consumed. "Yeah, there were signs at the sale and a name on the receipt that they gave me. Shay. No, that's not it. *Shaw.* That's it—*Shaw.*" As pleased as Cora was at her ability to remember the name, Elliott looked just as displeased by her answer.

"Cora, you need to stop this." He washed down another bite with a swig of beer and struggled to swallow quickly. "Stop with the ring stuff. Let it go."

"Why? Why does it matter whose estate sale it was?"

"Listen, you have to trust me on this. Hickory Falls is a different world from the one you're used to. *Everybody* knows *everybody*, and there are certain families you stay clear of. The Shaw family is one of them."

Cora started to laugh at the absurdity of Elliott's warning, but quickly realized he was serious. She couldn't imagine anything sordid about Beverly and Ruth's family; sure, Ruth was a little quirky, but Beverly had seemed the quintessential Midwest farm wife, complete with grumpy husband and loving cat.

"Listen, I know you're bored and trying to find something to fill your time here, but this isn't it."

"Elliott, these women were as nice and harmless as can be. What skeleton could they have in their closet that can't be disturbed?"

There was something about the look that Elliott gave her then that sent chills through Cora. He was either annoyed or angry, neither of which she deserved. Cora put her pizza down and sat back, a signal that she needed a response.

"All I know is that, growing up, my mom told me repeatedly to steer clear of the Shaws. And no, not because they weren't members of the country club, if that's what you're thinking."

"Um, I wasn't thinking that."

Elliott rolled his eyes as if it wasn't a far-fetched possibility. "I'm not sure exactly why, but there have always been whispers about them. Nothing specific enough for a kid to figure out, but there were always hushed conversations and warnings that I knew better than to disobey. Especially about the lady in the woods."

"Good grief, Elliott!" Cora couldn't help but laugh. *"Lady in the woods?* What are you talking about? This is the most interesting thing I've ever heard about this town and you're only now telling me?"

Elliott didn't find any humor in the conversation. He began to rub his neck the way he always did when he was tense or eager to change the topic of a conversation. "Look, I've been looking forward to our getting together all day, so let's just drop it for now. Please forget the whole ring thing, okay? Keep the things, sell them, donate them—do whatever you want, but please stop making the rounds and interviewing these people like you're researching some exposé. Enough."

And just like that, Elliott was done. A basketball game on the screen nearest them was closer than they'd thought it would be, and the bar had started to come alive with cheers and jeers that spectators hoped would help their favorite player land a three-pointer. Elliott joined in the roar of the bar crowd and started yelling at the referee on television about what he claimed to be an egregiously bad call, and Cora returned to her pizza and glass of wine.

Try as she might, Cora's conversations with Beverly and Ruth weren't easily forgotten, and they continued to run through her mind even as the warmth of the wine and comfort of a full stomach embraced her. These were the times when she wished she had a parent to call and talk to. She had built a wall around herself over the years and was proud of her independence, but she was struck at times by a loneliness that still made her feel unsettled and unsafe. This was one of those times. And as much as she would have loved to heed Elliott's warnings and drop the entire ring thing, she knew she couldn't let it go that easily. She wasn't actually betraying him by asking a few more questions, she reasoned.

He might have asked her to stop, but she wasn't the type to get distracted by a game on television and forget about something. Cora thought about books weeks after finishing them. She liked to talk about movie plot holes for hours after watching them, and drove Elliott crazy with conspiracy theories for true crime documentaries that she believed really hadn't been solved in their entirety. Elliott should have known better than to believe that she would—or even could—drop the "ring thing" with a mild scolding over a greasy pizza dinner. Elliott's attention might have already turned to missed three-pointers and a crowd of angry drinkers at the neighborhood pizza joint, but Cora didn't work that way.

Elliott might have asked her to drop the issue, but Cora had never agreed. If anything, his warning to stay away from the Shaw family had only piqued her interest in a ring without an owner and a family with their share of secrets. She had come this far, so she had to see what Hazel had to say about a special ring that nobody wanted to claim.

Chapter Seven

Cora was eleven years old when she saw her parents' brains spread like lumpy spaghetti sauce on the street. It had been impossible to identify the remains as from one or the other, so her child's mind had categorized the image of blood spatter and clotted flesh as belonging to both her mother and father, sparing neither victim nor Cora the lasting memory that her protectors shared an unspeakable end.

Cora's love of art, music, and sand beneath her toes came from her mother, and her ability to do math problems in her head and need to put things back in their proper place was a gift from her father. Her love of colorful baubles definitely came from her mother's side, jars of useless trinkets a long-standing sore subject between her parents when they were alive, the kind that results in seemingly playful bickering with resentful undertones.

Cora's grandmother found herself to be a mother figure again at age sixty-five, doubtful that she had done such a great job the first time around. She tried, though, to avoid the mistakes that she had made with her daughter, but it was hard. Cora liked what she liked, and it was never the types of things that stores suggested preteens were supposed to want. Losing her parents in a car accident was difficult enough, but having it occur two blocks from their home with the evidence laid bare on the street for all to see was not something that she could help her granddaughter cope with, not when Cora never really shared how much she had seen. Trips to the mall weren't going to help this type of trauma, so she simply let Cora find her own way, figuratively walking a few steps behind if her granddaughter teetered too close to an emotional cliff or started wandering off the beaten path as she sometimes did, lost in her own thoughts and memories.

"Hey, kiddo. How've you been?"

Cora was always taken aback at how old Margaret, her grandmother, sounded on the phone, wondering if she had always sounded that way or if her move away from California had aged her. She had to remind herself that her grandmother was in her eighties now, and a few coughs during a conversation were to be expected.

"Hey, Gram," Cora said. "Just wanted to call and say hello. Nothing real new to report from here." Cora looked at the laundry waiting to be folded on her bed and propped her legs up on the pile of warm clothes instead, working her toes into the towels that had come straight from the dryer.

"Are you settling in? Are people there nice to you?"

Cora smiled at the question, one that had been asked in various forms over the years with each new life chapter. When she'd returned to school after the accident, her grandmother wanted to know if people were being too sympathetic or not sympathetic enough. When she'd taken her first serious art class in high school, her grandmother wanted to make sure the 90210 crowd wasn't acting like they were better than Cora, even though not a single student lived anywhere close to the 90210 zip code or gave Cora a second look. Even now, well into her twenties, Cora was always being asked how she was being treated by others, a fact that made Cora wonder how her sweet little Gram had been treated in her own life.

"Everyone's lovely, Gram," Cora said. "It's really a sweet little town, but an adjustment obviously from life there. I'm fine—just trying to figure out my next steps."

"Well, your next step is getting married. I already have my dress and it's not returnable, so you need to go through with it." The coughing started again, but Cora wasn't worried this time because it was due to a belly laugh. Margaret and Elliott had developed a unique and special relationship. She liked to tell inappropriate jokes to make him uncomfortable, and he liked to praise conservative politicians to return the favor, both affectionately tormenting the other. Before Elliott proposed to Cora, he had asked Margaret for her permission. She had declined, which is exactly what he had expected she would do, so he asked daily for an entire week before she relented with a smile and a hug of congratulations. When they'd decided to move to the Midwest so Elliott could join his father's dental practice, he had insisted that they tell Margaret together. And when he promised that she would always have a place in their home, Margaret responded, "Nonsense. I'll expect to be put up at the nicest hotel in town, thank you." Regardless of how she really felt about Cora's life decisions, her grandmother had never been anything but supportive and encouraging. Margaret was tough yet lovable, demanding but also entirely selfless. Cora missed their evenings spent on the deck, with a glass of wine, complaining about their days or laughing about the ways they themselves had made someone's day difficult.

"I found myself a little adventure at an estate sale," Cora said.

"Oh, did you? Hope it was a long lost Picasso or something."

"Well, nothing quite that exciting. I found a diamond ring and wedding band in the bottom of a jar of buttons and other odds and ends. I'm trying to figure out who they belong to so I can give them back."

"Well, that's idiotic. Why on earth would you do that?" her grandmother practically shrieked into the phone. Cora could picture her eye roll thousands of miles away. "Good grief, child. It's like the universe hands you something good, and you lose sleep trying to give it back. Just keep the damn things, or sell them and put the money toward your wedding." The exasperation in her voice had added another layer to an already gravelly tone, Cora's choices in life exhausting in their complexities. She had taken after her mother in so many wonderful ways: she was an art lover with natural ability and a desire to learn more. Her headstrong, purpose-driven nature from her father was something her grandmother struggled to appreciate, or at times even understand. To her, it was like taking a painting of the ocean and slapping a bright yellow buoy into the water, to warn against swimming.

"It's all good, Gram," Cora reassured her, numb to the feeling of disappointing her with yet another bad decision. "It's all good."

From experience, Cora should have known better. Her grandmother didn't want to hear about mysteries or diamonds found among a colorful jar of baubles. She would only question her decision to buy the jar in the first place and tell her she had plenty of buttons if she wanted them.

Her grandmother was a five foot one, silver-haired package of contradictions. She wanted Cora to exhibit the artistic side of her daughter yet questioned the energy spent pursuing artistic ventures. *Some* artistic ventures, that is. If Cora decided to paint with only crushed peas and grape jelly, her grandmother would have applauded her originality and dedication to the craft. But if her granddaughter decided to build a three-dimensional replica of Notre Dame out of toothpicks, she would most likely have been met with a smirk and "it's been done." You never quite knew what you were going to get with Margaret Haley, but chances are it wouldn't go your way. Cora never knew if it was genuine disagreement or simply her grandmother's unfiltered and unbridled need to offer a contrary view. She understood that if she had actually found a Picasso at the estate sale, Margaret would have probably extolled the virtues of Degas under her breath, just to be difficult.

"How's your art coming?" her grandmother asked, the question that Cora dreaded but always knew was coming. "What are you working on?" It really wasn't a question. Margaret assumed her granddaughter was always working on something, and if she wasn't, shame on her for wasting her talents. It was a conversation that could have told itself.

"Just looking for inspiration," Cora said, responding the same way she had ever since leaving California. They didn't have a "I'll tell you when I start something" type of relationship. Art, to Margaret, was what kept the soul alive, and she was going to make sure Cora took that breath until she herself took the last of hers.

"You've dedicated your life and education to art and could find inspiration in a dead sea horse floating in the water, but you can't find inspiration in a place that is entirely new to you?" Cora could hear the disappointed head shake, the words flung with little thought as dismay took over. She was no longer talking to a person on the other end, but rather to a palpable emotion that wanted to reach through the phone and shake her. This conversation was neither new nor a surprise, just another round in an old, ongoing rebuke to express the same emotion. Last time, it had been "you could find inspiration in coffee grounds;" and the time before—which Cora found particularly creative—"you could find inspiration in expired milk." The thing was, the diamond ring had tossed a little detour in Cora's path, and it was inspiring her in its own way.

Cora then did what she always did to avoid a conversation she didn't want to have. She asked her grandmother about the weather and the ripeness of tomatoes at the farmer's market. She focused on the latest efforts of the preservation society to revitalize the boardwalk, or brought up the seagulls that Margaret both hated and fed whenever she was on the beach. Cora had mastered the art of small talk over the years, her ability to turn the tides away from the shore almost poetic in its gracefulness and ease. She asked her grandmother about things that she loved to discuss—local politics, annoying tourists, or her latest art class—one time hitting the jackpot with a story that involved all three in a salacious affair involving a city councilman, a yoga instructor, and an unsuspecting bystander who would never again look at downward dog the same way. Cora listened patiently as her grandmother complained about a beach trash problem that, if one believed her description, had resulted in not a square foot of beach left unaffected. She talked about stupid small things that Margaret could go on and on about. Cora responded with "uh-huh" and "that's horrible" when appropriate, all the while looking at the small velvet bag on her nightstand and plotting her next move.

She listened to her grandmother say, "Good God, take them with you" as she retold the horror of discovering a used condom on her morning walk, mentioning only briefly that it might not actually have been a condom—she hadn't wanted to get close enough to it to make sure. While her grandmother talked, Cora slipped the diamond ring onto her pinky finger and whispered, "How horrible," into the receiver.

Tilting the diamond this way and that under the lamp by her bed, she felt sorry for the orphan ring, a once-loved heirloom, forgotten among buttons, marbles, and other junk, in an old glass jar. Wedding rings take on a new life and purpose when slid onto a finger; this one's journey was disrespected once it was tossed aside with trinkets from the dime store.

Diamonds, she thought, are a form of art. Like snowflakes that spin in blustery herds of whiteness, an individual diamond's story is unique and precious to its owner. Cora compared the diamond in her own engagement ring with the one next to it, the aged diamond a tinier but more mature, worldly version of her own.

Margaret had moved on to a new topic, a neighbor who didn't understand the unwritten rules about lawn upkeep and the size of rocks suitable for landscaping. Cora had become lost in the way the light bounced off the diamond and fluttered around the room, a flame on the verge of dying.

"How horrible," she whispered again.

Hickory Falls

~

September 10, 1949

If Lewis Shaw had been seen walking down the street, he might have been mistaken for an escaped convict on the run. He'd steal a quick glance over his shoulder as if suspicious of being followed, and his steps were quick and precise, so quick that he almost tripped a time or two over his own feet as he sprung from the curb into the crosswalk and waved to oncoming cars in thanks for letting him pass. In reality, they didn't have much choice.

Lewis was on a mission, and he only had an hour to complete it. He wasn't walking so quickly just because of a time crunch; he had told his wife that he was leaving at four o'clock, but snuck out the back door of his shop fifteen minutes early. Like a cat burglar leaving a crime, Lewis glanced around to make sure he wasn't attracting the attention of bystanders, albeit his only crime that day was stealing a few extra minutes of alone time in search of a cold beer on an unusually hot afternoon.

Evelyn didn't try to be difficult. At least that's what she told him. She simply had a way of wanting things "just so," a description that his young wife used like a medical condition that she couldn't control. Lewis tried to satisfy her, even putting in ridiculous hours making furniture that he sold at a flea market an hour and a half away to help pay for an engagement ring that even the wealthiest women in Hickory Falls admired. She had a way of pleading with him without begging—his favorite meal prepared here, an ice-cold beer handed to him there; kind gestures were always a prologue to a story and followed by a request. Most recently, Evelyn had been pouting about the faded floral wallpaper in their kitchen, something that never seemed to bother her until her friend Janice got new wallpaper with images of parsley, thyme, and tiny cloves of garlic. He had heard all about it over dinner the night before. He tried to be patient, explaining that his job as a woodworker—as popular as his custom-made furniture was among the locals—didn't provide for much excess.

The baby, now already almost five years old, only brought additional stress and expense. His sweet little Beverly had arrived way earlier than they had planned. Evelyn had shrugged through happy tears when she told him she was expecting years ago, waving off his questions about the purported effectiveness of birth control as she discussed her plans for the baby room and remodeling that would have to be done. Lewis had never asked her about the pink plastic container that held her diaphragm in the bathroom drawer, a piece of plastic that hadn't seemed to move from its position in quite some time. Such talk was uncomfortable, even between a married couple, because he expected her to do her part to uphold their agreement to wait to grow their family for a while. Talk of small pink plastic containers was like peeking into a woman's purse—Lewis would never dare. Once informed about the pregnancy, he believed a confrontation would be pointless and the equivalent of proclaiming that he wasn't happy about the baby. He was, of course. He had always wanted to be a father, and although the timing and circumstances were less than desirable, forcing Evelyn to explain her betrayal would bring with it an emotional waterfall in which he would surely drown. Not to mention, everyone knew that expectant mothers were to avoid stress, so he simply couldn't risk it. He was now responsible for both a wife and child and could never forgive himself if he caused harm to either. So, Lewis embraced the news with all the joy and excitement expected of a first-time father and buried his worries deep into the corners of the brain reserved for such things.

Baby Beverly's arrival—as blessed an event as it was—had dealt a financial blow to Lewis that he had never fully recovered from. Evelyn had approached motherhood with the same zealousness—and lack of practicality—with which she approached all other things in life. Her expectations and plans for Beverly were influenced by the pages of glossy magazines that she became obsessed with buying at the dime store, as well as conversations with other Hickory Falls mothers who had been parents six months or longer than Evelyn and therefore felt qualified to dish out advice on the toys, clothing stores, and extracurricular activities that would somehow guarantee their little ones' favorable lot in life. Once the expense of baby items had ended, Evelyn had filled Lewis's evenings with talk of ballet classes and private voice lessons in a nightly cycle that was only briefly interrupted by a cold beer with friends who didn't ask him too many questions.

He needed one of those cold beers right about now.

Lewis again held up his hand to warn a truck that he would be crossing, jogging as he reached the middle of the crosswalk and realized the truck had no intention of slowing down. Evelyn allowed him a one-hour break in the afternoon to spend as he pleased, rolling her eyes that a man who "whittled away in a workshop" could need any such time. Regardless of the eye roll, Lewis made his way to the tavern off Hyde Street every day at four PM, a cold beer poured and waiting for him when he walked through the door. Lewis would drink at least four beers during his time there, laughing with the other regulars about the ball and chain at home, before rushing off precisely at five PM to make the seven-minute walk home. Today he had found an extra fifteen minutes, a real treasure of a time heist.

Just one block away, Lewis could practically taste the suds and hops, slowing his pace only slightly to brush off the sawdust from his overall pants. He was covered in a layer of fine wood pulp, tiny grains caught in the hair of his forearms left unprotected by his flannel shirt sleeves being rolled up to his elbows. Catching sight of a mirror propped up next to artwork in a shop window, he stopped to brush more sawdust from his dark hair, his hand feeling the two-days' beard growth on his chin and cheeks. He felt too young for gray hair but knew it was there, patches of silver along his jawline a daily reminder of days flying by too quickly with too little purpose. It was a thought that gnawed at him relentlessly. Although he knew he had so much to be grateful for, he couldn't help but feel like his life was like the same record played over and over, a melancholy tune that built up to a brief crescendo as he ran to the neighborhood pub for a few minutes of relaxation and freedom from expectations that he never seemed to satisfy.

A gold border on the window caught his eye just then, a painted trim to the shop window, glowing in the late afternoon sun. Taking a step back, Lewis realized he had never really taken notice of this storefront before, its copper awning providing a welcome relief from the heat. Two owls had been carved into the top corners of the heavy wood doorframe, his woodworker's eye drawn to the intricate details of their wooden wings and the masterful carving of eyes that somehow looked upon him as if the creatures were alive.

Lewis was so preoccupied by the details of the carved wooden owls that he didn't even see her in the window, a woman with long dark hair piled on top of her head and secured with what looked to be a wooden stick. They noticed each other at the same time, when she turned to take the stick from her hair and let it fall freely down her back. She was running her hands through it when they made eye contact, the sun shining through the window like a spotlight and revealing her bright green eyes.

She swiveled to face him from what he now saw was an easel, a paintbrush still in one hand. They stood frozen like that for a few seconds, both staring at the other as if time had stopped. Her shoulders suddenly loosened as if she had been holding her breath, and then, pushing her hair back from her face, she smiled. For a moment, Lewis did nothing. For those few seconds, he was not a sawdust-covered worker with calloused hands and a wife who was preparing to ask for new wallpaper. In those few seconds, the universe transported Lewis back to a time when he could pause to see life's beauty and didn't have to keep one eye on his watch while he guzzled a beer. Lewis brushed off a bit more dust from his hair and raised his hand in a silent hello.

And he smiled.

Chapter Eight

~

"These damn gravel roads," Cora muttered, turning the radio down to concentrate. Although many people do the same thing when they're lost, it really didn't make any sense. The sound of Billy Joel's fingers on the piano did nothing to impact her ability to read road signs. The signs themselves were the problem, some faded and others missing entirely, Cora left to translate the written directions from a notebook page provided by Ruth without the actual landmarks that she based them on. It was only when she saw a mailbox with a fake chicken perched on top that she was able to confirm she was anywhere close to her destination.

Take first right after chicken mailbox.

Cora had never been so happy to see a chicken sitting on top of a mailbox in her life. She turned the volume back up, disappointed that the piano man had been replaced by a hair band ballad, turning onto the first right she saw after passing the farm. She assumed it was a chicken farm but had learned it wasn't safe to assume anything, since moving to Hickory Falls.

Gated driveway after fallen tree but before deer crossing.

Cora wondered how long a fallen tree must remain before it's considered a navigational marker, and was pretty sure that, despite her deep roots in the area, even Ruth wouldn't be able to predict wildlife sightings. She had no choice but to follow the obscure directions, however, getting her answer about a half mile down the road when a blackened mass appeared in the distance. The giant rotted tree wasn't far off the road, beer cans and a makeshift firepit nearby signaling its use as a popular teenage hangout. Cora could only assume from its tar-like exterior that it had been a victim of a lightning strike.

Another quarter mile and she saw a rusted gate marking the end of a driveway, a deer crossing sign farther down the road. Ruth's eccentricities luckily did not extend to her map drawings, which had proven to be nearly perfect in their use of the landscape.

Cora turned down the gravel drive and saw the house almost immediately. It was a cottage, really—a small white wood Shaker home with an arched doorway and window shutters painted a tasteful gray-blue. Nestled in the woods like this made it look enchanting, a little house that either welcomed the lost or housed the witch of the forest, depending on the type of story. The house was surrounded by trees on all sides, and a small clearing behind it was home to a body of water too large to be a pond but too small to be a lake. A few ducks startled by her arrival turned in unison and swam in the opposite direction. A squirrel standing on his hind legs atop a rock nearby wasn't as bothered by her presence. It looked intrigued by a new visitor yet prepared to make a quick getaway if need be.

Cora parked in the gravel roundabout and made her way to the front door, careful not to disturb a few sleeping cats sunning themselves on the porch. Yellow day lilies and overgrown rose bushes were fighting for real estate along the front of the house. The thorned roses towered over their competitors and leaned just enough over the lilies that it looked like they were about to pounce.

Apparently, there was no need to knock. Cora's presence had been made known thanks to her tires on the gravel and the closing of her car door, both as loud as gunshots in the quiet woods. The front door opened just as Cora approached.

"Well, hello there."

The woman who greeted Cora did so with a skeptical smile. She resembled neither Beverly nor Ruth, yet there was something familiar about her slight head tilt and guarded stance. Her salt and pepper hair was cut into a chic bob, with just enough salt to make the pepper interesting. Like her half-siblings, she was a petite little thing, her black capri pants and sleeveless turtleneck revealing the muscle tone of a woman half her age. She was classy and chic, warm and familiar, although it was her eyes that really took Cora aback, the vibrant green a shade she had only ever seen in nature. "Come on in and make yourself at home," the woman said.

The house was quite small, the kitchen and living room practically on top of each other, but in a way that was inviting rather than cluttered. What little space the house had was maximized with floor-to-ceiling bookshelves on which old photographs, ceramic treasures, and leather-bound books filled an entire wall on both sides of the rough stone fireplace. A well-worn green couch faced the fireplace, flanked by floral chairs on both sides with a cedar chest in between that was piled high with books and art canvasses. Some of these were blank and others showed the beginning strokes of a sunset or waves of an ocean. Bottles of paint were scattered around here and there, and a painter's palette full of both vibrant and muted colors glowed brightly in the sun shining through the picture window. Cora wondered if she had interrupted an afternoon painting session.

"You must be Hazel," Cora began, unsure whether to stay or apologize for the interruption and offer to leave. When the woman gestured for her to sit in one of the floral chairs, the decision was made for her.

"And you must be Cora." Hazel turned her attention to a teapot that had started to sing in the kitchen, filling two mismatched mugs with steaming water and dropping a triangular tea bag into both. She carried them to the living room and handed Cora a white mug with the image of a large bear on its side, the word *Mama* written above the artwork. The scene was like something out of a children's book. The only thing missing were birds at the windows eating directly out of Hazel's hands or a pot of porridge prepared for three bears. Surely, this quaint and sweet scene was not the "lady in the woods" that Elliott had warned her about. The woman in front of her looked about as dangerous as the squirrel who Cora could still see was keeping watch on its perch by the giant oak tree out front.

"Be careful now—it's hot." Hazel took her place on the opposite floral chair, the women sitting across from each other as if in a casual job interview.

"Thank you—this is lovely," Cora said. "I'm going to assume this mug was a gift from one of your children?" Hazel looked confused for a moment before clueing in to the Mama Bear reference on the mug and nodding in understanding.

"Yes, from my youngest. She's away at college." Hazel smiled but clearly didn't intend on offering more personal information.

"Well, I don't want to take up too much of your time, so I'll get right to the reason for my visit." Cora sipped the tea to show her appreciation for the hospitable gesture, and then placed it on the coffee table. "I believe Ruth filled you in a bit about my estate sale find. Although I appreciate the offer to keep the rings, I didn't feel right about doing so until I checked with you first. Neither Beverly nor Ruth recognized them, even though they were included in their mother's estate sale contents. I thought they might be your moth—your family's." Cora stumbled along the last words, uncomfortable acknowledging the possibility that the rings belonged to a woman whose relationship with the family patriarch was confusing at best and perhaps even scandalous. All Cora knew was that the three women she had met all shared the same father, but his marital situation was less predictable than what would have been expected to be the case decades ago in a small town.

"May I see the rings?" If Cora's nerves were showing, Hazel paid no mind, her attention now fixed on the small bag that emerged from Cora's purse. She took the rings from Cora and traced them delicately with her fingers, saying absolutely nothing for what felt like minutes. With the rings in one hand, she covered them firmly with the other, turning her head to the ceiling with her eyes closed. A single tear escaped down her cheek, her lips trembling slightly. The energy in the room had shifted; Hazel brought the rings to her heart and continued looking upward, another tear falling.

Picking up the hot mug of tea again, Cora didn't know what to do. She felt like she was witnessing something private; any sudden move on her part might disrupt emotions that she didn't understand. She froze in place, setting her mug down only when Hazel's eyes opened and she looked down again, peering into her hands and smiling as if embarrassed.

"I'm so sorry," she said. "I had no idea that I was going to have such an emotional reaction."

"So, you recognize them?" Cora asked, aware of how stupid her question sounded, but excited that the mystery might actually be solved. "Are those your mother's rings?"

Something flashed behind Hazel's eyes at the mention of her mother, a flickering light that was there one second and gone the next. "I can't be sure. It was so long ago. I was so young." The protective wall that had come down momentarily was once again standing firm, Hazel regaining her composure and now smiling politely at the stranger sitting across from her. She steadied herself in her chair and straightened her back the way someone does when they need a minute, but her grip remained on the rings, and her bright green eyes now seemed to shine even brighter.

Cora was confused again. *What* was so long ago? *What* had happened when Hazel was so young? She didn't dare ask, though, already uncomfortable upon seeing a family dynamic unfold that she had no place being part of. There was a story here, a story of sisters who lived in three completely different reality bubbles and who didn't cross paths much. Cora was certain of that. It really was like being in a fairy tale, one in which characters danced around bubbling cauldrons of personalities. Here Cora was with the lady in the woods, drinking tea and trying to avoid asking questions to reveal secrets that were none of her business. Here she was, a peripheral character in a story that was unfolding right before her eyes.

"Listen, you clearly need to take these," Cora said, grabbing her bag and readying herself to leave. *Enough.* Elliott's words echoed in her head as she stood to signal her intended departure. She had accomplished what she had wanted, and it was time to close the cover on this fascinating story and let the main characters battle one another among its pages.

"I'm not sure what the story is, and it's really none of my business, but these rings obviously mean something to you—they belong with you." Cora felt better instantly, a weight lifted from her shoulders as she prepared to end a journey that had taken her down a rather winding and twisty road. She had done the right thing. Her persistence had paid off, and she would now return to the beautiful baubles back home, the contents still well worth the five dollars that she had paid.

She was anxious to get out of here and back to town, the tiny cabin in the woods suddenly appearing isolated as the sun dipped behind the late afternoon clouds, and shadows began to dance within the room. She glanced out the window, hoping to see the friendly squirrel still keeping watch, but it had long since abandoned its post and lost interest in the afternoon distraction.

"What did my sisters tell you?"

Cora sat back down. There was something about Hazel's tone that told her it was not yet time to leave, that their conversation had not ended. Hazel locked eyes with Cora, and her green-eyed stare was not something easy to break or turn away from. Her words weren't accusatory or angry; they merely seemed sad, as if the unspoken answer had already added a heaviness to her heart.

"I'm sorry—I'm not sure I understand." Cora said. "Beverly and Ruth didn't have anything to say about the rings. They didn't recognize them. Ruth wasn't sure you would either, but thought it might be worth a try."

"No. What did they tell you about my *mother*?" Hazel clarified. She was now gently transferring the rings from one hand to the other in anticipation. Or perhaps agitation. Her gaze turned to a point on the wall above Cora's head, but in a way that suggested her eyes were actually riveted on a memory of some sort rather than a painting in the room.

"Oh. Well, Beverly didn't mention anything about your mother, and Ruth just told me that the marriage between your mother and father didn't work out, and your father remarried Beverly and Ruth's mom." Cora hoped she had relayed that correctly, the details a little muddy in her mind. "I really didn't want to pry," she added. "I certainly didn't intend to dive into your family's history. It sounds a bit . . ."—she struggled to find the right word—"*complicated.*"

Hazel smiled and looked again at the rings, but it was a loaded smile, the kind that speaks volumes without saying a word. She nodded in understanding and took a deep breath, wiping away another tear that had escaped and lay suspended in a perfect teardrop on her cheek.

"Well, what Ruth told you isn't exactly an accurate description of what happened," Hazel said. "But it doesn't surprise me that that's how it was remembered or relayed to you. Her description is certainly a much simpler version of events, and we like to keep things simple and neat in Hickory Falls." She hesitated, contemplating how much more to say. The energy in the room, which had continued to shift unexpectedly with every turn of the conversation, was suddenly icy still, as if even the droplets of condensation in the air were awaiting Hazel's next words. Even Cora, who had been prepared to leave five minutes before and put all of this behind her, felt the tiny hairs on her arms stand alert with anticipation of where this conversation was going. Hazel sat there in silence, as did Cora. The sun was now fully slipping behind the horizon and casting dark shadows in the room where only a short time before light had shone.

"Ruth's choice of words is an interesting one, but I'm not surprised, especially when she was relaying the story to a stranger." Hazel's face softened as she looked at Cora once again. "No offense."

"Oh, none taken. I *am* a stranger." Cora was, in fact, a stranger, and was feeling more and more like a voyeuristic one as she sat there waiting for Hazel to elaborate on a private family saga that Cora had absolutely no business knowing. Was it horrible that she was now curious? As though she were reading a well-written novel, Cora found herself eager to turn the page and discover the next secret. She sat and inwardly hoped that Hazel would confide in her about a story that Ruth had found reason to minimize and Beverly had refused to acknowledge at all.

"I suppose my heart's hardened over the years because of all this, but a little sensitivity on their part would still be nice." Hazel stood up and walked over to a small lamp on the side table, clicking the vintage switch a few times before it finally relented and cast a faint glow across the room. The eerie lighting that played on the room's shadows did nothing to calm Cora's rapid heartbeat and a nervous twitch that was threatening arrival in one eye. The tremor was her tell—she might fake confidence in every other way, but her eye would always remind her that it was never fooled. Her thoughts flashed to Elliott in that moment. If he knew where she was and the conversation unfolding, he would not be pleased.

Cora had no idea what Hazel was referring to concerning her siblings' lack of sensitivity or hardened hearts "because of all this," but didn't feel right asking. She thought it best to stay on the sidelines and simply listen.

Hazel continued to stand next to the lamp, fingering the design along its green glass base. Now illuminated, the vase's vintage glass was the same color as Hazel's eyes.

"I find it odd that Ruth told you that my parents' marriage didn't work out," Hazel continued. "They were still very happily married when my mother disappeared."

Cora sat there in disbelief. She rubbed her eye, the twitch now an annoying distraction. One side of her brain questioned whether she had heard Hazel correctly, but the other half had fully processed what had been said. Still, it wasn't the type of thing that a person hears without questioning.

"I'm sorry. *Disappeared?* Your mother disappeared?" The most basic of questions was all she could muster, the heaviness that had been lifted a short time earlier returning as she sunk more deeply into her chair. Her heart was racing, and she thought of Elliott again. He had warned her not to dig.

"I was six years old," Hazel began. "I came home from school that day, excited to tell my mother that my artwork had been chosen for display in the hallway. I had drawn a raccoon, creating the fur exactly like she had taught me to, so it looked a bit disheveled and uneven, and I was so proud." Hazel was somewhere else now, memories of raccoon drawings and painting techniques at the forefront of a story that Cora was both afraid to learn and desperate to hear. She sat in absolute silence, allowing Hazel the time and space needed to continue.

"I was merely a child. I didn't understand when my dad told me that she was gone, vanished in the middle of the afternoon. Her gardening tools were still there, next to the tomato plants. The straw hat that she wore outside was found in the neighboring field, blown there perhaps, or dropped when she made her way through the corn. Nobody could tell us anything. Nobody could give us answers. Honestly, I'm not sure how hard they tried. Small towns, you know."

Cora waited for her to continue, but Hazel looked exhausted, drained from the memories. Cora wanted to stay and comfort her, but was also eager to leave, the heaviness in the room like a wet blanket that made it hard to breathe.

"Hazel, I am so sorry. I had no idea. I didn't mean to intrude." Cora simply couldn't imagine a little girl losing her mother in such a way. The most trusted and beloved person in a child's life, gone during the course of a school day, vanished into thin air, with nothing but unanswered questions filling the space in Hazel's heart where her mother once had been. How devastating for a child. How devastating for the adult that the child had grown into.

Hazel waved the apology away and smiled, this time one of genuine appreciation. "You couldn't have known, and you haven't intruded. Bringing me these rings and taking the time to find out who they belonged to was one of the nicest things that anyone has ever done for me."

"So, they *are* your mother's?"

"I simply don't know, dear. I was so young that I don't remember what her rings looked like. There's something familiar about them, but I can't be sure. We'll have to ask the one person who will know for sure."

"Oh, well, of course," Cora said. And just like that, she steadied herself for another chapter to the story. Perhaps there was a friend Hazel could ask, a friend of her mother's, who might have remembered the rings or even another family member, although Cora didn't know if she could handle news that there was yet another sister. She prepared herself for those options but couldn't have prepared herself for what Hazel said next.

"We'll have to ask my dad."

Just when Cora had come back down from one emotion, another hit her. Hazel must have seen the confused look on her face and laughed. "No need to do that math in your head. Yes, he's still alive. He's turning one hundred this year. He lives in the Hickory Falls Nursing Home, and his brain probably works better than mine. He was born in a time when only the strong survived. I tell him constantly that he'll outlive us all because he's too stubborn to die."

Hazel placed the rings back into the velvet bag and resumed her tea drinking, the ability to move elegantly past ugly memories something she had seemingly mastered over the years. Although Hazel's pleasant mood seemed to have returned, Cora's had now taken a sudden shift into a dark place. She needed to leave but hated to do so with so many questions, none of which were appropriate to pose during an initial afternoon tea.

How strange that Beverly or Ruth hadn't mentioned that their father was still alive and could help identify the rings. Beverly's failure to even touch upon Hazel's existence was bizarre, as was Ruth's description of the marriage "not working out." Then there was Ruth's rather ominous warning to make sure Beverly didn't find out about it if she talked to Hazel.

Strange. Bizarre. Ominous. The exhilaration that she had felt with her bauble jar find had taken a turn.

Although she had nagging questions, one was at the top of Cora's mind: If these rings actually turned out to belong to a woman who had disappeared, why on earth would they turn up in another woman's estate sale almost fifty years later?

Chapter Nine

"I'm sorry, but there's no way that's true. No way."

Anxious to prove Cora's story a work of fiction, Juliet practically flew off the curb onto Main Street, her black leather boots crunching glass pieces from a discarded bottle into even smaller shards on the street. "There's no way there was some disappearance in Hickory Falls without my Mimi knowing about it, and there's no way my Mimi knew such a story without telling me. Mimi knows everything."

Cora followed Juliet, trying to keep up with her pace. Her friend's reaction to Cora's recent story update had been surprising. Rather than the intrigue Cora felt when she shared Hazel's recollection of events, Juliet met the allegations with judgmental doubt, which made Cora wonder if she had broken some small-town code about never pretending to know more than the locals do about the goings-on in their town. She had agreed to visit Juliet's grandmother, Mimi, to get her reaction, but quickly realized that the offer was really more of a demand than an invitation. Now she followed Juliet toward her grandmother's shop to share what she had been told and, according to her friend, probably learn that Hazel in the Woods liked her share of psychedelic mushrooms and fanciful stories.

"Good grief, slow down," Cora said. "Mimi will still be there when we arrive, but my latte's in danger of being completely gone." She stopped to sip the milky foam oozing out of the plastic cap, their frenzied pace sending valuable droplets of caffeine-fueled goodness to and fro, the drink sloshing over the sides. Juliet didn't respond. She was too busy flipping off a car that cut the corner a bit too sharply.

Cora had explored this part of town a dozen times and felt a tinge of excitement that they were heading straight for a shop that had caught her eye every single time she'd passed it. The copper awning had aged beautifully and was every bit as much a work of art as the paintings displayed in its front windows. Juliet forcefully pulled the heavy door open, and Cora smiled at the wooden owls perched on each side above the door frame, guarding the entry like gentle, big-eyed gargoyles.

Oh, what those eyes have seen, Cora thought as she followed Juliet into the art gallery and toward the woman sipping champagne behind the desk.

"A little early for that, isn't it?" Juliet asked, nodding toward the glass of bubbles.

"Nonsense. I live on Parisian time." Mimi took another sip, her lipstick leaving small stains around the rim of the glass. Juliet's grandmother was every bit as her friend had described, waifish in appearance and quite startling, with her dyed black hair secured tightly in a severe bun along the nape of her neck. She looked like she belonged in a ballet class, clapping her hands in strict instruction to the miniature dancers who had not yet perfected their arched points or who dared drop their pose before allowed to do so. Then again, she looked just as natural in an art gallery setting, although Cora's first impression was that she wouldn't ever want to be on the receiving end of one of her critiques. This small woman drinking bubbles was, in fact, quite terrifying.

"This is Cora. Cora, this is Mimi." Juliet made the introductions as she dragged two barstools from the wall and positioned them in front of the desk. Confused as to whether Mimi was actually her name or simply what Juliet called her grandmother, Cora simply acknowledged her with a smile and took a seat. Mimi took another sip of her champagne and looked Cora up and down, raising an eyebrow when she reached her faded black sandals that had seen better days. Cora shifted uncomfortably in her chair.

"So, here's the deal, Mims," Juliet began. "Cora found a few rings at an estate sale and has been trying to track down the owner ever since. She's been handed a story from the family that's going to make you laugh, but I need you to tell her what's up."

Cora didn't appreciate the cynical introduction, but Mimi interjected before she could add her own spin on the facts.

"Who's the family?" Mimi asked. Her directness made Cora feel like she was in an interrogation, the kind where the detective already knows where someone buried the body, but enjoys the song and dance while they deny it.

Juliet and Mimi looked at Cora, waiting for her to respond.

"Oh, sorry . . . um, the Edmond family," Cora answered nervously. "No, wait—that's Beverly's married name." She laughed a little, but neither Juliet nor Mimi laughed with her. Rumors are apparently serious business in Hickory Falls. "The Shaw family," she continued. "The estate sale was for Evelyn Shaw."

Juliet might not have noticed, but Cora saw Mimi raise an eyebrow again, this time like an involuntary reaction to something she hadn't expected to hear. She took her champagne glass and finished it off, pausing before placing it on her desk.

"Tell me what you know." It wasn't a question so much as a demand. If this was fun and games for Juliet, it was not for the woman who was now staring a hole through Cora. Mimi swiveled her chair to directly face Cora, and waited for an answer.

"Well, in a nutshell, I found an engagement ring and wedding band in a jar with other things from the sale. I've met with the three daughters—Beverly, Ruth, and Hazel—to see if the rings belong to anyone in their family." Physically uncomfortable by the weight of Mimi's stare, Cora decided to just rip off the Band-Aid and get right to the heart of the story. "I know that they all share the same father, but he left his first wife, Evelyn, for Hazel's mom at some point and then later went back to Evelyn. Ruth told me that his second marriage simply didn't work out, but Hazel said her mom disappeared." Such an abrupt and emotionless retelling of the story sounded absurd even to Cora's own ears.

Juliet's head whipped toward Mimi, waiting with anticipation for the laugh that she was sure would come. What she saw instead was a heaviness overtake her grandmother's shoulders, and wrinkles appeared around her eyes that hadn't been evident a little time ago. It would seem that Cora's revelation had made Mimi age right before their eyes.

"Oh, girls," Mimi said softly, "why would you do this? That was such a horrible time."

"Wait, this is *true*?" Juliet whisper-shrieked. "Are you kidding me? How can there be a missing person case in Hickory Falls and I've never heard of it? There's no way."

"Juliet, calm down." Mimi wasn't having the drama. "This isn't something that you gossip about. Goodness knows, there was enough gossip going around already. This was a horrible thing that happened." Mimi turned her gaze toward the stained-glass window behind her desk and lost herself briefly. When she turned back around, Cora thought her eyes looked watery, tears kept at bay, but only barely. "At the end of the day, a beautiful woman disappeared and has never been found. That's not gossip—it's someone's life. I've never spoken of it with anyone. I was in between Beverly and Hazel in age, not knowing either very well. I was probably twelve when it happened. I remember my heart broke for that little girl. For the entire family."

"Well, what actually happened?" Juliet asked, her initial demeanor now softened. "Did she really just vanish? Nobody knows what happened, even after all these years?"

"Oh, there was a lot of talk and speculation. I mean, Lewis Shaw left his wife and daughter for another woman. That was a *huge* scandal back then, and I remember my mom and her friends talking about the affair over afternoon coffee, calling that woman every name in the book, in hushed voices, of course. The scandal quieted down after a while because they got married, had Hazel, and were living like a normal family. But Evelyn still lived in town with Beverly, and those types of things just didn't happen that often. I mean, if they did, one of the parties would leave the area to spare the other the shame. The talk never completely went away, of course, and when Hazel's mother disappeared years later, people assumed she had moved on to someone better. Another married man, they guessed, in some other town. It was easier to explain that way."

"Well, you don't believe that, do you?" Cora asked, more forcefully than intended. "I mean, her garden tools were still there where she had been working. Her hat was found in a field. You don't go out to garden one day and decide in the middle of picking tomatoes that you're going to leave your husband and daughter on the spot. That's simply ridiculous."

"You clearly got those facts from Hazel," Mimi said, not unkindly. "Yes, I remember my mother and her friends dissecting the evidence like it was a mystery. I mean, it was, I guess. But a hat blown into a field isn't exactly a rare occurrence around here, and the salacious talk resigned itself to more rational theories after a while."

Mimi looked at Cora with both kindness and concern, and pulled the bottle of champagne from a small refrigerator under her desk. She poured herself another glass, this one to the very rim, and sipped the bubbles before responding. "But, no, I never believed that this was simply a matter of a woman skipping out on her family to start a new life somewhere. Hazel, from what I remember, was very loved and cared for. If a mother is separated from her child, it's like she loses a limb. Mothers just don't do that—they *can't*. I've always thought there was more to the story, but you don't dare talk about that around here. There were too many loose ends that weren't going to end up nice and neat, no matter what you did."

"What other rumors were there?" Cora asked. "I mean, other than that she just ran away and abandoned her family."

"She was an absolutely gorgeous woman, and even at twelve years old, I knew what men thought of her around town. She was exotic and artistic. She was this dark-haired anomaly among a town of bleached-blonde beehives. She fell in love with the wrong man, but there were other men after her, one of whom was the town doctor with a rather vengeful wife. No, girls, this is a story that needs to die."

"What do you mean, 'others after her'?" Juliet asked. "The town doctor? His wife? Do you think they were involved? Oh my God, do these families still live here?" The weight and implications of this dark story on her hometown was now hitting Juliet, her mouth agape in shock.

"Oh, honey, there are some things that you just don't put out into the universe," Mimi said. "I was a child at the time and only knew what I was able to pick up from my hiding place during mother's afternoon get-togethers. Let's just say she was a beautiful woman who caught the eye of many, including happily married men in rather prestigious positions."

Cora wasn't ready to let this alternate theory go, but Juliet cut her off before she could beg Mimi for additional information.

"Didn't anyone think it was a little strange when he went back to his ex-wife?" Juliet asked. "Don't you think that's weird? If you divorced, you probably did so for a reason. Why would you ever get back together? I mean, the guy left you and you take him back?"

"It was a different time. In fact, I remember that people thought Lewis and Evelyn getting back together was good news, a family reunited and a mother figure for Hazel. Back then it was all about the family unit and an uncomplicated life. Lewis had chosen a complicated path, and it didn't end well. Of course, anything that I heard was from the stairway landing, where I hid when my mom and her friends were talking over coffee in the kitchen, but that's really how I learned most things back then. I remember them talking about the girls, Beverly and Hazel, and how it was good that they would grow up as sisters in the same house. Complicating factors weren't welcome here. They're still not. Juliet, you know should know that about

Hickory Falls." Mimi then turned to Cora. "You're learning that the hard way."

Unfazed, Cora wanted Mimi to talk as long as she could. "Let's go back to this guy who was interested in her," Cora said. "The town doctor. Did anyone talk about the fact that this woman probably didn't disappear on her own, that someone might have hurt her?"

Mimi smoothed her hair, her brow furrowed with unspoken thoughts. "Like I said, there were a lot of rumors. Men seemed to have an unnatural attraction toward her, an obsession almost. Again, this is from the mouths of my mother's gossiping hen group. Who knows what was true. I remember them lowering their voices when talking about the more salacious stories, like the one about the prominent town doctor who pursued her quite openly. But that's enough, girls. It's best to forget about all of this and focus your time on something more appropriate."

"She's asked me to go with her to visit her father," Cora said quietly, almost fearful to share this tidbit after Mimi's warning. "Hazel invited me to meet with her father, Lewis, and show him the rings."

Mimi didn't look up from the glass, preferring to study the bubbles' movements rather than make eye contact. When she finally did, her eyes had turned cold and her face serious. She leaned across the table and folded her arms on the desk, staring at Cora so sternly that she was completely unnerved.

"You be careful with this, do you hear me? Small towns bury their secrets deep and don't look kindly on people digging for them."

Cora nodded but couldn't manage a reply. Juliet stared at the two of them, her gaze bouncing, like a ball in a tennis match, between Mimi and Cora, waiting for one of them to speak. Finally Cora broke free of Mimi's gaze and nodded toward her champagne. "Got another glass?"

"Make that two," Juliet said, leaning back on the barstool and shaking her head in disbelief. "Who would have thought that Hickory Falls had these kinds of secrets."

"If you knew about them, they wouldn't be secrets, now would they?" Mimi said, opening up one of her file drawers to pull out two more champagne flutes. As she filled them, the air in the room lightened, the three women toasting in acknowledgment to a story shared among them, a bond that only secrets can form. They each raised a glass, but Cora stopped short of drinking.

"What's her name?" she asked. "I've heard about Lewis's wife, Hazel's mom, this exotic and beautiful woman who disappeared from everyone's lives without explanation, but I don't even know her name."

Mimi raised her glass even higher this time. "Clarity. Her name was Clarity Shaw."

Chapter Ten

~

"You're not the only one who's good at research," Juliet teased. "And by research, I mean buying Mimi another bottle of bubbles and helping her drink it. By the third glass, she's quite loose-lipped. When it comes to information, she's better than any encyclopedia."

Cora might not have approved of her friend's methods but certainly wanted to hear the results. She followed Juliet closely down a narrow path that was almost impossible to see in the dark, only the crunching of leaves on either side letting her know that she had strayed too far off the worn dirt walkway. The sudden temperature drop meant Cora was in no way dressed appropriately for a field trip. She clutched her long cardigan more tightly around her, both to keep warm and to save it from getting caught on the twigs and low-lying tree branches that seemed to hover more closely with every step. "Where are we going? And again, why can't we go in the daytime?"

"Everyone knows that it's more fun to visit a cemetery in the dark."

"Wait—hold up," Cora stopped on the path and looked around as if the darkness would somehow take pity on her and reveal her surroundings. "Juliet, I'm *not* going to a cemetery. At *night*. For *no* apparent reason."

"Oh, there's a reason, and a good one, but you're not going to know what it is unless you hurry up. I'll leave you here." Juliet had already gotten to the top of a small hill and quickly disappeared over it, along with her phone's flashlight. "Hurry up or you'll be lost forever." Her voice carried over the hill, and with it a low ghostly moan. She was enjoying this way too much.

"This is beyond ridiculous," Cora whispered to herself as she jogged a bit to catch up to her friend. "How about you fill me in on your quote research unquote while we're walking."

"Oh, here we are," Juliet said, pointing to an iron fence a hundred feet or so away. "Climb that sucker and we're in the graveyard." She was clearly ignoring Cora's request for more information.

At this point, they were at least a quarter mile outside town, and Cora was at Juliet's mercy to find their way back. This cemetery was certainly not like the one adorned with fresh flowers next to the church off Main Street. Cora had actually only recently learned from a podcast that the ones on church property are correctly referred to as graveyards; the ones on their own, like this one in the middle of nowhere and without a church nearby, are cemeteries. It was not a piece of trivia that she'd ever thought she'd actually need, but here she was plucking it from those shelves in her mind devoted to storing useless information. Regardless, she didn't think Juliet would be interested in hearing about the distinction. At least not now.

"Lovely. So glad that I wore my fence-climbing shoes. Oh, wait—I didn't." Cora was growing increasingly annoyed. When Juliet had suggested that they meet for a cocktail and adventure that evening, Cora was hoping more for live music or a new art opening at Mimi's gallery. Adventure, for her, had not meant trespassing under the dark of night for the first time since college. And even back then, she would have preferred live music or art. When she'd told Elliott that she was meeting Juliet for a drink tonight, he seemed happy to hear she was getting more comfortable in the town. She was pretty sure scaling a cemetery wall wasn't exactly what he had in mind.

Cora watched with a bit of awe as Juliet made her way over to the fence and hoisted herself up effortlessly, securing one foot on part of a spindle and throwing herself onto the other side. She planted both feet like a gymnast, arms raised to signal a perfect landing, and then motioned for her friend to do the same. Cora's rise and descent, however, wouldn't be quite as smooth. She fell twice trying to climb the fence and then toppled over its top edge and landed firmly on her ass with a less than graceful thud.

"This is stupid." Cora couldn't think of anything better to say as she wiped off dirt from her jeans and struggled to retain one iota of dignity. She checked her cardigan for holes, amazed that it hadn't gotten caught on something in the process. It took a minute for her eyes to adjust to what was now around her. The light from the rising moon shone across the landscape and revealed rows and rows of headstones, only a few of which still stood fully upright. Most of the stone slabs leaned forward or backward, chunks of them missing from years of neglect.

"Come on—I think they're down here." Juliet pointed to a vague area ahead. She navigated her way through the cemetery's occupants on her way toward a corner that somehow seemed even darker than the rest.

"*Think? They?* Are you ever going to tell me what we're looking for?"

Juliet was too busy examining headstones with her phone's light to answer. She would get within a few inches of a marker to decipher its name and then dart to the next. This part of the cemetery was incredibly old, many of the graves dating back to the Civil War. As they walked closer to the corner, the trees that lined both sides of the perimeter fence blocked out the moon entirely, along with any sounds of the outside world. It was as if, somewhere along the way, they had literally stepped back in time, leaving all of the comfort and safety of modern-day Hickory Falls behind. Cora's heart dropped when she walked by a small marker, where the image of a baby with a halo was etched into the dark stone, weeds covering the name.

"Here!"

Cora could now only see Juliet's phone skipping from one low headstone to the next along a line of markers. She hurried over, taking care not to trip over grave markers that, given their age, were often only bits of stone sticking out from the dirt.

"What's this?" she asked when she caught up with her friend. "Why did you want to find these?" She still wasn't used to how quickly the weather changed around here, the mid-Autumn temperature shifts feeling colder than anything she'd ever experienced before. Her cardigan did nothing to shield her from the crisp air. Their breath looked like puffs of smoke in the soft glow of their phones' flashlights, Cora's billowing out rapidly from the cold and Juliet's just as rapidly from excitement. Here they were in a cold, dark cemetery, pairs of glowing eyes from the trees above doing nothing to ease Cora's nerves. The entire scene was less than welcoming. She was eager to hear Juliet's story and get back to the warmth and comfort of her apartment. As soon as she had tossed herself over the fence and crossed the line into official trespassing, she had decided tonight's adventure was never to be shared with Elliott.

"So, like I said, I got Mimi talking a bit last night," Juliet began. "Clarity Shaw was obviously her married name, but after a while and a few drinks, Mimi remembered her maiden name: *Grey*." Juliet cast her light onto the graves—five of them total—all in a single line and sharing Clarity's last name. From oldest to most recent, they stood at attention in varying states of disrepair, the name *GREY* carved in all caps on the front of each.

"Okay," Cora said, now realizing the point of their trip. "So, this is her family?"

"Yes, but this isn't an ordinary family plot." Juliet got down onto her hands and knees, clearing muddy residue, weeds, and moss from some of the headstones. "Don't you notice anything *unusual*?"

Cora stepped forward to examine each a bit more closely. The graves were all by themselves in the farthest corner of the cemetery, as if they wanted their space or others wanted to distance themselves. The markers were identical—all made of a thick black stone—with the names and dates carved crudely by hand. Clearly comprising multiple generations, the dates had to be among the oldest in town, some even predating the Civil War beginnings of the town, improbable as that seemed. As neglected as the stones may have been, flowers had been laid in front of each one, long enough ago that the petals had dried up, but recently enough that the roses' thorns still shone sharp. How strange the sight was—five roses, now black in color, placed in memory of women, some who had been gone over a hundred years.

"They're all women," Cora suddenly noticed. "There are no men here."

"Exactly. And they all have the last name Grey. All women, buried side by side, with no men in sight. What—none of them married? That seems unlikely. And look at their names. How odd is that?"

"And the roses. Who would have left these?"

Juliet shook her head in disbelief, scanning the surrounding area as if the owls might not be the only ones watching.

Cora studied the marker closest to her and the most recent.

Enid Grey.

The inscription under her name was difficult to make out. Certain letters had worn smooth since her 1942 burial, but Cora could make out enough to decipher what it said.

To live. To have lived true.

She skipped to the next.

Phoenix Grey. 1898. To rise and lift others.

And then the next.

Clio Grey. 1890. To bring glory.

And then the next.

Harmony Grey. 1880. To bring peace.

"These are amazing," Cora said softly. "Given the dates, some might have been sisters. Others, maybe mothers and daughters. What do you think it all means?"

"Well, I mean, we were on our second bottle of champagne when Mimi really started talking, but she remembers a lot of hushed conversations around town about the Grey family being into strange things."

"Define 'strange.'"

"They had their own way of doing things."

"That doesn't help."

"I don't know," Juliet said, sounding uncomfortable and even a little embarrassed. "She mentioned spells and stuff."

Cora stood up, laughing. "Good grief, we're actually talking witches now?"

"I'm not saying it; I'm just saying that's what Mimi told me. Besides, why aren't there any men here? It's all strange. Your description of Hazel didn't exactly sound *normal*. I mean, she lives in a *cabin*. In the *woods*. *Alone*. Where's her husband?"

"I have no idea, and it didn't occur to me to ask. She mentioned a daughter, though. Seemed pretty normal, if you ask me. Maybe she simply likes the quiet. Who knows? But I don't think the lack of guys out here means anything. Clarity's husband didn't disappear—*she* did."

Juliet didn't have a response for that.

"I find the entire thing fascinating and more than a little odd," Juliet finally said. "And I'm more than a little ticked that you uncovered some Hickory Falls mystery that I didn't even know about. I'm totally into history and all of this witchy stuff, so I don't know why Mimi didn't tell me before."

"Maybe because there's nothing to tell." Even as she said it, Cora found herself doubtful. She didn't want to read too much into anything but couldn't deny feeling something when she'd met with Hazel, especially when she'd handed her the rings. Hazel had shown a strong reaction to them, although she claimed not to know for sure that they were her mother's. Even as she tried to brush all of this off when speaking to Juliet, there was something about the row of five graves that gave Cora pause. They weren't normal by design for the time period or way of life. Husbands were laid next to wives. Couples stayed together. This was unique and a bit strange.

Casting one last stream of light on the most recent marker, one dated 1948, Cora spotted something peeking out from the weeds. It didn't look like it belonged there, a lighter color than the surrounding grass lying next to it that was growing in odd directions. Unlike the part of the cemetery that they had walked through, the weeds in this remote area were high, and the grass had been mowed haphazardly by a caretaker who probably didn't devote much time to upkeep in these far corners. Cora walked over to the area and knelt down, smoothing the weeds and parting the grass to see what it was hiding. The moon had moved high enough in the sky to find some space to shine between the trees, and Cora was thankful for the additional light. She found a flat rock wedged into the dirt, and traced her fingers around it. It had clearly been there a while, long enough to have altered its surrounding landscape, but didn't look random. By the light of the moon and her phone's flashlight, Cora cleared off the front of the rock to reveal a single word had been carved crudely on its face. Both time and weather had somehow spared letters that were still so clear they looked like they could have been etched the day before. As cold as she had been a few moments before, Cora was now dizzy from a heat that rose from her chest to her cheeks, to her head, her eyes stinging and ears ringing from a sight that she wasn't prepared for. On the rock was a single word and the remnants of a rose.

Clarity.

Hickory Falls

∾

June 15, 1950

By all accounts, the flea market was a success. All of Lewis's furniture sold except for a side table that people kept saying was "too large for the space." Evelyn would be pleased with the money. Although he had hinted that many women worked outside the home to help make ends meet, Evelyn had always shushed away the idea. Her job was taking care of Beverly, and his was to make as much money as possible and not comment on her spending.

To "help," she circled flea markets within a three-hour radius in the newspaper's calendar section and folded the paper neatly on the arm of his living room chair. Sometimes, she would cut out the calendar notices and tape them to the bathroom mirror or put them on the table next to his side of the bed.

Evelyn was always helpful that way.

* * *

The driveway really couldn't qualify as one except for its path that led from the gravel road to the house, tire tracks visible in the packed dirt, tall grass growing between the tracks and on both sides. The grass in the middle lay at a different angle from being dragged under the truck, the billowy blades like a calm green ocean leading up to the tiny cabin in the woods.

The truck leaned this way and that as it made its way up the short drive, pulling to an angled stop in front of the house. Clarity jumped out and made her way to the back of the truck, lifting out a sizable oil painting that had been protected between the layers of a blanket.

"I can't believe I sold eight paintings today," she said, her long dark hair swirling in the wind of a darkened sky. "Can't say that I'm surprised this one didn't sell, although I did enjoy the gasps and whispers when people walked by." Lewis was now standing beside the truck, too much of a gentleman not to walk her to the door but too much of a married man to feel right about doing so. He found the painting difficult to look at without blushing, the nude female form abstract enough to be allowed at the flea market, but too anatomically correct to be mistaken for anything other than what it was, even with the bluebirds that had been painted to cover the most private of parts. Lewis smiled to be polite but looked elsewhere, a mooing cow in the distance in need of his attention.

If Clarity noticed his modesty, she made no point of showing it, choosing instead to hold the painting up in front of her, and inspecting it like she was a buyer seeing it for the first time.

"Let them gasp and whisper, I think it's lovely. I call it *Blue*, both for the birds and the look of melancholy on her face. I didn't intend that expression, you know. It was almost like the paintbrush took over and created her itself. Yes, I'm rather glad this didn't sell. I'd like to keep it."

Lewis couldn't tell if she was talking to him or herself, her tilted head and serious examination of a painting that she had created suggesting a monologue that there was no need for him to weigh in on. He was fine with that; he really didn't want to have to comment on the painting of a nude woman covered in bluebirds. His house was decorated in landscapes, a pastel sailboat drawing navigating the walls of his bathroom, all of which had been chosen by Evelyn and hung at precisely eye level. The paintings in his house couldn't make a grown man blush, although, if Lewis had been perfectly honest with himself, he might have blushed at a landscape painting if Clarity was the one holding it.

Satisfied with her personal critique, Clarity hoisted the painting under one arm and carried it awkwardly toward the front door, her hair and long dress swept violently to one side as another wind gust surprised them. She had to hang onto the railing for balance, so confident that Lewis was coming that she found no need to look back.

"And I'm so glad we made it here before the rain hits. I'd hate for this or your table to get damaged." Clarity fumbled in her large knapsack with her free hand and, after pulling out a hat, an apple, and a notebook, emerged with keys and unlocked the door. "Come in while I look for that sheet of plastic. You'll need it for the ride home, to cover the table if the rain comes."

Lewis stood there, his attention still turned toward the cow that had long since stopped mooing. He had told himself that he was doing nothing wrong this entire time. They were simply two creative souls who enjoyed chatting about their work and projects. It was a friendship that had developed both slowly and within minutes of their first meeting, although Lewis would eventually confess to walking by the art gallery daily for weeks before developing enough courage to actually walk in and talk to her. And Clarity would finally admit that she saw him, a blur outside the window, walking quickly enough to avoid detection yet slowly enough to catch a glimpse inside. Such honest disclosures wouldn't happen until much later, though, after the nice-to-meet-you chitchat had subsided, and Lewis's occasional drop-ins at the gallery became anticipated—and welcomed—by both. Lewis asked her questions about art, and she learned about his woodworking, two people happy to have found someone interested in their craft and familiar with the unique way that an artist's mind works.

Until now, Lewis had admired Clarity as if she were a beautiful woman in a magazine. There was no denying her attractiveness. Her long dark hair and light green eyes were a startling combination, a beauty as objective as the sky's blueness and chill on one's skin from an early morning frost. Like the women in those magazines, Lewis simply gazed upon Clarity with a certain admiration, but from a safe and comfortable distance, never actually believing that those women would leap from the page and start engaging with him. Even as they spent more time together chatting at the gallery or traveling to flea markets to sell their work, Lewis never considered Clarity as actually *real* or something attainable. Although he kept their friendship a secret, he always viewed it as harmless. Yet here he was, standing outside her home as she waited for him to enter. It was as if the beautiful woman from the magazine had suddenly come to life and reached out her hand to welcome him into her world.

Clarity had come to the flea market at his suggestion that day, a genuine and innocent gesture on his part to help her sell her paintings in a bigger venue. She had talent, but it was the kind lost on those in Hickory Falls, who hung reproduced paintings of the Last Supper and bowls of fruit on their walls. Clarity painted differently. She described her process in terms of emotion rather than color or subject, most of her paintings taking ordinary things or people and distorting them to capture how she felt at the time.

Clarity would talk about specific artists she admired, and Lewis would merely nod, as if he knew them, always making a mental note to look them up in the library the next time he passed by. Chagall was a name that she mentioned often, the artist's dreamlike paintings something that Clarity admired yet intentionally tried not to emulate out of respect for his unique approach.

When Lewis had eventually looked up the artist for more information, he was struck by the vibrant colors of his paintings and their almost childlike qualities. He could understand why Clarity was drawn to the whimsy of his paintings, but thought hers were much better. Lewis thought everything she did—every word spoken and canvas painted—was perfection because it was hers.

Yes, Lewis had told himself that this was all innocent, but here he stood outside her home—her private and safe place—and his excitement at seeing this part of her betrayed any reassuring inner voice that worked overtime to cloud his true feelings. It was here that she slept and dreamed. Here she curled up with her books and scolded the rascal of a cat that she had shared so many stories of. By opening this front door, there was an entire layer of Clarity, self-exposed in a way that casual conversation in trucks and afternoon chats in art galleries could not. This little cabin in the woods made Clarity more *real*.

Lewis stood there, a man torn between a life that he had wanted and one that he'd never known was possible. In one, there were paint-by-number landscapes and meatloaf every Tuesday. There was comfort in the predictability and safety of defined expectations and responsibilities. In the other, there was none of that, yet it felt both much more natural and terrifying. Lewis stopped the charade of looking toward a cow that had long since disappeared and made his way to the front door.

Chapter Eleven

⤔

Sometimes, a person just needs a thunderstorm.

Cora was still getting used to these Midwest storms, dark skies in the middle of the day that brought whistling winds and flying debris. The first time a thunderstorm rolled in, she had run down to her building's basement and huddled in the corner, waiting for the other tenants, sure that a twister was on its way to swoop them all up before spitting them out in the middle of some distant cornfield.

She had waited for what seemed like an hour, only to emerge embarrassed when one of her neighbors walked off the elevator with her laundry basket under one arm and a Diet Coke in her free hand, looking more than a little concerned to find the new girl hiding behind a stack of empty produce boxes in the dark. Elliott had snort-laughed when he heard the story, now a favorite whenever he introduced Cora to new friends and family members. He always began with, "Honey, I'm sorry, but I have to tell them about your first *tornado* experience . . ."

This storm, however, was welcome because it was a way for Cora to cancel all plans without actually admitting that she wanted to cancel them. No yoga-in-the-park class today. She couldn't possibly be expected to run to the store, not in such a torrential downpour. And that lightning! Metal-tipped umbrellas posed their own hazards in such conditions. No, Cora was going to have to stay home today in her fuzzy pink pajama pants and matching slippers. There was always laundry to do and the refrigerator to clean out, but the time didn't feel right for those things either. She had learned to embrace these Midwest storms for what they were—opportunities to isolate oneself without excuse or explanation. Today, there was really nothing for her to do except chill on the couch with coffee and search the internet for information about a missing person case from over fifty years ago.

A giant ball of thunder rolled across the sky just as Cora was sitting down with her laptop. It shook the windows and caused little ripples to form on the surface of her coffee cup on the table. She found the sight of the tiny ripples unsettling, as if danger had somehow found its way inside walls that were supposed to protect her. Storms she was getting used to, but the unexpected waves of thunder were still a surprise in both volume and frequency. And because her apartment was on the fifth floor of an old, renovated warehouse, the rain and wind seemed like they were on top of her, threatening to rip off the roof with every boom and burst of energy. She waited for the thunder to quiet before opening her laptop and wakening it from its sleep.

She started with the most basic of search terms:

Clarity Shaw

The first results featured diamond websites, the irony not lost on her as she scrolled through blurbs describing clarity, color, cut, and carat—the four prongs of a diamond's analysis. She deleted that search and started another.

Clarity Shaw Hickory Falls

This one turned up Evelyn Shaw's obituary as the first result, the photo of an older woman in a pink ruffled blouse next to her name. Cora clicked on the link.

> *Evelyn Rose Shaw left this earth peacefully, surrounded by loved ones, on May 3, 2019, at age 96. The daughter of Henry and Beatrice Lancaster, Evelyn was born on June 1, 1923, and was a resident of Hickory Falls her entire life.*
>
> *After finishing her schooling and earning exceptional grades, Evelyn married the love of her life, Lewis Shaw, on May 15, 1943, and welcomed daughters Beverly and Ruth in 1944 and 1962, respectively. Lewis adored his wife, showering her with flowers and gifts simply to brighten her day, and is now lost in the grief of her absence. Theirs was a love story for the ages and one that had no comparison.*
>
> *Evelyn was a pillar in the community, always there to help others in need, spending her time volunteering at the local school and library, and serving as a longstanding board member of the Women's Gardening Club and the Hickory Falls Preservation Society. She was admired by her peers, trusted by her friends, and beloved by her family. The Shaw family has lost its brightest star, but she will continue to shine brightly above us.*

Cora skipped the details about her service and the in-lieu-of-flowers instructions, allowing her first impression of the obituary to simmer for a moment. It came across as quite desperate in its need to portray Evelyn a certain way. No doubt she had been a wonderful woman with a family who loved her, but Cora had never read an obituary so intent on bringing that emotion home. Rather than a loving note in tribute, there was an undercurrent to these words, as if this post in the daily paper provided an opportunity to officially document who Evelyn was so the record was clear. Then there was Hazel, who was not mentioned at all. Evelyn had presumably raised her as one of her own since Clarity disappeared, but Cora realized that maybe that wasn't entirely true. Maybe the role of stepmother was one in name only, a loving relationship not always implied. The tale of Cinderella might have been more fact than fiction in that respect.

Cora closed the link and opened the search screen again. The chance that news stories from decades ago had been preserved online was low, so her only hope was that the Clarity Shaw case had been discussed sometime more recently. She knew the odds were slim, but as another rolling ball of thunder rattled her windows and threatened to destroy her roof, she took a sip of her coffee and gave it another everything-but-the-kitchen-sink try.

Clarity Shaw unsolved disappear missing mother Hickory Falls

Cora was prepared for another dead end and was shocked when a book excerpt popped up that looked like it might be on point. Holding her breath, she clicked on the link, which took her to a preview of an eBook titled *Murder, Mayhem, and Mystery in the Midwest*, hoping the content would be less cheesy than the title. Two pages were available to view online for free, with the last paragraph on the bottom of the second page including a few of her search terms.

Unsolved Mystery—The Disappearance of Clarity Shaw
Clarity Shaw, a 28-year-old mother in a small Midwest town, disappeared without a trace while gardening in

*her backyard in 1960. Locals are tight-lipped about the
tale, the missing woman referred to as a witch or gypsy by
some who are now too old to remember many details. The
police report is only a few paragraphs long, describing her
tools left beside the garden and a summer hat found a half
mile away, but it's the blood droplets*

Cora couldn't believe what she was reading, but it ended there.
The free excerpt ended mid-sentence. She couldn't hit the "Buy"
button fast enough, the ninety-nine-cent eBook taking forever to
load and open. She scrolled down to the bottom of page forty-two,
searching for the words *blood* and *gypsy* to guide her way, finally
narrowing in on the right paragraph and continuing her read.

*on the grass that suggest this "gypsy" might have never
walked away like many claimed. It seems the Shaw family
was a complicated one. There was a messy divorce and
resentment from a first wife, and some residents recall
rumors of threatening confrontations by a jealous doctor's
wife who didn't appreciate his open affection for Clarity,
described by all as an exotic beauty who stuck out on the
streets of the sleepy town. Even all these years later, the town
continues to take a don't ask, don't tell approach when it
comes to this mystery, closing their eyes to what appears to
be certain murder.*

That was it. From there, the book began a summary of a 1953
kidnapping farther up the Mississippi River, sightings of the teenager a regular recurrence along the same stretch of highway along
mile marker forty-five. Another wave of thunder rolled overhead

as Cora sat so lost in thought that she almost didn't hear the buzz-
ing of her phone.

"Hello?"

"Cora, thank God, I've been trying to get a hold of you. Where
are you? Why haven't you picked up?' The panic in Elliott's voice
snapped her out of her mental daze.

"I'm home—why? What's wrong?" If Elliott had been trying
to call, either the storm or her concentration on the online stories
had drowned out the sound of the phone.

"You need to the get to the basement. Twisters have been spotted just west of town."

"You're hilarious, Elliott. Thank you for taking this opportunity to remind me of one of my more embarrassing times. I'll spare
myself the humiliation today."

"Cora. *Listen* to me. Get down to the basement *now*. Don't
take the elevator. We've taken all of our patients into the storm
cellar of the building. The sirens are going off."

Cora swiveled to face the large windows behind the couch
just as the sirens started to shriek their warnings. The sky had
turned a deep green, and everything had suddenly stopped, like
Mother Nature had hit the "Pause" button. There was no rain,
no birds singing, no wind. The green and gray clouds were falling like a blanket over the town, either to protect it or swallow it
whole.

Cora ran toward her apartment door, phone still in hand,
Elliott's voice now so far away.

"Cora! Cora!"

She sprinted down the hallway as fast as her slippers allowed,
the overhead lights flickering for a second as she rounded the

corner toward the stairwell. There was no movement in the other apartments or on the stairs, and Cora's rubber-soled steps were almost completely silent on the metal stairs as she jumped down by twos. Elliott was now gone; any cell reception that hadn't been impacted by the storm had been suffocated within the concrete walls of the stairwell.

When she finally reached the basement, every other tenant was already there, turning her way when she burst through the door, out of breath and terrified. Two children had buried their faces into their parents' sides in a panicked embrace, muffled sobs heard on top of the whispers of other tenants, all staring upward as if waiting for the ceiling to disappear. Cora took up residence along an empty portion of the wall, her fuzzy pink slippers now on top of plywood sheets left there from some renovation project. She wondered why they were all whispering, as if the storm could somehow sense fear and target it more closely.

An older gentleman whom Cora had seen a few times in the lobby put one finger to his lips and pointed upward with his other hand, the first to hear what sounded like a train whistle far off in the distance. The room followed his lead, falling into silence; even the children's cries had been displaced by the sound of a train growing louder as it traveled toward them. Panic had become resignation. A few people turned toward the concrete walls and knelt down, covering their heads with their hands, children protected under the cover of their parents' arms. Others stood together along the perimeter, some wide-eyed while their neighbors whispered prayers and crossed themselves repeatedly. Cora turned to face the wall, not so much for protection, but to stop the visual. She relied on the locals to help her find her footing in Hickory Falls; if they were terrified, she didn't know what else to be.

It was there that Cora knelt, in fuzzy pink pajama pants and slippers, cold and alone in the corner of a horror movie basement when the lights went out and the train arrived.

Hickory Falls

October 15, 1951

Clarity was well aware of her reputation in Hickory Falls. She found the stories quite entertaining when she was lucky enough to overhear one, tales of the goings-on at her cabin in the woods far more interesting than what actually happened there. Truth be told, the people of Hickory Falls would be incredibly disappointed to learn that her evenings were spent sipping tea and cleaning cat hair off her couch rather than crafting hexes to toss onto unsuspecting shoppers at the farmers market.

Among her favorites was a rumor that she was one in a long line of Grey women who dabbled in witchcraft. How marvelous and mystical, she thought, to have some hidden knowledge of the universe. Clarity assumed it was her long hair that refused to be tamed that helped to support her image as such, or maybe her dresses that were so nonfashionable they were laughable. Then there was her isolation, miles out of town, that did nothing but add to the talk. Reality, she realized, was much more boring than the stories people fill it with.

The truth was, she had never figured out how to control her curls, so she simply let them fly. She didn't have the money for fashionable dresses, so she had to make her own. And the tiny cabin in the "haunted" woods was actually quite charming in its simplicity and a gift from one of her grandmother's carpenter friends, whose memory she retained only a sliver of.

The mid-October wind had picked up a bit, adding a chill as it sent fallen leaves into frenzied flight patterns throughout the air. Clarity wrapped the green velvet cloak around her a bit tighter, bunching up its fabric around her neck with one hand while she carried a wicker basket full of orange- and red-colored chrysanthemums in the other. She made her way quickly down Main Street, aware that she looked every part the witch that so many people suspected her to be as her hair danced crazily behind her, and her cloak flew like a cape in the wind. A green velvet cloak might not be to everyone's taste, but she hadn't been able to let this one go when she spotted it at a recent flea market a few towns away. Intricate white and pink flowers were sewn along each sleeve cuff and around the edge of a hood that wouldn't stay in place. Most importantly, it was heavy and warm, and she was going to need all the warmth she could get as she rounded the corner off Main Street and headed out of town.

The houses grew farther apart as she walked, whole pumpkins and those carved by Halloween-excited children lined many of the porches, a tissue paper ghost flying in the wind on one door, secured only by what looked like a hook clinging to the top of its head. Although it was only midafternoon, the clouds overhead had smothered any sunlight, and the darkness only seemed to grow as Clarity walked by the last house on the street and stepped onto the dirt path that led to her final destination. She had walked this path many times before, but usually in nicer weather, the bare tree limbs and crisp leaves underfoot a reminder that the harshness of winter was soon to come.

Clarity switched the basket from one arm to the other and picked up the edge of her cloak to keep it from snagging on the rocks and a few fallen branches, startling a squirrel gathering nuts in the process.

"Don't mind me, little one. You'll need those nuts for winter."

The squirrel froze in place and stared straight ahead, the way squirrels do in hopes of becoming invisible. When it realized that she was continuing to walk its way, the squirrel stuffed another nut into its already-full cheeks and scurried up the nearest tree.

The walk was less than half a mile but felt much longer on this particular day, parts of the walking path almost completely dark thanks to the clouds and giant trees that still managed to offer shade without any leaves. She really hadn't wanted to visit today, but it had been a while, and she felt guilty. If she didn't go, nobody else would. She was the only one left.

"Thank you, hill," she said, grateful for a brief reprieve from the wind as she made her way up the terrain that protected her from the elements. She tried to enjoy it while she could, knowing from past experiences that any weather was magnified once she reached the top of the hill. The good news was she was almost there. The hill was the final landmark. Clutching her hood around her face in anticipation, Clarity reached the top and steadied herself from the wind gust that awaited her, lowering her head and letting her hair cover her face as another layer of insulation.

Relieved to have arrived, Clarity glanced around her to assess whether anything had changed since her last visit. It was a funny tradition because nothing ever did, but she did it all the same.

This time, however, she did spot something in the distance that confirmed a rumor she had heard around town. Long metal poles stuck out of the ground every ten feet or so on the far side, signaling truth to the rumor that the town planned to build a fence around the old cemetery. Why they would do such a thing was lost on Clarity. A fence around a cemetery? Who were they trying to keep in—or out? This particular cemetery predated the town and held more history than any of the buildings that boasted to have some historical significance in Hickory Falls. She couldn't understand the bother. These souls had lain peacefully for decades; let them rest.

"Hello, Edward," Clarity said, addressing a grave as she walked by. She didn't know Edward, nor anyone in his family, but greeted him every time she visited the cemetery. Engraved under his name was "GOODBYE," which Clarity thought was quite beautiful in its simplicity. According to the dates on the marker, Edward had lived to be ninety-two years old before he passed away in 1904, a truly remarkable feat for the time, so Clarity liked to think that he was quite ready to go when the time came, and content to wave farewell.

"You're looking lovely today, Sophia," she said passing another grave. Sophia wasn't one that she spoke to on a regular basis, but she didn't want anyone there to feel left out. Clarity walked with a purpose toward the far corner of the cemetery and stopped in front of a line of grave markers identical to the ones next to them. This was her family—the Grey women. People undoubtedly found it odd that the women in her family were all buried side by side and memorialized with the Grey name, regardless of marriage status at the time of death. Clarity found it odd as well when her mother had brought her here for the first time and explained the family tradition. They did so—not out of disrespect for their husbands or other family members—but out of respect for the bond between the Grey women and the significance of their role in the family unit, and because of the sanctity of tradition. Women in her family, even when minimized in the views of modern-day society, were always treated as powerful, intelligent, and strong creatures.

As her mother, Enid, had explained to her, women's lives on earth were devoted to growth in family, community, and spiritualism. In death, the Grey women would lie together in unity and help guide one another to the other side.

"After we take our last breath, we reconnect and celebrate our time here," her mom explained. "Women are nurturers. We devote our lives to making people feel safe and comfortable, so we lie side by side in death and celebrate our love for one another. As Grey women."

When Clarity was young, she thought of it as a tea party, a description that her mother had loved and adopted. Thereafter, when she came with Enid to distribute flowers and well wishes to her family members in the cemetery, they would always refer to it as "meeting the ladies for tea." Clarity even recalled a few times when her mom had packed a blanket and cookies for the occasion.

Yes, Clarity was well-aware of her reputation in Hickory Falls, as well as the reputation of those who came before her. They lived and loved uniquely, believed in the magic of nature and the power of love's tightly woven bond. They were misunderstood and at times even feared, but others' judgment never swayed them from living their lives in the truest form. As her grandmother once told her, everyone has a reputation. The key is to own it if true and to resist adapting to reputations that are not. The key was drowning out the chatter and always listening to her own inner voice.

Clarity took the flowers from her basket, and brushing off any foliage that had fallen on each marker, adorned her mother, aunts, grandmother, and great-grandmother with a touch of orange and red. She sat down on the grass and took an orange from the bottom of the basket and started to peel. Looking from one marker to the other, she popped the first orange slice into her mouth and began their tea session.

"Hello, lovely ladies. How are you all today?"

Chapter Twelve

It just didn't seem right to be standing there, picking out oranges.

Cora tore a plastic bag off the roller and struggled to open it, fighting with the plastic before dramatically tossing it aside and grabbing a new one. It wasn't healthy to take out her frustrations on helpless fruit bags, but she had no training in post-tornado trauma and was doing the best she could. The storm might have passed, but her nerves had been sucked up into its cyclone and spit out somewhere far away, leaving her with only a thin layer of emotions left to tackle the day-to-day issues like seams of plastic bags that are suctioned together. She only had a small reserve of emotional stamina left and couldn't waste it in the produce section of the local grocery store.

Cora had been lucky, or at least that was the word used by the reporters who had been canvassing the town in colorful rain parkas embroidered with their station's logos. Her apartment building, an old warehouse along the river's waterfront, had been spared with the rest of the historic downtown area when the tornado spun off the bluffs and flew over them before settling back again on the outskirts of town. There had apparently been more than one twister, a small and destructive army of spinning storms that had destroyed properties, crops, and one overpass that left a car dangling over its edge.

When Elliott could finally get to her apartment, they had watched the news in horror for the rest of the day, Cora too frightened to look outside and see the reality of the aftermath of nature's wrath. She watched the news coverage like it had happened in another town, far away. Sure, there had been storms in California, but it hadn't been until she moved to the Midwest that she'd realized how cruel and unforgiving Mother Nature was. Almost immediately after the twisters had ripped through, forever changing some people's lives, the sun had started shining as if to say, "Who *me*? I didn't do anything."

Cora had yet to choose an orange. Some were too hard, others damaged or knotty in spots. She examined each orange like a precious gem, tossing them back onto the pile one by one. She felt guilty grocery shopping so soon after the storm. There were people tiptoeing through rubble to find anything worth keeping from their prior lives, and here she was, filling her cart with Gouda, grapes, and a red wine that she had chosen based solely on its label. She had told herself that it was okay to go out, that she still had to eat. Her package of smoked almonds wasn't going to sustain her for long, but she still felt strange being here in the supermarket with its fluorescent lighting and light rock from the eighties accompanying her down the aisles. Truth be told, she had decided to come in part to get away from the news and the neighbors gathered in the hallway, sharing stories about recovery efforts or accounts of people who had not yet been heard from. The people who were still *missing*.

Missing. That word seemed to be haunting Cora lately.

She chose four oranges randomly and twisted the bag shut, suddenly in a hurry to get back to her apartment. There was a lot more she needed, but she really didn't feel up to the thought process that went into cooking actual meals. Cora could easily survive on roasted red pepper hummus—her favorite—and cheese and crackers. Toss in popcorn and a few cans of soup, and she was good to go. She grabbed a bag of sea salt chips from the end of an aisle before taking a sharp left toward the check-out, driving a bit recklessly by shopping cart standards, and ran into a cart coming from the other direction.

"Oh, good grief, I'm so sorry!" Cora was still so shaken by yesterday's storm that she found even this tiny collision unnerving. "Totally my fault." She felt her face flush and her stomach lurch, both rather severe reactions to such a minor event.

"Oh, hon, aren't you a little pile of nerves." The woman picked up a bag of pasta that had fallen from her heaping cart and tried to get it to balance on top again. It took a minute for Cora to process who was in front of her. Seeing someone out of context has a way of reverting them to virtual strangers. "My grandbabies are coming to visit me, so I'm afraid I've bought enough food for ten families here. Makes it so hard to steer!"

"Beverly!" Just as the color of her cheeks returned to normal, Cora became flushed again, but this time out of embarrassment. "Oh my gosh, now I feel even worse. I'm so sorry. I'm very distracted today." She pulled her ponytail a bit tighter and ran a finger under each eye to remove any lingering mascara from the day before. It's always at those times in life when a person feels the most vulnerable that they end up running into someone and are forced into polite chitchat. Not only that, but the universe must get a giggle from setting up such run-ins in grocery stores.

"Honey, we all are. God bless those families who lost so much yesterday, especially those who lost so much more than their possessions. It's so terrible." Beverly's eyes started to water. She touched her chest, a gesture that Cora assumed was to feel Evelyn's ring on its long gold chain. It was such a sweet thing to do that Cora felt her guard drop a bit. Beverly didn't care what she looked like on the heels of such a town tragedy. She was only here buying groceries for her grandbabies and trying to cope, like the rest of Hickory Falls. Cora spotted a large tub of chocolate-chip ice cream in Beverly's cart and felt comfort in knowing that some methods of coping are universal.

"Are you and your husband okay?" Cora asked, shocked that she hadn't thought about Beverly's old farmhouse, out there in the open, or Hazel's tiny cottage in the woods. "The whole thing was so scary. I've never experienced anything like it. It was exactly like what you think a tornado will be, but ten times worse. I hope you and your sisters made it through without losing anything. On my way here, I drove by so much stuff on the streets and in parking lots. It's hard to know what belonged there and what flew in from somewhere else."

Beverly smiled warmly at the question. "So sweet of you to ask, but we're all okay. The winds were pretty harsh at the farm and did some damage, but it's nothing that we can't fix with a bit of elbow grease and time. When one of those storms whips through, you really just have to say a prayer and let God decide what will be spared. He's the only one in control."

"I've never been so scared in my life," Cora repeated, an image of her parents' car accident suddenly flashing across her mind. "Well, it was one of the scariest moments, at least. I'm glad you're all okay." She said the last bit realizing that Beverly had never really confirmed that Ruth and Hazel were fine, but assuming she wouldn't be here buying pasta and fruit juice if they weren't.

"Oh, I can imagine how scary it was for you being new to these parts. I'm not saying that I don't find them terrifying, but I've lost count of how many storms I've lived through over the years. Some have a bark much bigger than their bite, but others aren't satisfied with leaving until they've left a mess of the place. It's simply what one expects living in this part of the country." Cora smiled and looked at clock on the wall as if she had somewhere to be, a gesture that Beverly must have noticed. "So, listen, hon." Beverly came around her shopping cart and took Cora gently by the arm, steering her to the side of the aisle before she had a chance to leave. "I've been wanting to talk to you about something since I heard. Ruthie told me that you went to visit Hazel."

Whatever emotional stamina Cora had left drained from her body. Ruth was the one who told her *not* to tell Beverly that she was going to talk to Hazel, so it was unexpected that she herself had spilled the beans. These sisters apparently couldn't keep secrets from each other, which was either a good or a bad thing, depending on the side of the secret one was on. Regardless of how she'd found out, Beverly now knew and clearly wasn't pleased. Her pleasant smile remained, but it was more the kind that parents have when scolding their kids in public. The smile was for others; the message for Cora had a sharper edge.

"Listen, I don't want to get involved in any family drama or anything," Cora explained. "Since I talked to you and Ruth, it just seemed like the right thing to do. You know, doing my whole due diligence and all." Cora laughed nervously, completely failing in her attempt to make light of the situation. It was true; she didn't want to get involved in any family drama, but every time she tried to put a cork into this mystery's bottle, another bubble seemed to pop up and shoot the top right off. Like the scolded kid in the candy store, she was trying to explain her actions.

"Oh, honey, there's no need to apologize." Beverly's face softened and she now seemed more concerned than upset, biting her bottom lip before continuing. She smiled and nodded at a woman passing by, waiting for her to round the corner before taking up their conversation again. "Families are complicated, and mine is no different," she said. "We've had our ups and downs, missteps and misadventures. We always find our way back to one another, but that doesn't mean the history isn't painful sometimes. My dad made some missteps; he went through some things when he was a younger man, dealing with the stress of being a new husband and father. That time period was a really horrible one for all of us, and I just don't like to revisit it."

Cora felt terrible. She liked Beverly. She liked all three sisters and didn't want to hurt any of them. She had spent many a night over a glass of wine, pondering if this little quest was more for them or her, a harmless little adventure to fill her time and pour a little excitement into her life. She had always convinced herself that it was truly for the good of the family because the rings had to be returned, but now doubt was creeping in again because harm had been caused. The rings were opening old wounds and the kind that Hickory Falls residents didn't like to admit existed. Here she was, standing in the grocery store next to organic spaghetti sauce, unsure of her next move. She didn't want to hurt any of these women but had so many questions about Clarity's disappearance.

"Beverly, I never intended to pry into your family's history—please know that. I just wanted to make sure that Hazel didn't have a connection to the rings before I agreed to keep them."

"And did she?" Beverly's eyes looked on the verge of tears again. Cora had taken all of this too far. She was now making sweet little women cry. "You know, never mind that," Beverly said before Cora had a chance to answer. "I don't even want to know. That was all such a long time ago. Hazel's been through a lot too, goodness knows. I mean, what kind of mother leaves her only daughter? But you know, her mother was one of *those* women." She said the last bit in a whisper with a bit of side eye just as a cart pulled up to them, and the woman driving it touched Beverly on the sleeve.

"Oh, Helen, how are you?" Beverly said, startled. Her voice had returned to a normal octave.

"Oh, Bev, I don't want to interrupt, but I just want to make sure you are all okay out there after the storm. Good heavens, it was a rough one." Helen looked like what a Helen should look like: gray hair curled into a classic school-secretary style, with pearl earrings and a camel-colored cardigan.

"Oh, we're fine, we're fine." Beverly said. "It was a nasty one, though. I hear the Kennedy's lost their entire fence, and most of their cows decided to leave on some cross-county adventure. They're finding them everywhere. One was wandering around the Higgins grocery store parking lot fifteen miles away in Scott-sworth!" Helen didn't know what to do with such information, waving her hand in the air in silent reprimand of cows gone wild.

"Well, you take care," she said, glancing at Cora to signal she understood she had interrupted a conversation. "So sorry to interrupt."

"Not at all. Coffee next week?"

"That would be wonderful. I better get home now. Roast won't cook itself." Helen wheeled away, but not without first giving Cora a quick full-body glance. She was clearly curious about the disheveled young woman talking to her friend, and a bit disappointed that she had not been introduced. Cora waited an appropriate amount of time before returning to the topic at hand.

Those women, Cora thought. She considered her options. She could bid Beverly goodbye and continue her shopping, or she could follow up and see what she could find out. She figured she had come too far to retreat now. "I'm just curious. What do you mean that Clarity was one of *those* women?"

"Oh, you know dear. A bit of a *hussy.*" Beverly said the word with such disdain that Cora was a bit taken aback. *Hussy* wasn't exactly a word that one heard anymore, but she understood its meaning from a different time. Even if she didn't, the way that Beverly spoke the word with such righteous indignation was all any listener would need to understand the context. "She wasn't from around here—just moved here to find someone, and once she did, moved on when she found someone better. She broke up my family and almost succeeded in breaking up another because she set her sights on the doctor in town. Thank goodness he didn't fall for it. No, I suspect she found some wealthy married man in another town and simply moved on."

It was a lot of information, spoken with barely a breath taken.

So, Beverly considered Clarity to have been a gold digger of sorts, preying on men and moving on when better opportunities presented themselves. She clearly believed that Clarity had left of her own freewill, abandoning her husband and daughter.

There were so many things that Cora wanted to say but didn't dare, not in the middle of the spaghetti sauce aisle. *What about the blood? Why wouldn't she have taken Hazel? Why the tools left behind like she was in the middle of gardening?* These were all loaded questions—and not the kind to ask a woman who had lived with a very specific narrative of an event all of her life, a narrative most likely told to her from those she loved and trusted the most. No, a person doesn't start to chisel away at someone's reality when all they have is a bit of research and a nagging hunch.

"I understand, and believe me, I'm only trying to do the right thing here. I'm sure the whole thing will be wrapped up soon. Either the rings will find their rightful owner, or I'll keep them and treat them with the respect they deserve." Cora maneuvered her cart back into the driving lane and was relieved to get going again. This day would never end.

Beverly made no motion to move, however. She continued to stand alongside her cart, weighing something that she was about to say. "I merely want to make sure that you're not involving my father in any of this," she said. "He's almost one hundred years old. He's lived more life than most have the honor to, and I want to make sure the energy around him is full of love and positivity in the time he has left. I don't want some of the worst years of his life brought back up. He doesn't deserve that."

Cora had nothing left. She was exhausted and anxious to get home so she could eat the Gouda and drink the wine. That was all she wanted—cheese and wine and maybe a reality TV show that required no thought.

"Of course, Beverly. " She glanced at the clock again to signal she was needed somewhere soon, and began to turn toward the exit.

"Will you?" Beverly didn't move from her position and again took hold of Cora's arm to regain her attention. "Do I have your word that you will drop this?"

Cora forced a smile. Being asked not to burden an elderly man with questions was one thing, but being asked to drop the ring issue entirely was another, especially when Beverly had shown no interest in the rings at all and really shouldn't care. Cora couldn't help but feel a bit protective of Hazel right now, her waves of emotion during their conversation holding steady in Cora's mind and heart. "Yes, perhaps."

Cora smiled in goodbye as she left Beverly for the checkout line at the front of the store. She thought about the clothes that she had forgotten in the dryer, and the new art-heist documentary that she had wanted to watch on Netflix. She thought about dinner with Elliott's parents tomorrow night and whether post-tornado trauma was a legitimate reason to reschedule. She thought about the mildew that she couldn't get off her shower door and the library books she had forgotten to drop off that morning. Cora thought about all of these things as she made her way out of the store, to keep herself from thinking about the plans she had with Hazel to meet Lewis this week, a meeting that she had pretty much promised Beverly would never happen.

Chapter Thirteen

~

"The chicken cordon bleu is always a good option, maybe a few baby carrots on the side with spinach salad. Don't you think, Wade?" Lydia refolded and smoothed the napkin on her lap and took a sip from her glass of chardonnay, leaving a red lip stain on its rim.

"That's an option, but you need to offer steak as well. I don't care what anyone says, people love red meat. They come to a wedding to drink themselves into oblivion and eat. People always remember the food. I can't recall a single wedding ceremony that I've ever attended, but I can tell you which receptions served the good stuff."

"Well, except for ours, of course," Lydia chimed in, shooting a warning shot her husband's way. "You remember our wedding ceremony."

"Of course, dear," Wade said, winking to Elliott as he cut another bite of his porterhouse steak and dipped it in his mashed potatoes. "What do you kids want? Our opinions don't really matter." Cora spotted Lydia deliver another warning stare his way, but he didn't seem to notice. Wade, sharply dressed in a starched shirt and tie, was too busy rearranging his mashed potatoes on the plate and preventing his tie from dipping in the gravy to pay his wife too much attention. A new song streamed through the speakers overhead; Cora couldn't place it at first, but then realized that it was an instrumental version of "Staying Alive" by the Bee Gees.

Despite standing in her closet, lamenting the lack of country-club wear she appeared to own, Cora looked every bit the part of the dentist's future wife that evening. She wore an off-the-shoulder black cashmere sweater, with her hair swept up into a loose bun; and her mother's single strand of pearls—the nicest jewelry she owned—showcased both beautifully. She didn't love the country-club setting, but didn't loathe it either; she enjoyed the people watching as families strolled through the mahogany doorway and greeted one another as if they hadn't just finished their latest tennis match in a tie-breaker third set and seen each other an hour before. The music fell somewhere between elevator tunes and dentist-office-waiting-area music, soothing piano accompanying the delivery of silver trays and iced teas. It was all very civilized, and after the stress of the week, Cora was perfectly fine pretending to be civilized for an evening. Although part of her had hoped the evening would be canceled, she now welcomed the distraction. She was tired and her pasta primavera was better than anything she could have whipped up at home.

"You know, we've been talking about options and really like the thought of getting married outside somewhere," Elliott said, focusing on his plate of food so he didn't have to lock eyes with his parents. "Nothing too big or fancy. Maybe just a ceremony in the arboretum and a party after. There are some really great venues in the warehouse district." The waiter arrived with another whiskey on the rocks and switched it out with Elliott's first. His timing was a welcome interruption as Elliott took a stiff sip and pursed his lips from the burn.

Wade paused for a second, eyebrows raised in thought before he uttered "hmm" and shoved another forkful of red-meat-and-potato goodness into his mouth. He didn't really appear bothered by the idea, perhaps just surprised that something like that was even a possibility. Cora wondered if he had ever been to an outside wedding ceremony or if the towering white stone church that overlooked the town on the bluff was always a given in this town. She really wasn't worried about Wade's reaction; if he drank and ate well, of course, and they played his favorite James Taylor tunes at the reception, he'd be fine.

Then there was Lydia. Cora walked an emotional tightrope with her future mother-in-law, teetering to one side when she felt accepted and toward the other when she felt like the quirky art girl from California who would never fit in. Regardless, she constantly felt off balance with Lydia, as if a strong wind or wrong word could send her plummeting from the tightrope to her death below.

Just then, Cora felt something for Lydia that she had never felt before—sympathy. She tried hard not to laugh at the expression of the woman sitting across the table from her. Lydia just sat there and smiled, the kind of smile that wants desperately to convey everything is okay when every emotion on her face suggested otherwise. She started to blink rapidly and took another drink of her chardonnay, this one much more robust than her first. There Lydia sat, a woman who found herself on a train moving entirely in the wrong direction, but too polite to call the conductor and ask to be let off. She pretended to enjoy the strange landscape passing by. She was finally able to utter a single word.

"Outside?"

"I really think we can come up with something that everyone loves," Cora said enthusiastically. "Maybe an outside ceremony and reception with music that we all love, a cool drink bar, and maybe even some amazing chicken cordon bleu." The last bit was a hail Mary because Cora had never tried the dish.

Elliott put a hand on top of hers to signal that it was okay. He wasn't flustered a bit and didn't want Cora to be either. "Listen, more than anything, we just want to have a fun wedding. We want to welcome everyone in attendance and feel thankful that they're all there. I do *not* want to stand in a receiving line while one of you whispers the name of some guy I've never met or a lady from one of your social clubs. *Small. Intimate. Special.*" Elliott looked at his parents as if addressing a child on the verge of a tantrum. His words were chosen carefully and with intent—anyone present could have read between the lines to know that a firm message was being delivered, and he expected it to be heard.

"Honey, I know you both want something small, but Hickory Falls is—"

"Oh, it's fine," Wade cut his wife off with a wave of his fork. "Nobody in Hickory Falls is going to give a damn if they're not invited to the wedding. Let them do what they want. If there are fewer people, it's a bigger budget for food and booze." He pointed his fork at Elliott in an *aha* gesture, Wade's thoughts already on the better cuts of steak they would be able to provide. "Kids do things differently these days, dear. Not everyone wants that God-awful two-hour ceremony where everyone falls asleep or sweats to death in their suits."

"Well, suits would still be worn," Lydia announced in a panic. "Suits would still be worn, wouldn't they?"

"Mom, it's fine—don't worry. It's not like we're going to show up in Hawaiian shirts."

"Oh, how great would that be? So comfortable." Wade was now really getting into it, which caused Lydia to panic even more.

Lydia finished her glass of wine in one gulp and smiled again, staring blankly out the window on a train that was carrying her farther and farther from her destination. Cora smiled back, hoping to express her appreciation for their understanding, but not really sure if it had been received. The strong, independent side of her told her that she needed to be welcomed for who she was, but there was still that part that yearned for acceptance from her future in-laws. Wade was clearly not an issue. He was now jokingly suggesting that they forego steaks altogether and go for the pig in the ground thing, an image that was able to push Lydia completely over the edge.

"Well, I was going to wait until coffee and dessert to go over this, but I guess we could do it now." Lydia pulled a black binder out from under her chair with the sad resignation of someone whose careful planning had been for nothing. "These are simply a few things that I pulled together after you two got engaged. You know, thoughts on caterers and floral arrangements. Songs that have been played at every wedding since, oh, I guess as far back as anyone can remember. I've provided the beginning of a guest list, though I'm still working on it. You know, just a few things, if you find them helpful."

Cora accepted the binder, her wrist giving out from the weight and knocking over an empty water glass. "Oh, wow. Thank you so much. We will do everything we can to incorporate some of these wonderful family traditions." She could feel Elliott's stare but resisted looking his way. He might feel comfortable drawing firm lines in the sand with his parents, but she didn't. They were going to be her family and had been nothing but kind to her since she moved here. Lydia had even insisted on paying when they went on a shopping spree, a gesture that Cora chose to believe was centered around kindness rather than dismay at her fashion choices. The black sweater she was wearing had, in fact, been bought that day, and Cora felt good when she saw Lydia smile upon seeing her.

In a continued effort to avoid her fiancé's amused glare, Cora leafed through the binder, pretending to have an intense interest at what lay beyond each color-coded tab. Lydia wasn't kidding; at the beginning was a typed and table-formatted list that read like a *Who's Who* of Hickory Falls. Most of the names had a distinguished prefix or suffix of some sort, *Dr.* and *Esq.* being among the most common, but a few she was going to have to look up. Elliott was the fourth generation of dentists on his father's side, which made up a fair share of those represented, but it was clear that Lydia's family was equally accomplished. The "starter" guest list was seven pages long, two columns per page, in what could easily have added up to three hundred and fifty people. A family tree was next, a piece of artwork that had been printed off in heavy cardstock complete with green leaves with red berries adorning the end of each tree branch. Registry suggestions followed, a list of wedding vendors—with some favorites highlighted—and the contact information for every reputable baker in a fifty-mile radius. This binder represented every stressful decision and attention to detail that Cora had been desperate to avoid in the wedding-planning process, and she could have panicked at the sight of it, the title of its bold font staring back at her, but she didn't. Truth be told, this wedding binder must have taken Lydia hours if not weeks of her time and would be incredibly helpful.

Wade and Elliott had changed the topic three bites ago and were now talking about a recent dental hygienist hire who wasn't turning out too well. Lydia was trying to look at ease but had resumed her routine of refolding her napkin. Her green wrap dress looked exquisite on her, not to mention very expensive, but she didn't come across like some of the more snooty of women at the club. Lydia was stunning without trying too hard, her porcelain skin the product of dedication to sunscreen and a daily moisturizing routine rather than surgery, and she managed to keep the color of her auburn hair natural looking. Some might say that the black binder was about control or a need to dictate arrangements, but others might say it was simply the efforts of a mother who wanted to be involved in her only child's big day. Cora waited until she looked up and mouthed "Thank you," with her most genuine of thankful smiles.

Lydia did not smile back.

Hickory Falls

~

December 22, 1951

There was snow and then there was *snow*, the difference being delicate flurries or getting dumped on. This storm definitely fell into the latter category. Lewis watched snowflakes the size of quarters fall steadily, aware that his trip home was growing more treacherous with every minute that he stayed. If he got stuck out here, he'd have a hard time explaining why. His prior stories about searching for wood to use in projects wasn't as believable when the world outside was covered in two feet of snow. He was only making it worse prolonging the inevitable, but the crackling fire had sucked him in, and the warm whiskey had dulled his senses enough to blur the lines of reason. He knew all of this, but yet he stayed.

"I can't believe you did this." Clarity stood in the living room, the glow from the fireplace making her oversized white sweater look like it had been adorned in flames. A log suddenly shifted under the weight of its neighbor, sending embers onto the hearth before settling into its new position. "How did you pull this off?"

She stood, hands on hips, staring at the bookcases that Lewis had built on both sides of the fireplace, the shelves reaching to the ceiling like tree branches growing toward the sun. Lewis had come up with the idea as a Christmas gift when Clarity's piles of books kept tipping over in the living room. She also really needed a place to display her smaller works of art. The size of the tiny cottage didn't really allow for big furniture pieces, so he'd decided to build something that looked like it had been there the entire time. Something store-bought didn't really seem like Clarity anyway.

"I built most of it in my shop and installed it when you were gone this morning. I have to tweak them, but I wanted them set up by the time you got back from your show." Clarity's reaction was exactly what he had wanted—complete disbelief and joy. The late hours had been worth it, her smile worth every nail and ounce of glue that held together his biggest project to date. She had already started arranging things on the shelves, admiring and commenting on each book and knickknack placed like they were old lost friends.

"The single nicest thing that anyone has ever done for me," Clarity said, walking over and wrapping her arms around his neck before planting a giant kiss on Lewis's lips. When she buried her face in his neck, he felt his entire body relax and sink into hers, letting go, for the moment, of every emotion that one can feel when they're living two different lives and walking a tightrope between. At that exact moment, Lewis was happy, but he knew it would only last until the door opened and he left to travel the road home that had now become dangerous both literally and figuratively.

He hadn't wanted this to happen, but nobody does. Lewis found it hard to believe that anyone would intentionally choose this route in life, the dark divide between his family life and time with Clarity as deep as the guilt that formed it. He had a mutual respect and love for Evelyn, and there was no end to his love for his daughter. His family was envied by churchgoers who couldn't get over the adorable hats that Beverly wore proudly or the hours that Evelyn spent establishing herself as a do-gooder within the community. When one thought of an ideal family, Lewis's was the one most often pictured, complete with Sunday ham dinner and biscuits made from scratch. How despicable of him to want more; how unforgivable to feel overwhelmed by his wife's demands for a better life. Isn't that what he was supposed to want to provide? *More?* More clothes, more opportunities, more status. Just *more.*

Here, however, in the tiny cottage being devoured by snow drifts, he was simply *enough.*

"I wish we could spend Christmas together," Clarity said, snapping him back to the present. "I know that's not possible," she said, hugging him tighter and cutting him off from the start of a reply. "It's only a wish. You need to be with your family. I can imagine how magical it is to experience Christmas through the eyes of a child."

Clarity's words tore at Lewis's heart because he knew that she meant them. She didn't want to take Lewis away from his family, even though she desperately longed for her own. She asked him about Beverly but was careful not to ask too much, mindful that his role as parental protector was sacred and not to be entwined with his feelings for her. Here in the woods, hidden from the world, they had a connection that neither could explain and rarely tried to, cherishing their time together as a fleeting little beacon of joy that burned too brightly to last for long. Clarity described their relationship like fireflies that lit up the sky on warm summer nights, darting here and there to avoid being caught, but shining brightly enough to feel seen.

Wrapping his arms around her, Lewis stayed focused on the Christmas tree in the corner, its strands of popcorn and cranberries like a scene from a postcard, with the snow falling as a backdrop in the window. Clarity had made the hand-blown glass bulbs, each a different ethereal hue that added to the magic of it all. On the top was a silver star that they had found in a flea market months ago. At the time, Lewis remembered thinking that Christmas was so far away and that by the time that star got placed on the top of a tree, things would be clearer and decisions made. He wasn't this person; he wasn't the type of guy who betrayed the people he loved and escaped to another life. Six months ago, when this star had been bought and carefully wrapped for safekeeping, he'd told himself that the holidays would bring answers, yet here he stood, watching snowflakes fall and wishing he could hide himself among them.

Clarity pulled herself away and walked into the kitchen, her signature move when emotions ran high and she didn't want to address them. Lewis saw her wipe a tear away as she fumbled with coffee cups that didn't require straightening, the sound of Frank Sinatra singing "It Came Upon a Midnight Clear" coming softly from the phonograph. Lewis watched as she stood mesmerized by the falling snow outside the kitchen window, her long dark hair useful for hiding tears that she didn't want him to see. Clarity hadn't wanted any of this either. Their relationship was like the fire crackling a few feet away from Lewis, slow-burning embers that had been in the right place at the right time to spark a genuine flame.

Lewis allowed himself to imagine this as his life, a life in the forest, with its smell of pine needles and snow drifts along the windowpanes. He felt an inner warmth take hold, a combination of exhilaration and whiskey enveloping him in a comforting hug. Lewis draped his coat, which he had thrown over his arm, back on the chair and sank into the weathered couch, tossing his shoes off to feel the stinging heat of the fire on his feet. He didn't mind the pain; it was nice to feel something in such a literal way. He had told himself that his secrets were to avoid causing pain, when they were in fact self-serving and to spare the need to answer for his actions. A man can tell himself all sorts of things to justify bad behavior. *Life is short. I deserve happiness. If nobody is hurt, it's okay.* Those excuses will build on each other until the words become meaningless, however, a pile of empty letters that no longer form words that matter. Lewis had told himself all sorts of things to explain away his indiscretions and decisions, but in his heart he knew what he had to do. This was a season for love and forgiveness, and he could only pray that he was worthy of both.

The time had come.

Chapter Fourteen

Cora pulled into the stately entrance, giant concrete columns bordered by manicured peony bushes on each side welcoming visitors to the Hickory Falls Retirement Village. She always found the village reference a bit strange, images of old people living in mushroom-shaped houses in the middle of a forest a vision that her younger self carried around for years.

Nestled between Main Street and the town's riverfront park, this was no forest retreat, but a stately complex with a mansion-like facade for its entrance and circle drive. It welcomed prospective residents with images of grandeur and a lifestyle they deserved in their golden years. Wrought-iron tables and chairs were scattered among the front lawn in the shade of hundred-year-old oak trees. Cora couldn't help but notice that nobody was sitting at them except for a few squirrels who were in the middle of a discussion on top of one of the tables.

A group of men with chainsaws was busy slicing pieces of a tree that had fallen in the yard, presumably from the recent storm, the severity of the sound cutting through the peacefulness of the grounds like a sharp knife. The squirrels didn't seem bothered; they were living their best life and chatting the way that animals do when they think nobody is watching. A groundskeeper looked up and waved as Cora made her way up the drive, but then promptly returned her attention to an overturned flowerpot that was lying on its side and spewing red and yellow petals. From the look of the similar overturned pots lining the drive, flowers in retirement villages were among the innocent victims of the storm.

Cora spotted Hazel standing under the entrance's canopy, and waved as she pulled into one of the parking spots designated for visitors. Her heart raced a bit as she fumbled with her keys and perched her sunglasses on the top of her head. She really didn't want to be here and didn't know why she was, accepting Hazel's invitation only because she couldn't think of a good enough reason to decline. This entire ring thing was a family issue, a personal one that involved scandals, hurt feelings, tension, and town gossip dating back decades. Now that it also involved a disappearance, Cora was even more eager to sever ties. She had decided that this was it. This dive into the Clarity Shaw mystery would be her last, and whether the rings belonged to the missing woman or not, she would leave them with Hazel and drive away from the entire thing today. Of that, she was certain. She was already dealing with the guilt of lying to Beverly about being here. She couldn't handle all of this. There was a wedding to plan and in-laws to win over, and her time was best spent doing both.

"Hello, dear." Hazel welcomed her with a waving hand, the other wrestling with a few hairs dancing across her face. "What a windy day. Dad's just had lunch, so we don't have much time before he takes his afternoon nap." With that quick introduction, she pulled open one of the heavy entrance doors that welcomed visitors into the village. It had gold-etched lettering on its glass and the hint of cleaning products lingered beneath the scent of lavender air freshener.

"Hi, Sue." Hazel walked up to the front desk, and the gray-haired woman behind the counter smiled and glanced at Cora long enough to make sure she was with Hazel and not a stranger taking advantage of the open door. "We're just popping in for a quick visit after lunch. Beef stew today?"

"Hamburgers," the woman responded.

"Oh, that probably didn't go over well."

"No. The man really likes his beef stew. But I made sure he had a good-sized piece of strawberry shortcake for dessert, to ease the disappointment."

"Ah, well, I appreciate that. We won't be long."

"No problem. He might be a bit tired because Beverly was by to see him this morning. He's quite popular lately." Sue returned to her work and her cup of coffee, a few drops of dark brew falling from the side of the cup and onto the papers she was filing. "Oh, dang it. What a mess."

"How was he after Beverly's visit?" Hazel asked, her smile now a bit faded. "Everything go okay? You know how she's been with these birthday plans. He couldn't care less about a big party, but she insists."

"Oh, give the man some cake, and he'll be fine." Sue was too busy blotting the papers with a tissue to respond with anything more.

Hazel made her way further into the belly of the main building; leather couches, silk floral arrangements, and a stand-alone popcorn maker designated it as a common room space for movie nights, card games, and old people get-togethers.

They walked past two women sitting at a corner table, nibbling on cookies and sipping tea from flower-patterned cups. One of the women wore a hat, and Cora wondered if it was an afternoon tradition.

Hazel walked at a pace that was hard to keep up with as she weaved through the furniture toward a door on the far end, flashing a card in front of a black security system screen to gain entry. Cora followed her into a long dimly lit hallway with doors on both sides, each with a gold number and some with wreaths welcoming visitors. There were no mushroom-shaped houses here, only an apartment-like complex with bird-nest wreaths and a few chalk message boards identifying residents. Cora almost ran into Hazel when she stopped, her attention diverted for an instant to a door reminding neighbors of a happy hour and a sing-along later that day.

Hazel knocked lightly on a door with no wreath or message board, just a plate identifying its resident as L. Shaw.

"Hi, Dad—it's Hazel."

Hazel let herself in, and Cora was immediately hit with the smell of pipe tobacco. Surprised that residents were allowed to smoke in their rooms, she was relieved to see a diffuser in the corner of the room, sending a steady plume of muskiness into the air. This man might be surrounded by bird-nest wreaths, but he wasn't going to let anyone fill the room with lavender. Cora liked him immediately.

"How's it going today, Dad?" Hazel gestured for Cora to follow her and sit down on a small sofa facing a man nestled in his wheelchair, under a buffalo plaid blanket. He didn't look like he was nearing one hundred years old. His eyes were an astonishing blue, and his thin white hair was combed neatly from a side part. His face lit up as Hazel leaned down for a hug and a cheek kiss.

The room was nice enough—lots of natural light from giant windows overlooking a garden. A bit cramped with a bed, couch, and dresser, but the walls were painted a warm gray and full of framed photographs and paintings, some the products of finger paintings by grandchildren—or more likely great-grandchildren, at this point. The gallery wall facing his bed was the most eclectic: a canvas of a nude woman covered by strategically placed birds was the focal point, surrounded by smaller pieces that looked like they could be painted by the same artist, based on color and style.

"My mom painted all of those," Hazel said, noticing Cora's stare. "The bird painting was one of her favorites, and it's fun to see people's reactions when they come into his room." She laughed and grabbed her father's hand like two people do when only they share a memory or secret.

"It's beautiful," Cora said, hoping to sound sincere.

"Oh, it's not for everyone, but then again, neither was my mom. She was a living rendition of her artwork, wasn't she, Dad? Beautiful and a little misunderstood."

He seemed to lose himself in the painting for a spell, his smile one of agreement, but his eyes distant, lost in a memory.

"Dad, I want you to meet someone, a new friend of mine. This is Cora. Cora, this is my dad, Lewis."

Lewis smiled and nodded in understanding. "Hello, dear," he said softly, the same greeting she'd received when meeting his daughter. His eyes twinkled, the soul of a much younger man still evident among the deep wrinkles and sun spots. He again turned his gaze to his daughter, his eyes tired.

"How were the hamburgers for lunch?"

Lewis waved a hand in irritation, as if Hazel already knew the answer.

"Well, sounds like the strawberry shortcake might have helped."

He shrugged his shoulders the way old men do when they don't agree, but don't want to get into an actual discussion about it.

"So, listen, Dad—we have something to show you. It's really pretty remarkable, even if it doesn't end up being what I think it is. Cora found something that might be Mom's. I think I remember them, but I'm not sure if it's just because I'd love for them to be hers. Will you take a look for me?" Hazel paused, taking in a breath and searching her father's eyes for understanding before continuing. "I think she might have found Mom's wedding rings."

Lewis stopped smiling. Cora watched the color drain from his skin and the hollowness of his cheeks appear to deepen. He said nothing, searching Hazel's eyes for an explanation. When he found none, he looked at Cora. Hazel nodded silently toward her, clasping her hands nervously as Cora pulled out the small bag that now housed a huge mystery. She handed the rings to Hazel, who showed them to her father, picking up each one in turn so he could see them clearly.

Cora knew immediately. He saw a ghost in these rings, one that was as clear to him as if it were standing in the middle of the room, so grateful to finally be seen. Without a doubt—these rings had once belonged to Clarity.

Lewis struggled to speak, his hands twitching and his eyes glistening with tears. His breathing became labored, and Cora was concerned this was all too much for him. She started to lean toward Hazel to pull her back, but they were already on the same page. Hazel closed her fist to hide the rings and put a supportive hand on her dad's arm, steadying him in a feeble attempt to bring calm to the situation. But her father wasn't having any of it.

"Where did you get these?" His eyes were still kind, but his jaw was now set and his voice an octave lower. This was the question that she had been afraid of. This was the exact exchange that she had imagined hours upon hours the night before in her failed attempts at sleep. How could she tell a one-hundred-year-old man that she'd found his missing wife's rings in an estate sale of another wife? She simply couldn't. She should leave the rings and walk away. It was exactly what Cora would have done had she not felt cemented in place by his stare. Hazel stepped in to save her.

"She's new to town and just passed by an estate sale. She has no idea whose it was." Cora smiled reassuringly, but she was no liar. Her hands were shaking as she struggled to put the rings back into the bag. "Are you sure these are Mom's? How can you know?"

Lewis held out his hand, trembling as she placed the rings onto his palm. He delicately traced their details as if the slightest touch might damage them, even though they had survived among the dust and dirt in the bottom of a jar for years.

"These rings are your mother's," Lewis said, his voice steadied by a strength much greater than a man his age could possibly have.

"Well, this is amazing. The important thing is that they've found their way back to us after all these years." Hazel looked genuinely happy, her eyes jumping around the room to avoid her father's stare as he continued to search hers for answers. Cora sat there, stunned, eager for the time when she could make her escape and leave the mysterious details of this exchange behind. She didn't want to be part of this anymore. She wanted to focus on reception food that she didn't care about and debate whether people even signed wedding guest books anymore. She was relieved to be free of the rings. The rightful owner had been found, and her job was done here. The end.

"I know." Lewis's voice was so frail at this point that both Hazel and Cora struggled to hear him.

"What, Dad?"

"I *know.*"

Lewis's eyes began to tear up and his bottom lip trembled, but Cora sensed his demeanor change was due to anger rather than sadness. With an open palm, he patted one arm of the wheelchair harder and harder, a single tear now falling.

Hazel looked at Cora, concerned, her eyes pleading with her to help in a way that Cora didn't understand.

Lewis whispered something.

Hazel leaned in, and despite not wanting to get involved, Cora did the same. She needed to hear what he said.

Lewis stared at the painting behind them, his eyes fixed on the centerpiece of the gallery wall.

"I know who took your mother from us."

Cora felt sick. Hazel's eyes grew wide and confused. She shook her head to stop her dad from saying something that she either wasn't prepared for or didn't want to hear, but he had opened a door and was ready to walk through.

"I know who killed your mother." Lewis seemed to transform before Cora's eyes. A younger man, full of anger and pain, could be felt in the room, someone willing to speak words that had broken free from their lock and chains. Lewis wasn't looking at either of them. His focus had shifted to the window, in search of a memory that had been buried for too long.

"His name is Jack Manchester."

*   *   *

Cora swung the front door open a bit too forcefully, almost knocking down an older woman who was walking arm in arm with a deeply tanned man in a pink and white plaid button-down shirt. She smiled, but it didn't stop him from giving her an annoyed look as she held the door open for them in silent apology as they entered. Cora made her way toward her car, navigating a maze of groundskeepers weeding the front flowers and a crew still grappling with the carnage left after the storm.

Jack Manchester.

She shouldn't have left the room so quickly, but there was something about hearing an actual name associated with this mess that made it a bit too real for Cora. Names accompanied people, and people lived actual lives that were affected by some silly rings found in the bottom of a jar bought for five dollars at an estate sale.

Cora didn't even notice as she made her way through a cloud of dust and wood chips shooting from the edge of a chainsaw biting through a branch nearby.

Jack Manchester.

Manchester.

Could it be the M *from the engraving inside the ring?*

Cora willed the thought away. It simply didn't make sense. The engraving of a wedding ring occurs before a wedding, not after, and a wedding band would never be altered to include the name of anyone other than a spouse.

Right?

Cora fumbled for her keys and repeatedly hit the button to unlock the door as she approached. She couldn't erase the vision of Lewis in her mind, his soft eyes changing so rapidly within seconds.

When she had excused herself so suddenly, Cora explained she didn't want to be involved in such a personal family situation, and that was definitely true. What she was now admitting to herself as she reached her car and entered its sauna-like interior was that she had left for another reason. Lewis's change in demeanor had been so drastic, so jarring in its intensity, that she didn't feel comfortable being there. She had watched as his hands gripped the handles of his wheelchair and his jaw tightened. The glisten of sadness in his eyes had hardened to a steely gaze. Cora had left for a lot of reasons, but there was no mistaking what she'd witnessed in that room.

Pure rage.

Hickory Falls

~

January 1952

Evelyn took the news worse than was expected because she found out on her own before Lewis had the chance to come clean. With as many blessings as a small town brings, the lack of true anonymity is a curse that residents bear because of watchful eyes everywhere. It was a pair of those eyes that caught sight of Lewis's truck making its way to Clarity's little cottage in the woods on more than one occasion. It would go against small town morals not to investigate further, so that same set of eyes followed him one day and saw a kiss exchanged in the doorway.

It was too bad for Lewis that those watchful eyes belonged to the biggest town gossip and long-suspected editor of the town's anonymous newsletter that shared none-of-your-business stories under the guise of neighbors looking out for one another.

Although there's never a *right* way to share such news, one would hope that a husband would tell his wife of his infidelities in private and with a level of sensitivity warranted for such a situation. Evelyn wasn't afforded such luxury; she learned about her husband's affair from the church ladies during their Wednesday afternoon sit-downs, whispered apologies shared and judgmental looks exchanged from women appalled at her husband's lack of discretion, especially given the unsavory type of woman with which he chose to commit such a sin.

One can imagine how Evelyn took the news.

Lewis's actions were bad enough, but he had done the unthinkable. He had made Evelyn the talk of the town. He had humiliated her publicly and without regard to her reputation or the long-standing impact his infidelity would have on her and Beverly. For a woman used to being a part of a group that spread such news, she had now become the feature story. With such horrific pain, she saw once-loyal friends distance themselves and less loyal friends change aisles in the dime store to avoid conversation. Evelyn suffered the plight of so many non-offenders before her—she was avoided, not for her own crimes, but because the entire situation made people uncomfortable. And for that, Evelyn could never forgive him.

Beverly had seen and heard it all from her position on top of the stairs. Her mom yelled words that she didn't understand, but she didn't need much context to know they weren't compliments toward either her father or the *woman* that her mom refused to mention by name. Evelyn had gone back and forth between heartbreak and anger, her declarations of love and devotion riddled with shouts of fury and, a time or two, the sound of china breaking against the floor. Beverly's little heart raced as she heard her parents in a heated exchange. The only words that she could remember her father uttering were "I'm so sorry," over and over again, and her mother begging him to reconsider before tossing another china saucer onto the floor.

It was all horrible and not something that a seven-year-old needed to hear, yet she stayed at the top of the stairs and listened to it all.

Although quick, the divorce was anything but painless, and Evelyn's demands like something somebody would read from a Hollywood breakup. She wanted absolutely *everything*, and Lewis's guilt made it impossible for him to deny her. Even when she insisted on alimony and child support that amounted to twice his annual income, Lewis was ready to make it happen until his attorney stepped in and explained the practical limitations of promising money he didn't have.

Evelyn didn't care; if she was going to be a divorcée, she was going to embrace her new position and better her lifestyle. She would wholeheartedly take up her role as victim and wear it like a war badge reserved for the bravest and most injured in battle. There was only one thing that a woman in Evelyn's position could do: control the narrative and make sure that she was viewed as the injured party, and not the kind that one avoids in dime stores. She was determined to be viewed as a victim that the society ladies admired for her grace in a storm. At least, that's how Evelyn thought all of this should work. In reality, she would get the house, car, and a small amount of money for essentials. She would walk with her head held high but was at the mercy of others in terms of admiration.

During divorce negotiations, Lewis agreed to everything except her proposed custody arrangement, which would have essentially turned him into a shadowy figure in Beverly's life, with no official involvement. At the time, male infidelity was not the most unheard-of problem, and Lewis could have walked away relatively unscathed financially, reputation fully intact. In fact, there were more than a few men who would have elbowed Lewis in con-gratulations if the opportunity arose, knowing winks exchanged between men being all too common in a time that turned a blind eye to such chauvinistic endeavors.

Lewis, however, was not like other men. He had taken his marriage vows seriously, as well as his breaking of them, and he wanted to serve a penance for the sin. There was the penance for which he would pay the price in the legal system, the one that he would face in society, and the one that he would serve internally. The last in this trio was sure to be the harshest.

Lewis and Evelyn eventually settled on shared custody terms and parted ways, only to meet up every Wednesday at a neigh-borhood diner for custody drop-offs or, in the auditorium for an occasional school play and awkward conversation. There was noth-ing normal about this new normal and Lewis navigated it the best he could, staying silent and taking the heat from whichever direction it was launched.

After their names were signed on the bottom line of the divorce agreement, Beverly walked a delicate line between loving her father and supporting her mother. Evelyn's pain emerged in different forms, some days with exuberance and talk of new beginnings, and other days with tears and stories about what could have been. It was difficult to see her in such a way, espe-cially for a daughter who adored her, and it was made even harder when her father introduced her to Clarity. This new woman was so different from her mother, more carefree and colorful, both in spirit and outward appearances. Beverly had to hide her excite-ment when visiting the little cottage in the woods that, to her, seemed like it was plucked right out of a fairy tale.

Like many kids from a divorce, Beverly felt guilt when she was happy, and responsible when her mother was sad, growing up too quickly and assuming the role of care provider and therapist whenever she was needed. Lewis and Clarity had waited to talk wedding plans until time healed some wounds, but there was not enough time in the world for such things.

Beverly was nine years old when they announced their plans to marry, and the only thing the little girl could think of was the devastation this would bring upon her mother and the tears she would try to dry before they hit the floor. Time couldn't heal news like this; there was no statute of limitations for a husband's about-face announcement that he wanted his happily ever after with someone else.

Their everyday lives were hard, but the day of Lewis and Clarity's wedding was the absolute worst. Beverly loved her dress, a vintage, rose-colored, knee-length design with a neckline that reminded her of what starlets were wearing on the red carpet. Clarity had found it in some boutique during one of her travels and told Beverly the color brought out the blue in her eyes. And then there was Clarity. Beverly had never seen a bride wear a navy blue dress. According to her picture books and the few weddings she had attended, brides were supposed to make their entrance wearing a dress of white, one that accentuated a tiny waist and ballooned into a cascade of tulle and lace that followed her obediently down the aisle. And Beverly was equally surprised to hear that it was even legal to be married outside. Her father's response that "God is everywhere" was a fact never once mentioned by her Sunday school teacher, who reprimanded those who missed a class or two.

Beverly had never felt prettier than that day, but tried to downplay every morsel of the event to her mother, who asked about the wedding while simultaneously saying that she didn't want to know. The entire day was exhausting for Beverly, the joy that emanated from her father met with resentment that he had taken so much from her mother. It was as if there wasn't enough joy to go around—her mother's happiness had been sacrificed for this union to grow, and for a girl caught in between, Beverly felt like she was shunning God to celebrate with the Devil.

When Hazel was born a year later, Beverly felt a sudden shift in any balance that she had worked hard to maintain. Like the seesaw on her playground, when she was up, someone else was down. But when *she* was down, she often crashed to the ground, forgotten completely. It was hard for a ten-year-old to compete with a newborn baby, and although Clarity claimed to welcome her help, Beverly would sit and watch the new little unit of three lost in their own world while commenting on their swaddled miracle. Beverly wondered if her parents had looked at her just as lovingly when she was a baby, but couldn't imagine Evelyn and Lewis cuddled together like this. Even if her little face had been looked upon with as much awe, it had now been replaced with the pimply skin of a soon-to-be teenager and the adolescent awkwardness that hung heavy on her shoulders.

And so, it would be for years—a back and forth in both physical location and emotions for Beverly—until that horrible day when her world once again shifted, and the joy that had been given to her father was stripped away by the Devil who came to claim his due.

Chapter Fifteen

Cora could have left it alone. She could have left Lewis and Hazel at the retirement community, bidding farewell with all of the pleasantries that come with saying goodbye to people one may not ever see again. Her role in the entire thing had been intriguing, but it was over. The rings were back with their rightful owners, and any talk of missing persons was best addressed by those who actually knew and cared about that person.

Cora strolled the aisles of the bookstore, trying to convince herself of that fact, but found herself in the mystery section and wondered if the universe was trying to tell her something. She believed in signs—not the ones that anyone could look for and latch onto in times of need, but those that were unexpected and more powerful in their presence. If the universe wanted her to be involved, it would send her something unmistakable, not merely land her in the section of a bookstore that was always among the most popular and situated accordingly in the store. No, she would need something more than a row of books that she'd had no choice but to walk by on her way to the coffee shop nestled in the back corner.

Cora sipped her latte and continued her stroll, thoughts of the last few days weighing heavily on her mind despite the random books she picked up and tried to concentrate on. She had left the meeting with Lewis and Hazel hastily, uncomfortable with the emotional charge of the room and feeling like a voyeur to a terribly private conversation. Hazel had told her there was no reason to leave, but Cora had insisted, the name of a suspect in the disappearance of a missing person more than she had signed up for on her quest to return rings that she now wished she had never found. She was having trouble sleeping because of the entire thing and needed to clear her head, but every time she tried, the strange facts of the situation crept up on her like a twist in a movie plot that she couldn't get out of her mind.

A *marriage*.

An *affair*.

A woman *missing*.

An *accused* person.

A family *divided*.

A woman's rings *discovered* . . . where they shouldn't have been.

It was this last part that she couldn't shake. Clarity's rings had been found in her husband's ex-wife's—and then once-again wife's—things, discarded in the bottom of a jar with worthless trinkets. Clarity had disappeared when she was gardening, so it wouldn't be unusual for her to take her rings off before playing in the dirt. Perhaps they had been left in the house and mistakenly discarded in the chaos of her disappearance. Or had they knowingly been put in the jar with the hope they would never be found?

Cora found it hard to believe that someone would go through so much trouble; if Clarity had been taken from the back of her house, her abductor wouldn't risk losing precious time by removing her rings and putting them somewhere. That just seemed nonsensical, but then again, it all did.

Cora hadn't even realized she stood frozen in thought in the middle of the self-help aisle. It was only the sound of her name that brought her back, a muffled *Cora?* seeking her out as if from a dream. The second one was louder and impossible to ignore—*Cora?* accompanied by a touch on her arm.

"Honey, are you okay?"

There was Ruth, a pile of books in one arm and a giant handbag draped over the other. Her glasses were a bright green that day, an odd choice given her pumpkin-orange sweater and leopard scarf. "Honey, you were somewhere else entirely." She laughed a bellowing laugh, the kind that fills the entire room and draws attention to someone whether they want it to or not.

"Oh my gosh, I guess I was," Cora responded, embarrassed by the concerning looks she was being given by a mother and her "ducklings" making their way toward the corner for children's story hour. A little girl who looked to be around five or six seemed especially judgmental, casting a quick glance up and down Cora's outfit before following her mother toward the cardboard castle that hosted the daily gathering.

"Just a lot on my mind, I guess," she said, trying to sound casual. "How are you, Ruth?" She had nothing against Ruth but couldn't seem to get away from this family. By now, she didn't know *who* knew that she had talked to *whom* about *what*, and really just wanted to chalk this all up to a crazy introduction into Midwest life.

Cora hadn't seen the youngest Shaw sister since visiting her condo weeks before, something that seemed so long ago given the events that had transpired since. She felt guilty that Ruth had caught her deep in thought about her family's shady secrets, as if her questions floated like thought bubbles over her head for the world to read. The encounter was an unexpected one, and Cora really just wanted to leave. Her phone saved her, the familiar chime of a bell alerting her to a message. Although her gaze drifted to her purse and the sound of the phone, Ruth either didn't notice or didn't care.

"That storm was a bad one, wasn't it?" Ruth asked. "I hope your building was okay. It's such a beautiful old place. I always hate to see historic buildings get damaged, but then again, they're often built the strongest."

Cora pulled out her phone and smiled in polite agreement, swiping the screen and reading the text excerpt that was visible without unlocking. It was from Hazel.

"Yes, yes, I agree completely. All is fine at home," she said, now in an even bigger hurry to leave. "Everything okay with you? I mean, with the storm and everything?"

"Oh, it's fine. We're used to storms like that around here, but they're usually more bark than bite." It took Cora a minute to place the phrase, but then she remembered Beverly using the exact same one to describe storms when they were in the grocery store.

"How's everything else?" Ruth's words hung suspended in the air, their trajectory and meaning determined solely by how Cora chose to answer. Cora had no intention of spilling the tea about her visit with Lewis, so she pretended Ruth's question was simply polite conversation that needed no substantive response.

"Oh, all's good. Busy wedding planning and stuff like that." Ruth's expression didn't change, a small smile frozen between laugh lines. "I'm so sorry, but I need to respond to this." Cora raised her phone to signal an important text and returned one of the books she was skimming to the shelf. "So nice to see you, Ruth. Take care." Cora maneuvered past a group of high schoolers huddled around a single book in the aisle. "Love the green glasses, by the way."

Ruth's smile had still not shifted, and she waved a cursory goodbye as Cora made her way toward the exit. Cora opened Hazel's text on the way out, the lengthy message an apology of sorts for the intensity of the meeting with Lewis. She'd had no idea it would go that way and was sorry if it had caused Cora to be uncomfortable. Hazel wanted to meet for coffee soon, an invitation that Cora had no intention of responding to right now.

Outside, the temperature felt like it had dropped ten degrees as storm clouds smothered the sun. Giant drops of rain began to fall, large and sporadic enough for Cora to run to her car without getting too wet. It was perfect timing as immediately after she reached it, the clouds buckled under the pressure and released a downpour that turned Main Street into a blurry mix of shapes and colors. Other pedestrians, too, raced to their cars, and some people huddled together under storefront awnings. A woman darted in front of Cora's car and made her way toward the bookstore. It was Beverly. Cora watched her enter the shop and wave to Ruth, the two sisters chatting briefly before taking their seats at a small table by the window.

The three Shaw sisters, all spotted or heard from within a tenminute time frame. Cora had asked for a sign, and this was it. Whether it was a sign to stay involved or leave well enough alone, she was going to have to decide for herself. Switching the wipers to high speed, Cora prepared to brave the elements and make her way back home. When she was about to pull from the parking space, she looked back at Ruth and Beverly seated in the shop's window. They had been joined by another woman, a figure made blurry by the rain. Cora lowered her passenger side window to get a better view while she tried to keep out frenzied rain drops eager to get inside and tap dance across her leather seat.

Cora squinted to get a better view. The three women were now talking to a young woman in an apron and gesturing while telling her their coffee orders. The face of the third woman was still unclear, but her mannerisms were vaguely familiar. It took Cora a few seconds to register what and whom she was seeing.

Lydia. Her future mother-in-law was sitting at the bookshop table with Beverly and Ruth, the three of them ordering coffee like old friends.

Cora didn't even notice the raindrops pooling into the crevasses of her passenger seat. She sat in stunned silence. Elliott had told her that his family had always warned him to stay away from the Shaw family, yet here Lydia was, meeting two of the daughters for coffee and conversation. There was nothing unusual about bumping into people in a small town. There was nothing unusual about grabbing a coffee and quiet spot to wait out the rain. But there was something that felt off about this little encounter, and Cora couldn't rectify the conflicting messages and information being handed her recently.

And then there was also something that Cora found a bit unusual about her conversation with Ruth in the book aisle. Talk of the recent storm was expected these days, accompanied by the common courtesy of asking if people's property and loved ones had emerged unharmed. It was normal for Ruth and Cora to have talked about such things, but it wasn't until she sat in her car, watching the three women engage in conversation with their cups of tea or coffee, that something occurred to her. Ruth had specifically asked Cora if her apartment building had been damaged in the storm, mentioning its age and historic nature. The strange thing was, Cora had never told Ruth where she lived.

Hickory Falls

November 1957

Clarity wasn't one to run to the doctor every time Hazel sneezed. She believed that the body was designed to fight off the occasional flu bug and virus, and there was a benefit in letting nature take its course. She had always been taught that viruses were best battled with herbal tea, cozy blankets, and extra-gooey cheese on sandwiches, so that was how she always approached Hazel's bouts with the sniffles and other viral visitors.

She snuggled up with her daughter, read her favorite books over and over again, and pretended like they were elephants blowing their trunks each time Hazel needed to blow her nose. Her three-year old couldn't seem to shake it this time, though, and her labored breathing and spiked temperature the night before were enough to send even the most chill mom to the doctor's front door as soon as it opened or, in this case, fifteen minutes before.

Clarity and Hazel now sat in front of the white house on Main Street that housed the office of the only physician in town, a holiday wreath on its front door and glossy black window shutters seeming to repel the snowflakes falling steadily. The car was getting cold, and she considered turning it on again to get a little warmth inside. Hazel was asleep on the seat beside her, with her yellow giraffe still clutched in one hand. The snow was coming down a lot heavier than when she had left home, Lewis upset that she wouldn't wait to go until he could drive them later that day. Trusting that inner voice, however, Clarity had insisted on taking Hazel first thing in the morning, her poor little girl radiating as much heat from her fever as their blazing fireplace.

Clarity checked her watch again. It was four minutes to nine, one minute later than the last time she'd checked. Just then a white Cadillac rolled slowly past and turned into the house's driveway, the crunching of snow under tires one of Clarity's least favorite sounds. She was relieved to see the doctor finally arrive, her irritation at waiting now outweighed by the relief that she felt upon his arrival. Given the forecast for snow increasing throughout the day, she had been afraid that he would simply cancel all appointments, and her poor little Hazel would have to suffer another day. That wasn't going to happen. This little girl needed help, and she would have strapped Hazel onto a dog sled if need be. Mother Nature should know better than to mess with a worried mom.

Before he even reached the front porch, Clarity was closing the distance behind him carrying a limp three-year-old with bright red cheeks. The sound of her boots in the snow must have surprised him, because he swung around, looking a bit shocked as he put the key in the door.

"Clarity, my word, you startled me," he said, pushing the door open and waiting for her to enter. "We've got a sick little one, I see. I hope you haven't been waiting long. It's getting brutal out there."

Clarity felt her body finally relax as she entered the warm office space, Hazel's care now in the hands of an expert. It was only then that she realized how scared she was for her daughter, the stress of the last few days now settling like a heavy blanket on her shoulders.

"My nurse isn't here quite yet, but let's get this child settled into my exam room. Nothing to worry about, Clarity. We'll get her feeling better in no time." He brushed snowflakes from the shoulders of his heavy coat before hanging it on a coat rack in the corner. "I'm going to run into the back room and get a few things ready. It's not freezing in here, but it could be warmer. I'll take care of that too."

"Oh, I'm sorry—do you mind?" He gestured to the empty maker and filters. "I'm in need of something to warm me up, and you might like a cup too."

"Of course, please."

He smiled at Hazel and then reassuringly at Clarity, and she could feel her heartbeat slow down by his calming presence. Doctors surely weren't this calm if they suspected a patient was horribly sick. They definitely wouldn't stop to make a pot of coffee if they felt they were in the presence of a medical emergency.

Clarity unwrapped the scarf from her neck with one arm while cradling Hazel in the other, the smell of disinfectant, the fir garland on the fireplace mantle in the waiting room, and coffee grounds somehow a pleasant combination.

"Dr. Manchester, I'm so glad we're here."

"Please," he said. "Call me Jack."

Chapter Sixteen

Mimi wasn't happy.

Cora watched her walk across the room—or rather begin to *pace*—and then return to her chair behind the desk. She was like a nervous dog waiting for the next startling noise.

"I told you to leave all of this alone," she said, a skinny finger pointing at Cora. *"Leave. It."*

After the meeting with Lewis, Cora hadn't known what to do. Because of a few less than honest answers to "How was your day?" inquiries, Elliott was under the mistaken impression that the entire ring thing was behind her. To say he was angry to learn otherwise would be an understatement, especially when she brought up his mom's secret meeting with the Shaw sisters.

She should have chosen her words more carefully, but felt defensive, so instead of simply asking Elliott why his mother would have met with Beverly and Ruth, Cora came across as accusing Lydia of hiding something from her family. The entire thing was a mess, and upon being told that Lydia and the Shaw sisters were on the planning committee for an upcoming church bizarre, Cora felt paranoid, foolish, and embarrassed that she had fallen so hard and swift down a rabbit hole.

Elliott was mad enough with the limited information he had. She could never share her cemetery adventure or admit that she'd met Lewis. Elliott would never understand her need to insert herself into such a family drama, feeling that, until recently, he had survived just fine knowing nothing about. Cora didn't disagree; the entire thing seemed ridiculous and an unimaginable breach into another family's secrets. She didn't want to be involved, but had a hard time extracting herself. She was hurting her relationship. She was angering women she barely knew in town. She couldn't believe she was in all of this, yet here she was, sitting across from Juliet's grandmother, steadying herself for another scolding.

"Mimi, please listen," Cora pleaded, the heated judgment she felt from the tiny woman across the desk almost smoldering. "I didn't *want* to get involved—I really didn't. I thought as soon as I gave Hazel the rings that my participation in all of this would end, but she invited me to visit her father, and I just couldn't say no. I stupidly thought it would be nice to see his reaction if he was reunited with Clarity's rings, but I obviously didn't know." Cora could feel her emotions begin to bubble over, and she hated this feeling, the tears in the back of her throat and shakiness in her voice betraying any sense of calm that she was trying to convey. Mimi sensed it too, because her face softened, and her shoulders fell from their on-guard position. The eyes that had just now been shooting daggers at Cora fell to a leather appointment book on her desk that seemed about as full as a calendar could get.

"The last thing that I would ever want to do is hurt this family," Cora said softly, encouraged by the energy shift in the room. "I'm going to lose sleep over this whole thing either way, so I figured I might as well lose sleep over trying to make sense of what happened to Clarity. I mean, would you be able to turn away?"

Mimi leaned back in her chair and stared at the ceiling as if the answer were somewhere among the ornate copper panels. She was weighing her response in a way that people do when they know a lot but are considering how much to share.

"I'm quite shocked he mentioned him by name," Mimi finally said. "In a town this size, there are things you say, things you whisper, and things you never mention." She took a sip of her tea, dunking the tea bag up and down lost in thought once more. "Then again," she continued, "if you've lived to see one hundred years, why the hell not just say it all?"

"So, you know who he is then? Jack Manchester."

"Yes, I know the name Jack Manchester. Let's put it this way: my school was Manchester Elementary. Everybody knew the Manchester name. They go back generations in Hickory Falls and were among the closest we had to an elite society. Doctors, dentists, lawyers—you name it. I think there was even a state Senator or two. Manchester money—and influence—built this town."

"Who was Jack, specifically?"

"He was the town doctor, and the only one for quite a while. A bit older than me, but I remember him and all of the Manchesters. You'd think they were the Rockefellers, the way they held themselves, but they were simply big fish in a very small pond. A good-looking family, I'll give them that. If you live in a small town and are both attractive and successful, you'll make a name for yourself quickly."

"What kind of reputation did Jack have? Why would Lewis even mention him in association with all of this?

The sound of the bell over the front door tossed them both abruptly back into the present. Mimi jumped up and made her way toward the entrance, a welcoming curator's smile now on her face. Cora was left wanting more. She had come to Mimi desperate for answers. Juliet was enjoying the salaciousness of the situation too much, so Cora had come alone that morning, hoping to fill in a few puzzle pieces that were now missing from the middle of the emerging picture. The rings' owner had been identified, but the mystery now seemed to have taken on a whole new category, and not one that she could navigate on her own. Sensing that Mimi wouldn't be back anytime soon, Cora checked her phone and felt her heart drop when she saw three missed calls from her future mother-in-law and two from Elliott, in addition to a text from him that simply read, *Forget something?*

"Shit," Cora muttered, grabbing her purse and heading toward the door. She had completely forgotten about meeting Lydia at a local florist to discuss bouquets and table centerpieces. She hadn't wanted to go, which was likely why it had slipped her mind. Cora couldn't care less about floral displays; she would have been happy with a wildflower bouquet picked on their way to the ceremony, but flowers were important to Lydia. Luckily, the florist was right down the street, and she would only be fifteen minutes late if she sprinted.

Mimi was standing behind an older woman near a piece at the front of the gallery, her arms folded across her chest and head tilted the way art connoisseurs do to show their appreciation. She sensed Cora behind her and turned briefly, just long enough for Cora to gesture silently that she had to go. Mimi touched the patron lightly on the arm and whispered something before excusing herself to meet Cora at the front door. She looked both tense and relieved that their conversation had fallen short.

Mimi walked Cora out the front door like she was an important client, and closed the heavy wooden door so only the carved owls were witness to their conversation.

"If you insist on pursuing this further, do your research," Mimi said. "Newspapers were quite different back in the day. Small-town prints were built on idle gossip that would get you sued for libel these days. If you want to learn about Jack Manchester, check out *The Whispers of Hickory Falls*. It was an anonymous gossip newsletter that wasn't around very long because it caused so much trouble. My mom and her friends would meet weekly to talk about it." Mimi started to head back inside, but Cora stopped her.

"Mimi, where am I going to find back issues of a gossip newsletter from decades ago?"

Mimi looked both ways down the sidewalk to make sure nobody was around, and Cora was beginning to get annoyed with her coyness.

"We're not making a drug deal, Mimi," she said, her patience wearing even more thin now that she was sure to get the evil eye from her future mother-in-law for being late. "This is a little silly. Just tell me."

"Check the Historical Society's archives," Mimi said. "But you probably shouldn't tell them what you're looking for." She disappeared back into the gallery and left Cora on the front step, processing this information, the wooden owls overhead perched like time-capsule sentries with secrets to tell.

Hickory Falls

⁓

April 12, 1958

People said her legs were twisted in unnatural positions when they found her, one foot pointed in the opposite direction of the leg that held it, the ankle snapped in two. The innocence of her fifteen-year-old features erased by hair glued to her cheeks with blood. People said that she would have died on impact, but that doesn't stop someone from wondering about her thoughts during the fall. She had roughly thirty feet to think about what awaited her on the rocks below. People said there must have been something strange going on, that two good kids like Ralph Swanson and Isabelle Jeffrey never would have trespassed onto the property unless they were lured there somehow. That's what people said, anyway.

The truth was, teenagers trespassed on the Grey property in the woods all the time. There were sizable hills—cliffs they might even be called—that surrounded the small lake out back. Kids liked to jump into the water from the top of a rock that had been worn smooth by erosion. This wasn't the first time that kids had scaled the wooden perimeter fence and made their way to the watering hole without the owners of the land knowing they were there. It was the first time, however, that a teenager had fallen to her death and split her head open on the jagged rocks below.

Nature, even the beautiful and serene kind found in secluded watering holes where the Romeos and Juliets of their time carve their initials into rocks, can be deadly if not respected. Rocks, once rough and gritty, can be worn smooth with age. Dirt, with its earthy smell and amazing little microorganisms, can be transformed into ice with early morning dew or the remnants of a light rainfall. Rational minds would conclude that a combination of the two were at fault that April morning, but rational minds tend to send their thoughts into the universe like bubbles to land softly. It's the irrational ones that shoot ideas into the sky with the reckless abandon of a blindfolded archer. Archery was a popular sport among Hickory Falls naturists, a fact that comes as no surprise.

Like an arrow sent flying toward the sun, the rumors took off immediately and were sharp enough to cut through actual facts. Although Ralph, himself only fifteen years old, was traumatized by the event and swore that Isabelle lost her footing on their way to the jumping spot, there were those in town who would insist there was something else in play simply because her death occurred on Grey property. Like certain locales in Salem, Massachusetts, or the house famous for its attic eyes in Amityville, there were some places that would never be allowed a happily ever after by these people. To them, a car accident in Salem would have been caused by forces unseen, and a bird taking a rest on the roof of the Amityville house was a beacon from beyond. The Grey property—one owned by an eccentric family who had never buckled to societal expectations—was similarly tainted, and there was no talking the rumor archers out of it.

In the days, weeks, and months following the accident, the talk of the town was unnecessarily cruel and relentless. Lewis tried to shield Clarity from as much of it as possible, particularly claims that the kids had been lured there by the "Shaw woman," as if she lived in a candy house with an oven preheated just for them. Amateur sleuths questioned how Isabelle could have fallen from that particular location, one so far from the kids' usual path, choosing to ignore Ralph's explanation that Isabelle insisted on walking along the cliff's edge to get a better view. With every plausible explanation Ralph provided, the townspeople came up with five outlandish theories, none of which ever pointed the finger at him. They couldn't; he was the son of the county judge, and Isabelle was the daughter of Lionel Jeffrey, the Hickory Falls mayor. If something unfortunate happened to anyone in these families, it was never by their own doing. Ralph's older brother, for instance, had failed his first semester at college but somehow got reinstated with passing grades after his father launched a media investigation into the quality of secondary-education instructors. Isabelle's mother had disappeared for a few weeks to "get off the drink," an infliction caused by her sensitivity to tannins rather than her insatiable taste for the fermented grape. Isabelle falling off the cliff on her own didn't fit such a narrative, so the people of Hickory Falls shuffled events around a bit to shift the blame to someone they were comfortable with. If people are convinced they're morally justified, their minds can do all sorts of things.

Lewis, Clarity, and Hazel were actually miles away at a flea market when the accident occurred. They ran their booth from sunup to sundown and hadn't been to the cabin in days.

Such facts, however, were no match for active imaginations and dramatic flair. There were some who, regardless of Ralph's account of events, would find a way to cast blame on the unusual woman from the unusual family whom nobody understood—nor made any effort to. Some said she didn't have to physically be on the property because she had put a curse on trespassers. Others said she *was* there that day, and her husband—a man with a known proclivity for lying when it came to his relationships—had simply covered for her. Then there were the ones really out there, who had Clarity hiding in a tree and orchestrating the entire thing by singing some alluring song known by witches to summon the innocent. It was all preposterous, but that didn't stop tongues from wagging or stories from flying.

Clarity had been devastated when she heard the news. Hazel was her entire world. She couldn't help but fast-forward to her daughter's teenage years and the fear that something like this would happen to her own child. It's every mother's worst nightmare, and she shared in the Jeffrey family's grief, although her wishes for them were passed along in silent prayer and thoughtful meditation. She didn't dare extend her condolences publicly.

Hickory Falls needed a villain, and Clarity Shaw fit the role beautifully. She was everything unheard of in women at the time in Hickory Falls: strong-willed, artistic, unique, and confident. It didn't help that she had chased teenage trespassers from her property before, concerned that an accident like this would happen someday. The townspeople chose to latch onto that image, the one of a woman with wild hair chasing innocent children off her land, rather than accept that she, too, had spent hours sobbing over the loss of such a young life.

Unfortunately for Clarity, the narrative was never going to lean in her direction, and right or wrong, the Shaw name was now on the lips of two very powerful families who had a reputation for publicly casting blame. Revenge of some sort was not out of the question, although it's referred to as *justice* in higher social circles to cast blame on those deserving judgment rather than the ones who wielded the proverbial gavel.

A quiet life, it seems, was not in the cards for Lewis and Clarity after all.

Chapter Seventeen

⁓

Cora might have rushed into the florist shop a bit too abruptly. She swung the glass door back on its hinges until its edge crashed into a giant ceramic pot holding a display of silk gardenias.

The sound of the door's metal frame colliding with ceramic made Cora cringe, and she hoped the pot would emerge from the altercation unscathed. The quaint shop was a symphony of calm—mellow classical music overhead complimenting the smell of all things fresh as a daisy, so her clumsy entrance caused the two women examining hydrangeas at the counter to spin around in surprise. Elliott's mother, one of those women, did not look pleased.

"Well, hello there," Lydia said. "What a dramatic entrance!" She smoothed one side of her bobbed hair on her way over to Cora. She was smiling the way people do when they want to avoid a scene.

"Marilyn, this is my future daughter-in-law, Cora. Cora, this is one of my oldest friends. She owns the shop and has been gracious enough to devote an hour to consulting with us on wedding flowers." Taking a quick glance at her silver Rolex, Lydia couldn't resist a subtle dig. "Well, I guess it's more like forty minutes at this point."

After repeated apologies, all of which were genuinely waved away by Marilyn and ignored by Lydia, Cora spent the next thirty-eight minutes pretending to be interested in the color, scent, and arrangement options of flowers. Apparently, flowers have auras that need to be taken into consideration. Choose the wrong combination of floral personalities and the entire wedding vibe could be compromised. At least one would assume so by the intensity with which Marilyn and Lydia analyzed the potential for the petals of a classic rose to clash with the prickly personality of a peony. Cora found the entire thing exhausting, but she put on a good face to avoid irritating Lydia even more.

By the time the appointment was over, Cora had chosen—or rather, Lydia had steered her toward—a tasteful globe bouquet of blush roses and tabletop pieces that featured a rather exotic-looking white flower with pink stripes. The flowers looked like blooming vaginas, but Cora wasn't about to tell Lydia that. She was fine with blooming vaginas if they got her out of the shop. This many flowers in one place was like too much of a good thing, and the intensity of the smell coupled with elevator music was giving her a headache. She was also secretly ashamed to have questioned Lydia's involvement with Beverly and Ruth, yet still in doubt of Elliott's quite innocent explanation. If Lydia didn't like someone, she didn't seem the type to put her personal feelings aside for planning committee obligations. In fact, she seemed the type to hand-pick the committee to avoid being put in an uncomfortable situation.

Cora and Elliott had plans to go to a movie that night, so she was anxious to wrap things up and finish running her errands as soon as possible. When Lydia said a brief farewell to Marilyn and walked a bit too closely behind her out the door, Cora had a feeling there was either a polite reprimand coming, or the sexual image of the centerpieces had just dawned on Lydia.

"Cora, dear, let's chat for a bit," Lydia said, looking relieved that the rain had stopped and her hair would be spared on her way to the car. She stuck her hand, palm-up, out from under the awning to make sure there were no hidden droplets in the air, and then walked briskly toward her car without concern for whether Cora needed to walk the same way.

"Lydia, I'm really sorry about being late. I didn't mean to put you in an uncomfortable position. Marilyn seems lovely, and I would never disrespect her time."

"Oh, honey, that's not it," Lydia said, stopping in front of a store and tugging lightly on Cora's sleeve for her to do the same. She began to look at a silver chandelier in the window of the antique store and tilted her head in piqued interest before remembering she had paused in the middle of her thought. "Marilyn's as gracious as can be and works with a lot of brides, so she understands the busy schedules of a bride-to-be." Cora breathed a sigh of relief that she had been spared an etiquette lecture. "I just wish you had mentioned having a busy afternoon so I could have prepared a bit better." Ah, there it was. "So, I hear you've been busy."

"Yes, well, there's lots to do!" Cora tried to play the role of excited bride-to-be but was afraid that Lydia would see right through her and know she hadn't touched a single wedding-related task for days. She wasn't a good liar and never had been.

"I'm not talking about wedding plans, dear. I hear you've been talking to the Shaw family." Lydia dropped this little bomb without looking at Cora, her gaze returning to the silver chandelier that looked remarkably similar to the one currently over her dining room table at home. A *statement* more than a *question*, Lydia's expression still suggested she expected a response.

Cora wasn't expecting this.

"Oh, don't look so surprised," Lydia said with a smile. "You aren't from here, and our sweet little Midwest towns are a bit different from the big cities in California. There's not much you can hide here." Lydia's perfectly capped smile tried to appear genuine, but her eyes betrayed her.

"I wasn't trying to hide anything," Cora explained, finding the choice of words troubling. "I only got to know the Shaw sisters because I found—"

"Oh yes. The *rings*, the *rings*. Yes, I've heard about your little find." Cora now realized that the meeting at the bookshop wasn't about centerpieces and raffles after all; it was about Lydia's future daughter-in-law poking around where she didn't belong, and Beverly and Ruth going to the very top to make it stop.

"I once found an actual loose two-carat diamond in a bin of jewelry auctioned off to benefit a women's shelter in Des Moines," Lydia continued. "What a find that was! I thought about having it put into a little necklace, but never got around to it."

Cora smiled. It wasn't exactly the same situation.

"Here's the thing. As lovely as it is that we don't have to spend much time sharing wonderful news because it has a magical way of spreading around here, less than positive news can spread like wildfire as well. The Shaw family has lived here for decades and have always had their share of scandals and secrets. I mean, Ruth's stint at the mental hospital was the talk of the town for years. Poor thing being talked about that way. And then, there's that cabin in the woods that really seems like it has a curse on it or something, what with that poor girl's accident and . . ." Lydia seemed to catch herself. "Well, you know how things go. What's that saying? Let sleeping dogs lie? Well, maybe in this case, let lost rings stay lost is more appropriate." She laughed awkwardly, the analogy a peculiar one.

"Accident?" Cora found the word an odd choice if Lydia was referencing Clarity Shaw's disappearance. "Was there an accident at the cabin?"

Lydia looked annoyed that she was being asked to elaborate, even though she was the one who had put the topic out there. "Well, yes, years ago. A teenage girl fell to her death along the lake under *very* suspicious circumstances. It was tragic and quite terrifying. I mean, we simply didn't know what went on out there. Some members of the Shaw family dabbled in things that good Christians don't even speak of." Lydia whispered the last sentence.

"Wait, so when was this? Was this when Clarity Shaw was there or before?"

Lydia's look turned from annoyed to concerned, but not the kind that accompanies genuine care. It was a look that is given to someone when a person is caught off guard and pondering next moves.

"Oh, I don't remember, but that doesn't really matter." Lydia shuffled through her purse to find her keys. "I need to bolt, dear," she said. "The Club's anniversary event planning committee tends to make questionable choices if I'm not there. I mean, they ordered standard cold cut trays for Sergeant Green's retirement party. Cold cuts! I mean, have you heard of *char-chut-er-ie* boards, girls?" Lydia laughed at the memory of such a disastrous near miss in her party-planning circle. To think that after years of fighting fires, Sergeant Green's send-off had gotten dangerously close to ham and turkey mayhem.

"Give Elliott a hug and kiss from his mother." Lydia started to walk off but turned around abruptly and pulled a folder from her Louis Vuitton bag. "Oh, I almost forgot. I finished our guest list last night and wanted to give it to you. This one is final. I mean, goodness, the more that I think about it, the more names that I add. I need to stop somewhere. I've asked Harriett to type out names, addresses, and the appropriate titles for each so there's no confusion when it comes to addressing envelopes." Cora had never met Harriett, but got the impression she helped Lydia out from time to time on life tasks that she didn't want to take on.

"Thanks, Lydia. I appreciate it." Cora took the folder with absolutely no intention of looking at it anytime soon. She was going to have to dig deep and resist the urge to drop a precious doctor's title from the invitation envelopes just to get a reaction. How horrible for them to be included among the little people.

Cora watched Lydia fast-walk to her car as she made her way back to her own car parked in front of the art gallery. Once there, she tossed the green folder in the back seat and tried to forget the events of the day—talk of flower auras, the Shaws, salacious gossip newsletters, and a mysterious Dr. Manchester would have to wait. All she wanted at this point was a movie with her fiancé, a box of Milk Duds, and a small bottle of wine that she planned to sneak into the theater.

She drove down Main Street, remnants of the storm now sliding off the windshield in shimmering droplets chasing one another to the edge. As the sun struggled to peek out from behind the clouds, a rainbow appeared in the sky. Sitting at the intersection's red light, Cora's gaze followed the rainbow's wide arch, and she wondered if anyone had ever gone in search of its end. She wanted to focus on the rainbow and Milk Duds, not Lydia's mention of mental institutions and tragic accidents. One can't say things like that and expect somebody's interest to fade; if anything, Cora now felt more devoted than ever to dig deeper into this long-standing mystery of Hickory Falls. She had peeled back the initial few layers, but there were so many more.

For now, all of that would have to wait. There was a box of chocolate-covered candy and a bottle of pinot grigio waiting for her. She would try to alleviate Elliott's concerns and reassure him that she would stay in her lane when it came to Hickory Fall's secrets.

What Elliott, Lydia, and the Shaw sisters didn't know wouldn't hurt them. At least for now.

Hickory Falls

~

August 16, 1958

Hazel walked into the kitchen, dragging the fluffy pink bunny by one ear. She took care of her stuffed animals as if they were real, talking to them and tucking them in at night with stories and promises of sweet dreams. It was only when traveling room to room that she tended to forget they were "real," dragging them by their appendages until she found her next landing spot, where she positioned them carefully beside her as if they hadn't hit their little heads on every wall corner and chair arm on their way.

"Where did she get that one?" Lewis asked with a smile, nodding toward the bottom half of the pink bunny disappearing around the corner. He winced slightly at the sound of the bunny's plastic nose hitting the wall. "It's like a stuffed animal zoo around here."

"Are you just noticing that?" Clarity asked. "I found Poop outside in the garden yesterday, suspended upright by a tomato plant. About scared me to death when I saw him." Poop was Hazel's favorite bear, a green-eyed fluff ball with white tuffs springing from both ears. His name was an accident, Lewis referring to it by its poopy brown color so often that they had all but forgotten its given name. George had never seemed to fit him properly anyway. George was too proper; this bear seemed to find himself getting into trouble all the time, so Poop was a better name.

"I actually considered leaving Poop out there to scare away the raccoons, but couldn't bring myself to do that to him." Clarity smiled, her dark waterfall of curls cascading over her shoulders and into her teacup. She took another bite of her blueberry muffin before realizing that it wasn't the one she had started on, so now she had two muffins, with a single bite out of each, on her plate. She shrugged at the realization. Blueberry muffins were her favorite, and she would have had two anyway.

Lewis's eyes rose from behind the rim of his coffee mug as he took another gulp, the difference in their tastes, coffee gulping and tea sipping, a source of constant entertainment and debate. "But the bunny. Where did she get the bunny that she's been carrying around lately? Poop will be jealous." His attempt at humor was thinly veiled by concerned curiosity because, although he asked, Lewis was pretty sure he already knew the answer, and he braced himself for confirmation.

"Dr. Manchester gave her the bunny," Clarity said, flinging her hair out of the way as she poured hot water into her cup while holding its ceramic lid in place. She added two cubes of sugar and a drizzle of honey into the cup without noticing that Lewis had put down his coffee rather firmly on the table. Or, if she noticed, she now tried casually to pretend she hadn't.

"Hazel, sweetie, come finish your muffin."

"*Again?* Didn't he just give her a new toy?" Lewis wasn't going to allow for a change of topic. Not this time. Hazel emerged from the next room, dragging her bunny behind her. One of its long ears was capturing any remnants left behind by the broom that Clarity had used earlier that morning to clean up loose leaf tea that had somehow been knocked off the shelf. In Hazel's words: "Maybe bunny did it."

Relieved to have her daughter in the room to deescalate the conversation, Clarity smiled at Hazel and gestured for her to come over to the table for a hug.

"Oh, he's just a sweet doctor. He takes care of all the kids in town and spoils them with little surprises." Clarity squeezed Hazel and brushed off bunny, picking bits of tea from the fluff in his ears. She then turned her attention to the larger of the two muffins on her plate.

"Don't you find that a little odd?"

Lewis wasn't ready to drop the topic. He found Dr. Manchester's interest in his wife and daughter far from normal. A lollipop here or there was one thing, but he had gifted Hazel with stuffed animals, books, and a paper doll collection that Lewis had seen in the toy shop window. It wasn't a cheap gift. A chance encounter isn't uncommon in such a small town, but Clarity and Hazel rarely went out anymore without a run-in with Dr. Manchester, who, oddly enough, always seemed to have a gift on hand for his daughter. It was unseemly and rose to a different level than mere coincidence.

And then there were the things that he had heard about Dr. Manchester, unsavory things that his wife or any proper woman didn't need to know. The Manchester family was from Hickory Falls, but Jack had left a few years ago to set up shop in another town when he married a prominent lawyer's daughter. Gossip swirled about his infidelities, including a concerning hush-hush story about Jack Manchester threatening his wife with a kitchen knife during a whiskey bender.

These were just rumors, of course, but Lewis had listened to them carefully, revisiting them when Jack Manchester showed back up on Hickory Falls with a new wife and a glossy new business sign. These were not the things that a man discusses with his wife over morning coffee and tea, but he was less than pleased that his daughter kept showing up with new toys and trinkets from the doctor on Main Street.

"Don't you think it's a little strange that he just *happens* to have a new toy for Hazel whenever he *happens* to run into you?" Lewis's attempt to appear casual was betrayed by his emphasis on the lack of likelihood of such a thing occurring.

"Oh, it's a small town. You can barely go out to pick up a daily paper without running into someone you know. I seriously doubt he walks around with bright pink bunnies, just hoping to run into Hazel. It was simply a coincidence. He said he was coming from the store, and they were giving them away with each purchase."

Clarity didn't understand that her husband wasn't only concerned about the attention Dr. Manchester paid to Hazel; he was also concerned with the attention the good doctor seemed to be paying his wife and the number of times she mentioned running into him around town. Coincidences evoke two different reactions: one can either find them everywhere or believe that there's no such thing. Lewis didn't believe in coincidences, not when they appeared this frequently and involved his wife, daughter, and paper dolls from the toy store window.

"I probably should start packing our picnic basket," Clarity said, getting up from the table and making her way toward the kitchen, teacup in hand. "Hazel's been looking forward to this all week. I told her that we'd bring bread to feed the ducks." He could hear the click of the radio in the kitchen, Elvis singing about a hotel at the end of Lonely Street. This was one of her favorite songs, and he only had to wait a few seconds for the volume to be nudged a smidge higher and the sound of Clarity's voice singing along with the King who was so lonely he could die.

They all needed this picnic and an afternoon in a private little corner of a sun-kissed field. It had been a horrible few months since Isabelle Jeffrey's death. The things being said were outrageous and overshadowed the truth of the situation—a young girl out to make memories with her boyfriend walked a bit too close to life's edge, both literally and figuratively, and died. No, they shouldn't have been trespassing, but whether the parents donning Hickory Falls PTA buttons liked to admit it or not, the watering hole on the property was the same one they had jumped into as teenagers, and the fence was the same one they'd climbed when trespassing on their way there. Not ones to invite trouble, Lewis and Clarity always asked the teenagers to leave when they caught them, explaining the risks and danger of jumping from the cliff, but they could never apprehend them all. Talk of Clarity running through the woods like a wild woman, with one arm raised to cast them off her property, was from the same dark fairy tales as those about Clarity's cauldron and secret spells. Same book, different chapter.

Talk was one thing, but threats were another. Lewis and Clarity had learned to ignore the rumor mill, choosing instead to focus on their lives together and avoid toxic situations. It wasn't difficult to do; they enjoyed spending as much time outdoors as possible. When they weren't working on one of their projects, they were traveling as a threesome to neighboring towns to sell their art and woodworking projects at flea markets and craft fairs. There, they enjoyed an anonymity that Hickory Falls couldn't provide, and when the urge struck them, they were even known to give themselves new names for the day, as if each town's city limit sign provided endless opportunities for a new identity. Over the summer, Hazel had changed her name to Lily, Cherry Blossom, Lavender Pie—and during their most recent trip, to *Turnip*.

Yes, talk was one thing, but coming home to threats in their mailbox was another. Lewis had found the note a few weeks ago, a message written in black crayon on typing paper. It might have been from one of Isabelle's grieving teenage friends, or perhaps from an adult who would stoop to such juvenile behavior, but regardless, the message was clear. There were people in town who held them responsible for Isabelle's death. More so than Lewis, they held *Clarity* responsible, a fact made clear when they came home with their daughter, Turnip, to find the word *Witch* spray-painted on the side of their shed. Lewis had been able to hide the letter, but he couldn't hide a word spray-painted in white against faded red siding. Clarity had panicked, concerned about Hazel's safety, but Lewis had reassured her that the people of Hickory Falls were cowards, hiding behind anonymous words and the power of graffiti. There was no real threat to their family. He had reassured her of this fact over and over until she believed it and he had actually begun to feel safe again himself.

If the good people of the town had only known the number of tears that Clarity had shed over Isabelle's death. If they had only known her pleas for a higher perimeter fence to keep this from happening again, but Lewis would explain that they simply didn't have the money. If they had only known that on the day of the funeral, Clarity had walked to the scene of the accident and tossed flower petals into the water in tribute to a sweet soul gone home too soon. Even if the people of Hickory Falls had known these things, Lewis doubted they would have cared. As he watched his wife and daughter hustle around the house getting ready, he decided that talk of toy bunnies could wait for another day. Clarity had been through enough.

Thirty minutes and one outfit change later, due to a poorly positioned mud puddle outside, the three of them made their way to Lewis's truck, arms full of blankets, a picnic basket, more toys than were necessary, and a bag of stale bread that Clarity had set aside for the occasion so Hazel could feed the ducks.

"What time are we supposed to pick up Beverly?" Clarity asked, tossing her things into the pickup's bed and readjusting a red handkerchief that had moved from its position on top of her head. She stood with one hand on her hip, looking effortlessly chic with her navy capri pants and a white blouse tied at her waist. "I hope she likes egg salad. Does she like egg salad?" Clarity suddenly looked worried, rethinking her entire basket. She did this a lot, overthinking Beverly's reaction, afraid that the slightest misstep might propel her into evil-stepmother territory.

"She likes egg salad," Lewis said. "Or maybe not. She's fourteen, so I can't really keep up with her tastes these days. And we were supposed to be there ten minutes ago." He hoisted the blanket and toys over the side of the truck, a fluffy pink ear peeking out from the bag. Waiting until Clarity and Hazel were inside the truck and ready to go, he grabbed the pink bunny and hid it in front of him as he jogged back inside yelling over his shoulder that he had forgotten something. Talk of the bunny could wait for another day, but Lewis was taking it upon himself to uninvite the little fluff ball and substitute a naughty bear in its place.

When he emerged a few minutes later, Hazel's face lit up at the sight of Poop, her green-eyed bear, who was dancing a little jig in her daddy's arms on the way to their picnic adventure. And in the background was a shed with a new coat of bright red paint.

Chapter Eighteen

The movie the night before had sucked. There was nothing that fancy special effects could do to save a story line that had no character development and a script that could have been written by a middle schooler. Even then, it would have gotten a C at best, but only for its sly humor that occurred during parts of the movie that Cora suspected weren't supposed to be funny at all.

Elliott had fallen asleep mid-movie, and she'd spent the second half thinking about the very things she told herself she needed a break from. Even her purse wine and snacks weren't enough to make the movie enjoyable, and she had gone through two mini bottles of wine and a box of candy, all wasted on a film that looked like it had been written in a day and edited by interns. So much for cinematic excellence and an escape from reality.

Cora now jogged across the street to avoid getting hit by a young man on a scooter who was too busy looking at a group of girls to pay attention to the road.

"Eyes forward!" Cora yelled as he sped past her and toward a busy intersection close to the local elementary school. She was sure he had heard her, because of his increase in speed and a middle finger at her reprimand, but at least his eyes were now on the road.

Cora jumped over a puddle, to keep her shoes from getting wet, and made her way toward the mahogany sign hanging from a bracket on a brick building ahead, its gold lettering announcing her arrival at the Hickory Falls Historic Society.

Cora tightened the lid on her coffee cup, to avoid any inadvertent destruction of historic documents, and made her way inside. She had never been to a historic society before, but pictured yellowed documents displayed under glass, and white-glove requirements. She would soon realize that her expectations had been clouded by the library-like images of similar places on television and film, historic societies on movie sets taking on some mystical quality. In Hickory Falls, the society was housed in an old home—appropriately enough—next to a yogurt shop with two small wrought-iron tables available on the sidewalk for guests. The white-trimmed shop with yogurt specials written in pink marker on the front windows stood in stark contrast to the dark house on the end of the street, which looked like it had refused to leave while the town was built up around it. Like history itself, the house was determined to stand its ground.

A bell signaled her entrance into the Historic Society, and a young woman looked up from behind a large desk. Cora wondered how someone her age could be drawn to such a job. Her question was answered when she noticed a calculus book, a coffee, and a laptop on the desk, and realized a quiet job that allowed time for study was actually a brilliant idea for any college student. There were no glass cases or white gloves in sight.

"Can I help you?" The girl looked relieved to have a distraction from the calculus problem in front of her. Her smile was genuine but tired, the kind given by somebody expected to be pleasant but with other things on their mind. Cora noticed a bright pink streak in the girl's hair and a small diamond nose ring.

"I sure hope so," Cora said. "Might be a long shot, but I've been told there was once a newsletter back in the fifties that shared town news. Not really a newspaper, but more of a society page that told the goings-on of people who lived in Hickory Falls. Any idea if that exists and you have copies?" She was prepared to be told no; college students who take reception jobs rarely taking any actual interest in the substance of their work.

The young woman seemed to perk up a bit. "That's so strange. You're the second person who's asked to see those this week." She got up from her chair and started walking down a spacious hallway toward an aisle where books, binders, and a few pages were displayed under glass. "Had a really hard time tracking it down the first time, so you're the lucky one."

Cora followed closely behind, surprised at the coincidence of someone else looking for the same obscure tidbits from a lost time. "Do you know who asked earlier or why they wanted to see them? Just curious."

"Not a clue." She stood on the bottom shelf and struggled to reach a dark red three-ring binder on the top, its color noticeably different from the ones beside it, since it had been recently nudged awake from its slumber, its binding no longer covered in dust. "Here it is: the complete collection of *The Whispers of Hickory Falls* newsletter. I have to admit, I now want to read these myself. I mean, two people who ask to see the same thing kind of makes it a bestseller around here."

Cora took the binder with her coffee-free hand and almost dropped it, five years of gossip weighing more than she would have thought.

"Thanks. I'll grab one of these tables by the window and put it back when I'm done."

"Take your time." The young woman disappeared down the hallway, back to her calculus homework and the quiet of the lobby. Cora changed her mind and sat in one of the leather chairs by a fireplace that had been filled in and plastered over. She assumed that once upon a time this room had been a parlor of some kind, the kind where guests are greeted and hosts pretend that they always spend their afternoons sipping tea below a window displaying stained-glass flowers. Confident she and the young girl were the only ones in the place, Cora was startled when a shadow on the windowsill began moving, a sleeping cat stirring to capture the best rays that sun could provide. *Of course there's a resident cat,* Cora thought. *How fitting.*

She began her review of the binder's contents, prepared to see long-winded stories with subtle innuendos, like a written version of women talking in whispers over lunch. But she wasn't prepared for the salacious newsletter that she found, a twisted little publication that rivaled any current gossip website. In fact, *The Whispers of Hickory Falls* was worse because it wasn't focused on celebrities living thousands of miles away. It talked about the secrets of people sitting in the church pew next to you, or living right down the street, and the person helping you choose the right wrench in the hardware store—all told with reckless abandon and without fear of being slapped with libel lawsuits. Cora couldn't believe what she was reading.

A certain someone, who often carries a bright pink handbag, enjoyed tuna casserole, peach pie, and coffee at Mitchell's Diner without paying last Tuesday afternoon. Neither a dime nor bite of pie was left on the table. Apparently, the same occurred at a small café right outside of town a few weeks ago . . . a shame.

Bubbles, the sweet beagle in the yellow house on Fourth Avenue, will soon be expecting a litter of pups because of the lack of a fence—or attention—of the neighbors and their mixed breed. Poor Bubbles. Please keep a careful eye on your dogs!

The pages were also full of news of bake sales and garage sales, fundraiser car washes and going-out-of-business discounts, but for the most part, *The Whispers of Hickory Falls* seemed to focus its attention on news otherwise unmentionable.

Our high school's graduating class of 1959 will be one less this year. It's being said that a young woman has been "sent away" to live with relatives for six months and will return at a later undisclosed time.

She flipped through the pages, some stories accompanied by photos of baby buggies and cars for sale, and a few patchwork quilts displayed in a story about the handiwork of one of the town's most sought-after seamstresses, known for her perfection of both the log cabin block design and seven-pointed star patterns. In the summer months, pages had been devoted to the preparation for the annual county fair. Parents of 4-H participants proudly displayed their children's craft and cattle submissions, while a few other "anonymous" sources questioned whether the blueberry pie recipe that had won for four years running was actually made with fresh berries and a homemade crust, as claimed, or rather store-bought berries and a ready-made pie crust. Oh, the horror!

Cora couldn't believe this dirty-laundry newsletter had been in circulation for five years before being shut down. How many lives had been ruined by its allegations?

Cora leafed through the newsletter as quickly as possible, elaborate descriptions of Christmas pageants and red ribbon ceremonies at the arboretum tucked in among bits of gossip and ads for lawn-mowing equipment for sale. *The Whispers of Hickory Falls* could be featured reading for some sort of anthropology class or sociological study regarding the mindset of a mid-century small town. Cora didn't know if she should be fascinated or appalled.

Without a clear idea of a time frame, Cora leafed through the binder, scanning titles, and tried not to get distracted by news of the church's offerings coming up short for the third week in a row. She was looking for anything that could have been related to Clarity, and stopped a few times when the word *witch* appeared, only to find out that these stories related to Halloween pageants; Mrs. Desirée Watters, who was apparently known for her amazing witch ensemble at the annual parade; and a few instances where proofreading did not catch the misuse of *witch* for *which*. Finding nothing of interest, Cora's attention drifted to the cat that was now staring with both suspicion and annoyance at her presence. Cats had a way of doing that, which is why she had always preferred dogs. They were less judgmental.

It wasn't until she reached the June 1960 newsletter edition that three words jumped off the page: *"do-good" professional.*

Cora woke up a bit and continued reading.

A certain young "do-good" professional has made these pages again. Already divorced and on his second marriage at such a young age, this certain someone was seen sharing a romantic drink with a blonde in a bar in a neighboring town.

There was something about the passage that made Cora take a second look.

"do-good" professional

"A doctor perhaps?" Cora asked the quiet room. She continued leafing through the pages, scanning the stories for any sign of an additional story about the mystery man. In an edition a few months later, three more words jumped off the page.

dark-haired beauty

Clarity Shaw didn't own the phrase, but Cora had a hunch that she had found something and kept reading.

And again, a young and handsome—oh, and married— "do-good" professional has been seen having a close and rather heated conversation with a dark-haired beauty, also married (who is known herself for breaking up marriages).

Cora sat back stunned. In the depths of her bones, she was certain the passage described an encounter between Dr. Manchester and Clarity Shaw. As silly as it was, she felt betrayed by a woman she had never met and afraid of a man she had never seen. The entry had been written the same month that Clarity disappeared. More than anything, Cora wanted to reach into the past and warn this "dark-haired beauty," Lewis's wife and Hazel's mom, of the dangers that lay ahead.

Run, Clarity. Stay away from this man and run.

Chapter Nineteen

Cora knew the task that lay in wait for her was bad when she scrubbed the toilet, cleaned her refrigerator, and pulled lint balls off sweaters—all to avoid doing it. Now that her toilet sparkled and the wilting lettuce had been tossed, she couldn't put it off any longer. She topped off her wineglass with the last of the cabernet and sat down at the kitchen table to begin the dreaded project:

The wedding guest list.

She found the entire wedding-planning process frustrating, not because of the work involved, but because of her lack of enthusiasm for doing it. It worried her sometimes. The giddiness that wedding websites told her she was supposed to be feeling had been lost somewhere along the way, if she had ever felt it at all. Cora wanted the marriage, but truth be told, she would have been perfectly happy with a courthouse ceremony wearing a vintage dress circa Carrie Bradshaw in *Sex and the City*, or even a jumpsuit and flowers picked fresh from the side of the road.

When she and Elliott had talked ceremony ideas early on, they had both gravitated toward small and quaint, somewhere outside, where the scenery set the stage and any emotions felt were genuine and not the result of candelabras setting the mood or, even worse, centerpieces with fake glass beads bought at the craft store. She hadn't wanted a binder separated into color-coded categories or appointments with florists to discuss whether a particular flower's aroma was too strong if large quantities of it were used to decorate. She and Elliott had talked about eloping, but it became clear that Cora's suggestion, made in earnest, was assumed to be a joke by her fiancé, a guy who was used to small-town ways and the pressure that came with a mother who would wordsmith their engagement announcement for the paper until you couldn't recognize either Cora or Elliott in the description.

She loved Elliott and couldn't wait until they were simply husband and wife—a partnership that took Taco Tuesdays very seriously and shared books and opinions on the important things in life. That part of her story would have to wait, however; for now, Cora had to address the guest list and suck up her bride-to-be obligations.

She shuffled the papers around on the table until she located the green folder that Lydia had given her and then sorted through a few more piles before finding her own guest list, if you could even call it that. Cora's list of guests was scribbled on the back of a cell phone bill, the list short and comprised of her grandmother and a few friends—long-standing friends who were good and loyal, the kind who will make a long trip without complaint, which is exactly why she felt guilty asking them.

She opened Lydia's folder and pulled out a color-coded spreadsheet of names, addresses, and "notes," including a key to the organizational system that explained what each color meant and corresponding order of priority.

Names in red—highest priority
Names in blue—second highest priority
Names in green—strongly suggest including
Names in orange—lowest priority (but would appreciate your including)

Cora laughed to suppress the urge to cry. She didn't know what to do with a list like this or the less than helpful deciphering code that essentially encouraged her to invite them all. Lydia's spreadsheet contained at least two hundred and fifty people, even though Elliott had told her they wanted fifty or seventy-five guests total. She didn't know what to do with this monstrosity of a list except to ask Lydia to send it to her via email so she could plug the few she would choose into her invite database. Elliott was going to have to address the number of people on the list; he was going to have to be the one to assume the risk of not inviting a "green" person; or, even worse, an orange person finding out they were orange instead of red, and at the bottom of the priority barrel.

The sound of the beeping oven timer startled her, the smell of slightly burnt pizza rolls a welcome emergency that demanded her attention.

Cora glanced at the pile of mail, magazines, and flyers waiting to be sorted, and she tried to convince herself that this task took priority over the guest list, before resigning herself to the fact that the list wasn't going away. The green folder had stared at her from the kitchen table over her morning coffee, lunch of leftover enchiladas, and afternoon ice cream. It wasn't going away and, like any monster, she needed to face it head-on to declare victory.

Now armed with a plate of pizza rolls, Cora returned to the table and readied herself for the task at hand. She scanned Lydia's list, this time marveling at the time and organizational skills required for such a work of art, and scanned the names to familiarize herself with the friends and soon-to-be family that she would shortly spend an evening with, hugging and thanking them for their congratulations. Most of the names were either completely unknown to her or sounded only vaguely familiar from dinners at the club where her in-laws mentioned them or greeted them at the table.

Harold and Hilary Swanson had stopped by to say hello during her last dinner-at-the-club appearance, Hilary's low-cut dress proudly displaying her ample décolletage that was new and "bought, not natural," a tidbit that Lydia had shared with their table after the couple was well outside of earshot.

The Pines—Greg and Marsha—were names that Cora recognized from her conversations with Elliott. Greg was the principal of the local high school and Marsha an art teacher there, both well-known in the community for their philanthropic bake sales and town-wide garage sales that donated all proceeds to a new women's shelter in a neighboring town. Nobody talked much about the nineteen-year age difference between the two, or the fact that Marsha had been a student of Greg's when he taught math at the high school years ago.

With the exception of those few, Cora didn't recognize most of the names on Lydia's list and wondered how she was going to survive an entire evening of small talk with faceless strangers. She grabbed a pen and added Mimi and Juliet's names to the list, thankful to have at least a few friendly faces in her corner. Juliet would come for sure, and Cora hoped that Mimi would come, even if only for a glass or two of bubbly and the opportunity to do what she did best—debrief Cora on who had attended her wedding and their interesting back stories.

Pizza rolls paired with a dark red made everything better, so Cora had relaxed a little. She refocused and began her list review again, starting at the top. As she continued with her list, a name at the top caught her attention. It was in the bright red category. She scanned the spreadsheet and noticed the same name over and over, each time typed in red to identify its owner as among the highest priority guests. How she had missed such a name the first time around she wasn't sure, but Cora suddenly sobered up on recognizing it now. She could actually hear the soft thumping of her heart as it struggled to make sense of what she was seeing, the blister that was forming on the roof of her mouth, from bubbling cheese, now numb.

Manchester.

Cora counted at least eight people with the name Manchester on the first page alone, another six on the second page, and more on the third, each staring back at Cora in a bold red font. O'Quinn, Elliott's last name, was the only name that appeared that often on the list.

Her chest grew heavy. She had to remind herself to breathe, her heart feeling like it had skipped a beat before settling back into a steady rhythm. Hyper-focused and tense, Cora studied Lydia's list more closely, identifying a method of organization that she hadn't recognized initially. The top of the chart was designated for family members, a few aunts' and uncles' names sounding familiar from stories told by Elliott or his parents, a few cousins' names now recognized as part of the same brood. Cora was pretty sure that Nathan O'Quinn was the cousin who went to summer camp with Elliott, his older brother Jake the one who spent time in rehab for prescription drug issues.

The O'Quinns were plentiful and painting much of the spreadsheet in red, but it was their Manchester counterparts who had caught Cora by surprise. She didn't recognize any of the names and only then remembered that Elliott once mentioned he was much closer with his father's side of the family than his mom's.

Manchester.

Cora continued to stare at the names on the list with a feeling of dread brewing like a slow-burning fire in her stomach. The red font that only a little while ago had signified one thing now designated something else, the color used for warnings and a hint of something perilous to come. She scanned the notes section on the chart for confirmation of what, in her heart, she already knew. Sure enough, Lydia had written little notes to accompany guests of significance. Aunts and uncles were designated as such by A and U in the note column, and Wade O'Quinn's parents were listed as GP for their grandparent status.

Cora's hand began to shake as she skipped over the O'Quinn names to focus on the others, searching for another set of GP designations, her finger tracing the names to match their description. When she found the designation, she knew the horror that waited for her at the end of the line—the names of Elliott's grandparents; Lydia's mother and father:

Jack and Joan Manchester.

Hickory Falls

April 2, 1960

The store and its price tags were not for those on an artist's salary. Clarity was more of a thrift shopper, an expert at finding treasures among the crowded racks of clothes and shelves of tarnished silver. Her artist's eye extended far beyond a painted canvas, pops of color in exactly the right places turning her day-to-day outfits and home decor into unique expressions of her taste. More than once, Hazel had been stopped on the street by a stranger commenting on her beauty that was only magnified by ensembles not worn by other little girls her age. Where other moms might be drawn to sequins and lace, Clarity was drawn to vibrant prints and lively patterns, mixing the two in a way that seemed both casual yet entirely intentional, and that people didn't dare try to duplicate. She had an energy distinctive to her, and although her inner voice typically directed her toward second-hand stores, in search of hidden gems, today it was leading her to the beautiful storefront windows with the smell of chocolate bursting forth.

Clarity walked onto the rolled-out red carpet—a bit too ostentatious for her taste—and through the grand front doors held open for her by a security guard. She held Hazel's hand tightly as they made their way past the glass displays of perfume decanters and sequined handbags, the women working behind the counter somehow making white cosmetic coats seem glamorous when coupled with bright red lips and wafts of flowery perfumes.

The air was thick with clouds of lavender and floral bouquets, the sound of women's chatter dancing among them and bouncing off the mirror walls. Crystal chandeliers hung from the ceiling, and little Hazel's eyes lit up as if she had crossed a threshold into a scene from one of her favorite books. The store and its things were beautiful, but it was really the storefront window that had caught Clarity's attention and drawn her in, the poshly styled mannequins arranged around a painting displayed on an easel. The window scene itself was rather silly; the thought of couture handbags lying next to painters' palettes and an artist wearing a strand of pearls, a comical rendition of Clarity's daily routine, yet it piqued her interest. The window scene is what had lured her in, and the smell of chocolate kept her there.

Six-year-old Hazel wanted to stop and stare at everything, including the women engaged in conversation with store personnel about the quality of cashmere scarves. She might not have the money to shop at such a store, but Clarity knew that the common passerby would never know that. She was confident in who she was, and confidence had a way of coming across as wealthy. Her fur-trimmed turquoise thrift-store coat had already earned her a compliment from one of the store employees. Not to mention, Clarity and Hazel were two unique beauties, with their light green eyes and dark hair, beauty itself a luxury that many often associated with money for some reason, as if the two went hand in hand. Hazel couldn't have been more entertained had she walked through the door of an actual dollhouse, her hand tightening on Clarity's with every new shiny item she noticed and waft of perfume she walked through.

Although Clarity was trying to make her way to the candy counter in the back, to buy Hazel a small treat of some kind, a green tiger-eye bracelet on display caught her eye. Hazel bumped into her mom from the force of her sudden stop.

"Oh, honey, I'm sorry," she said with a laugh. "Mommy saw something pretty. Look at this green bracelet. Isn't it beautiful?" Clarity believed in the powers of gems and stones, the world too vast and unbridled for her to ever feel completely in control of her own fate or destiny. She believed in the healing powers of nature and the energy that came with things that have been here much longer than any human form. The bracelet was beautiful, but there were other things to spend their money on these days.

Clarity's thoughts had recently turned toward having another baby, and then there was the issue of the house. Lewis hadn't wanted the family home in the divorce settlement, but Evelyn didn't want it either; she wanted to live closer to town and her friends "when she needed them the most," the latter a point that she raised as often as possible. Lewis had reluctantly agreed, and after he and Clarity married, he'd talked her into moving from the cabin in the woods to the farmhouse so they could grow their family. They would keep the cabin for weekend excursions and getaways. Even after putting every spare penny into renovations and repairs, however, the farmhouse had never felt like home, and Clarity was longing to move back into the cozy cabin. Truth be told, the garden would be the only thing she'd miss on the property, and even then, tomatoes had a way of growing anywhere. After the tragic accident on the cabin property, Lewis had thought it best to keep their distance, but Clarity's heart was in the woods, and in the woods it would stay.

Hazel looked at the bracelet under glass as if at a diamond, her little mouth forming a silent *ooh*, her eyes wide with interest. "You need to buy that pretty bracelet, Mommy," she said. "The green is the same green as your eyes."

"I agree."

The voice behind her made her jump, the man standing so close that her hair moved with his breath. Clarity turned quickly to see him directly behind her, hovering almost, and now moving even closer as a crowd of shoppers struggled to make their way past them in the narrow aisle.

"Oh my, Dr. Manchester, you *startled* me," she said, clutching her chest with a laugh. Clarity pulled Hazel over to the side and out of the line of shopper traffic. "I'd say it's a surprise to see you here, but I think everyone in town is here today. What a wonderful store and grand opening. I think you could find almost anything here." Clarity tried to sound casual, but couldn't shake the sound of her husband's voice suggesting that these encounters were a bit too regular to be coincidental. She smiled, however, eager to exchange pleasantries and then make their way to the smell of fudge being rolled out onto marble tabletops for cutting.

"Now, how many times do I have to tell you? Please, call me Jack." His smile put her at ease like it always did in times of high fevers and when she noticed little white spots in the back of Hazel's throat. Jack was popular among his patients for his comforting bedside manner, sparkling eyes, and a reassuring smile, a magical combination that signaled to worried parents that everything would be fine because he would take care of it. And he always did. Even when Hazel was in a miserable state and struggled to stop itching the tiny red bumps, Jack had welcomed the onset of chicken pox as if it were a long-awaited friend who meant no harm. If a parent could describe the perfect doctor for their children, Jack Manchester, with his doctor's bag full of magic tricks, would be the one.

"And how are you, Miss Hazel? I bet you're on your way to the candy counter." Clarity gestured for her daughter to answer, hugging her shoulders tightly when the child looked up at the doctor with a bashful grin because she was always a little shy around adults.

"Well, we wanted to support a new business, and buying a piece of chocolate might be a little more manageable than buying something like this," Clarity said, nodding toward the jewelry counter with a smile. "I mean, it would almost be rude if we didn't at least sample the fudge, wouldn't it, sweetheart?" Hazel clutched her mom's hand tighter and started bouncing excitedly in anticipation.

"Yes, Mommy, let's go. Let's go!"

"Well, I guess we better go," Clarity laughed, allowing Hazel to pull her in the direction of the intoxicating smell. "So nice to see you, Dr. Manch—I'm sorry—Jack. So nice to see you, Jack." Clarity almost added a little something about always running into each other, but thought better of it, afraid she would risk offending him in some way or come across as rude. But then she was grabbed, not tightly, but firmly, by her elbow. He looked just as surprised as she was at the gesture, releasing his grip and smiling awkwardly. Clarity drew away, trying to hide her shock, but the mere act of pulling her arm away from the man holding it warranted a certain level of alarm and a look to accompany it.

"Sorry, I thought they were going to run into you," he said, gesturing toward a pair of workers carrying shoeboxes on their way to the displays behind them.

Clarity tried to appear casual as she glanced in their direction, but knew it wasn't true. The workers were at least ten feet behind them and taking great care not to disturb shoppers. She laughed uncomfortably and grabbed Hazel's hand, nodding a goodbye because that's all she could manage at the time.

Clarity allowed Hazel to guide her through the maze of shoppers and toward the lacquered oak counter of the candy corner, the glass tubes lining its walls filled with every candy imaginable, and freshly made chocolate delicacies in individual doilies lining the display shelves. The sight and smells were almost overwhelming, but Hazel eventually chose a piece of classic fudge, and Clarity the same, but with walnuts. She tucked a few extra pieces snuggly into a box for the trip home.

Wrapped in the warmth of gooey fudge and the happiness of a five-year-old, Clarity let the encounter with Jack Manchester slip from her mind. There was too much to tell Lewis about that night. The scale and beauty of the store's chandeliers, growing in size since she had left the store; the potpourri of perfumes penetrating hers and Hazel's clothes; and Hazel's description of the chocolate counter made Lewis ooh and aah as if he struggled to believe that such a place was possible. Yes, thoughts of the coincidental encounter had been replaced with questions from Hazel asking when they could go back to the "pretty, pretty store" and a reminder that the price of eating fudge meant brushing her teeth really well that night. Clarity saw no need to tell her husband that she had run into Dr. Manchester *again* or allow him to speculate as to the reason for the awkward arm grab.

She didn't tell her husband because, unlike her other encounters with Dr. Manchester, Clarity couldn't explain this one away. She wasn't a good liar and didn't want to pretend—not with Lewis—and knew her true feelings would betray her if she even attempted to profess that it had all been in good fun. A *coincidence*. A *misunderstanding*. A *misjudgment* about a pair carrying boxes that were nowhere close to them. If Clarity was beginning to doubt such things herself, she would never be able to convince Lewis otherwise.

And, so, it was all forgotten, at least for a while. Clarity was good about things like that; she could compartmentalize events in her life, focusing on the positive and burying the worries under picnics, homemade raspberry scones, and fresh flower arrangements. It wasn't until a few days later that those worries clawed their way out of the dirt and reemerged, refusing to be ignored. Clarity had found a small white box tied with a red satin ribbon lying on her doorstep. She couldn't have known how little time she had left when she brought the box into the house and unwrapped it with Hazel, excited at what she could only assume was a sweet surprise from Lewis. This memory of her mom at the kitchen table just weeks before she disappeared would haunt Hazel for years to come. The memory of a red-ribboned gift and the smell of baking bread one that both killed her slowly and sustained her over the years when she missed the woman who, by her gentle smile and ready embrace, had represented all that was good in the world.

Sometimes really big things come in small packages, and not all of them are a welcome surprise. Hazel had shrieked that day when her mom had finally gotten the ribbon untied and the box opened. Given her own excitement, she hadn't noticed her mother grow quiet when she lifted the lid to reveal a green tiger-eye bracelet resting on its cotton bedding. Years later, when she was going through Clarity's things, Hazel stumbled upon this little box again and remembered that day, discovering a small handwritten note, tucked beneath the cotton, that must have terrified her mother.

To match your eyes.

Chapter Twenty

Cora unwrapped her sandwich, careful not to allow mayo to drip onto the manila folder that sat beside her on the blanket. She took a giant bite, only now realizing that she hadn't really eaten much since the day before and was starving. She would save the chips for later. She didn't want to risk bright orange cheese residue staining the papers. They were too important.

The riverside park was relatively empty except for a few mothers walking rapidly behind jogging strollers with bottles of electrolyte water balanced next to sippy cups in the cup holders. Cora watched as a barge maneuvered slowly toward a bridge, its concrete middle split into two vertical slabs parting like the Red Sea for river traffic. She would never admit it, but Cora found barges frightening in their size and the way they crept along the water. They didn't seem like they should be able to float, too big and bulky to be buoyant in any way. Yet here it was in front of her, navigating a narrow passage past a bridge with the grace and finesse of a sailboat.

She took another bite and wrapped the remaining sandwich back in its paper, eager to get to what she'd come here for. She glanced around, embarrassed at her paranoia. Even if people knew the contents of the manila folder, she doubted they would care, but it didn't stop Cora from looking around like she was in possession of a top secret file that others would steal if given the opportunity.

Even though the police station was willing to turn over the file with a small processing fee for warehouse location and copying costs, Cora still felt like she was doing something wrong having access to a crime investigation file. Although she didn't expect an inch-thick record regarding Clarity Shaw's missing person case, she thought it would amount to more than the three single pages, one of which was simply a checklist of police procedure. Still, three pages of information was more than she had when she placed her sandwich order a half hour ago, so it was progress.

She opened the file and began to read.

Official Report:

Monday, June 6, 1960

Call received from Mr. Lewis Shaw at 5:37 PM, claiming wife, Clarity, was missing. Officer Oliver Claymont traveled to Shaw residence at 1658 Cedar Lane to interview Mr. Shaw and take report. Upon arrival, Mr. Shaw indicates that one child is present in the home.

Mr. Shaw reported to have been alerted that something was wrong when he came home from a work trip to find his daughter alone in the house, which he said was highly unusual. Mr. Shaw walked the perimeter of property with officer and pointed out gardening tools in grass by garden in backyard and a pile of weeds nearby suggesting someone was gardening that day. Dark droplets were found on the grass near the gardening tools. Source not known. Nothing else unusual found outside. Mr. Shaw denied request to enter home, claiming he does not want his daughter disturbed.

Initial impressions: Mr. Shaw appeared distraught and anxious during questioning. A few small dark stains were visible on his clothes and his right hand was wrapped in a gauze bandage with blood stain visible. The bright color of blood suggests it was a fresh wound. When questioned, he indicated that he is a carpenter and cut his hand on a saw earlier in the day. He claimed he arrived home around 5:30 PM after spending the day in Orion picking up wood and other supplies.

Wednesday, June 8, 1960

Office Claymont followed-up with Schmidt Lumberyard in Orion to confirm Mr. Shaw's account of his whereabouts on Monday, June 6. Mr. Laney, owner and operator of the lumberyard, confirmed that Mr. Shaw was there that day picking up an order of wood, but believed he left by 3:30 PM. The lumberyard is an approximate 40-mile drive from the Shaw residence. Mr. Laney could not recall if Mr. Shaw had a bandage on his hand at that time.

A follow-up call was made to Mr. Shaw to request the clothing that he wore on Monday, June 6, but was told that they had already been laundered. Mr. Shaw indicated during that call that he discovered his wife's gardening hat in a nearby field. He again refused a request to search their home, claiming it would disturb his daughter's routine. Mr. Shaw appeared agitated at the request.

Mr. Emmett Mitchem contacted that day via phone. Mr. Mitchem and his wife are the closest neighbors to the Shaw residence. He was asked if he saw any unusual vehicles on the road that day, which he answered in the negative. Mentioned that his wife mentioned overhearing Mr. and Mrs. Shaw in an argument in town the day before, but described his wife as a "busy body" and that she got involved in business where she doesn't belong. Said the Shaws were quiet neighbors and mostly kept to themselves.

Monday, June 13, 1960

Received call from Mr. Shaw at approximately 9:15 AM asking that we investigate Dr. Jack Manchester as a person of interest. Mr. Shaw claims that Dr. Manchester has been stalking his wife and giving her and his daughter unwanted gifts. This information was not mentioned during the initial interview. When asked why, Mr. Shaw indicated that he was in shock and denial that his wife had disappeared.

Without additional credible evidence, we did not pursue a line of questioning with Dr. Manchester at this time.

Monday, July 11, 1960

Received call from Mr. Shaw requesting update on investigation of disappearance of his wife, Clarity Shaw. No additional update available.

Wednesday, July 20, 1960

Received call from Mr. Shaw requesting update on investi-
gation of the disappearance of his wife, Clarity Shaw and
update on our questioning of Dr. Manchester. Mr. Shaw
was informed that we have no further updates and do not
consider Dr. Manchester a viable person of interest.
Mr. Shaw became distressed and verbally angry, accusing
the investigation of being stalled due to prejudice.

That was it. Cora flipped the pages to look for more information, but there was nothing there. The entirety of the Clarity Shaw
file consisted of five entries over a two-month period, any active
investigation seemingly halted after Lewis accused local police of
neglecting the case. That was disturbing, but so were the refer-
ences to Lewis's bandaged hand and stained clothing, as well as
the failure to test the dark droplets by the garden. Then there was
Lewis's refusal to let them into the house and his failure to identify Dr. Manchester until later. She had hoped the police file would
hold some answers, but Cora was more confused than before.

Lewis, the sweet old man with tears in his eyes for his lost
love could not be involved in this. The thought seemed impossible, but the number of true crime shows that Cora watched
whispered in her ear that it was never safe to assume. She grabbed
the rest of her sandwich and closed the file, now left with two
big questions. Was Lewis hiding something or were the police
protecting someone? And, if the latter, could that someone be
invited to her wedding.

Chapter
Twenty-One

~

After Cora ordered her usual "double mocha, light on the whip, with caramel drizzle," she felt she was a little high maintenance on hearing Hazel order, "Coffee, black."

They carried their cups to a small table at the window and away from a book-club group gathering in the leather couch area. Cora had been here before during book-club nights and was surprised at how loud and rowdy a group of well-read moms could be. She had once watched a group pass around a tiny bottle of whiskey to add to their coffees, additional bottles pulled from their purses as the night went on. She spotted a copy of *Anna Karenina* on the table in front of them, impressed at their selection of Tolstoy for such a gathering. She loved the book herself but had to wonder how many of these women, clad in their puffer vests and cashmere sweaters, had actually read the book or, if they had, how many were affected by the protagonist's struggle during an age when women weren't afforded the luxury of self-decision for the sake of happiness. The book had affected her greatly, and she had never looked at the Russian author quite the same because, to write something so tragic, she knew that he must have felt such loss of self deeply within his soul.

Cora watched as the shop owner across the street struggled to balance a cornstalk against the doorframe, a few pumpkins sitting on a bale of hay inched a bit closer for additional support.

This was Cora's favorite time of year—pre-fall—the time leading up to sweater weather and bonfires, when everyone sheds their summer personas and waits patiently for the autumn colors to arrive. She was looking forward to fall in Hickory Falls because in the Midwest you could witness seasons changing rather than relying on the calendar to tell you they've arrived.

She sipped her mocha and waited for Hazel to say something, her request for "a chat over coffee" hovering like a storm cloud waiting to release. Cora's eyes again darted to the group of women assembling near them, one openly admitting that she had started the book, but "simply couldn't get into it" and suggesting something "a little less depressing" for their next book-club selection.

"Thank you for meeting me here," Hazel said, now catching sight of the reader's struggle. "I haven't had a chance to talk to you since you met my dad. You left pretty quickly, but I understand why. Here you are, simply trying to do the right thing and return a set of rings to their proper owner, and you end up in a conversation with a ninety-nine-year-old man accusing someone of murdering his wife." Hazel blew on her coffee before taking a sip, steam rising from her mug like smoke from a fire. She was dressed in a weathered brown leather jacket, her neck kept warm by a bright fuchsia scarf that bounced off the green of her eyes.

Cora's stomach dropped, and she could barely swallow the caramel coating her tongue. It was no secret that Clarity Shaw had disappeared decades ago, but *murder* was not a word that she had ever allowed herself to think or say. Yet, here she was, drinking coffee with a woman who wanted to chat about the fact that her father had accused a man of murdering his wife. And, it wasn't just any man—it was her fiancé's *grandfather*. Cora felt both disloyal and protective—disloyal to the sweet woman sitting across the table from her, yet protective of the man she loved who was probably, at that very minute, doing everything that he could to put one of his patients at ease. She felt nauseous. If Hazel noticed that she was uncomfortable, she didn't let on.

"Growing up, my mother was talked about almost daily. It was always about her habits, personality traits that my dad said we shared, or how a certain smell would bring back a memory for him. Her disappearance was rarely discussed. Even when I asked questions as a teenager or young adult, my dad would shut down." Hazel took another sip of her coffee, her shoulders sinking under the weight of the conversation and her eyes suddenly looking heavy and tired. "One thing that I always noticed, though, was my father would always refer to her as *taken*. The thought that she left on her own was never entertained. She was always *taken* by *somebody*. He'd catch himself before saying a name, though. It was like there was a name on the tip of his tongue, but something bad would happen if he actually said it out loud. That day in his room was the first time I heard him accuse Jack Manchester, but not the first time I had heard the name. This is a town quick to judge, but only in whispers. The people here have been eager to provide their two cents on any drama or scandal since horse and buggies lined the streets. Towns have energy and auras just like people do, and Hickory Falls has a complicated one. For every burst and swirl of color, there is a darkness."

Hazel almost looked surprised by what she had just shared, but relieved to have said it all. Secrets have a weight all their own. Some believe that when a person dies, they lose twenty-one grams—the weight of a human soul. Cora had to believe that secrets weighed much more, their heaviness so profound that they etch lines into skin and cause shoulders to buckle, buried secrets responsible for more premature aging than sunrays and burgers combined. Even now, after unloading these thoughts into the universe, Hazel looked lighter. Her eyes, following passersby as they walked past the shop window, shining brighter than only a few minutes before.

Cora no longer cared if others could hear their conversation. She was in this whether she wanted to be or not, and she owed it to Hazel to sit and listen without worrying about the outside world. Hazel was lost again; although her gaze was directed toward the pumpkin display outside, she was looking through it toward something much farther away that only she could see, a memory perhaps, or a feeling that had stayed locked inside for much too long. It was only in the presence of a virtual stranger—a mild acquaintance at best—that she felt comfortable sharing. Hazel fidgeted with her bracelet, the tiger-eye green stones like little magic balls around her wrist.

"That's a beautiful bracelet."

"My mother's. The green is the same as her eyes."

"Yours too. You must have your mom's eye color."

"That's what my dad said, but there was something special about hers. Mine might be the same color, but hers were different. I remember thinking there was something to them, a gold shimmer, that couldn't be found in nature. They were special."

"I'm sure." Cora wanted to allow Hazel this moment uninterrupted.

"It was impossible for me not to hear the rumors," Hazel eventually continued. "There are women in this town who made sure to discuss them when I was within earshot, the sordid story about the woman in the woods enticing the good doctor away from his family. There are a lot of people in town who still believe that she left town on her own when Dr. Manchester refused to leave his wife, determined to travel town to town until she found her next victim."

Hazel's eyes turned glassy from the painful memory, a single tear falling onto the coffee cup's saucer. It was only then that Cora realized how horrible it must have been for a child to lose her mother and then have to listen to hurtful speculation, especially suggesting that she had simply left her daughter behind in search of something better.

"Why didn't you leave?" Cora asked. "I mean, when you got older. Why didn't you move away from a town with such painful memories?"

"I couldn't leave my dad," Hazel said. "Even when we were all grown and he had built a life with Evelyn and their daughters, I couldn't leave him. When you share something like this, it weds you to a place. Leaving my father and Hickory Falls would be like leaving my mother behind in a way. I was so happy to leave that house, though. When Evelyn and Dad entered their nursing home, I was so happy to no longer have a reason to go there. Beverly can have it all." Hazel blew on her coffee before taking another sip, the shop owner across the street finally admitting defeat and shoving the cornstalk into the door's corner before slamming the door, to return inside.

"Wait, so the house that Beverly lives in now is the same house that you grew up in? The same house that—"

"Yes, it's the house that Mom disappeared from. I had to live in a house knowing that my mother vanished into thin air from the backyard."

Just then, an old pickup truck carrying a group of high schoolers in the back pulled up in front of the coffee shop, teenage girls dressed in HF Cheer Squad sweatshirts jumping out with "Homecoming Parade" signs clutched in their hands. Hazel smiled at the scene, girls scurrying away in groups of two or three toward shop destinations, a few making a noisy entrance into the warmth of the coffee shop and toward the poor barista, who sighed when he saw them coming.

"According to my dad, Evelyn insisted that she didn't want the house when they divorced, preferring instead to move closer to the town's center so she could be around her friends. We lived there—me, Mom, and Dad—until the world turned upside down. When Dad and Evelyn eventually remarried, he was ready to sell the place, but then she declared the house one of her absolute favorite places and insisted on moving back in." She paused to take a sip of her coffee, a new look taking over her face, one of confusion with a tinge of anger. "A bit strange if you ask me," she continued. "Why Evelyn insisted on moving back into a house connected to such a tragedy seems odd. Even cruel."

"I can't imagine," Cora said. "I'm so sorry." It was all she could think to say. There was nothing normal about this family, and her feelings about its members fluctuated daily. She had started to doubt Lewis, which she now regretted as she sat across from Hazel, who clearly adored him. She disliked Evelyn for pressuring him to stay in a home with such horrible memories, but the woman was considered nothing less than a saint by her daughter Beverly, and thinking ill of the recently departed seemed wrong. Cora felt both affection and pity for this family, as well as anger and disbelief at how certain things had been handled. They were their own Greek tragedy.

"Thankfully, Dad kept Mom's old house, the one that I live in now, and I moved in when I was eighteen," Hazel continued. "It's like a warm hug living there, there's so much of my mom in the cottage." She seemed to let her mind drift a bit before remembering why she was here, refocusing on Cora and giving her a forced, yet somehow genuine, smile.

"I can't imagine how hard that must have been on you, I mean, when your dad and Evelyn got back together," Cora said, careful in her word choice but interested in the impact that such a dysfunctional situation had had on Hazel as a child. "I don't want to pry. I'm just sorry you had to go through that. It must have been very painful and difficult for a child to understand."

Hazel's shoulders seemed to sink with the weight of Cora's words, her eyes now lost in the blackness of the coffee in her hand. She looked like she, too, was considering her next words carefully, their conversation one between two well-intentioned souls desperate not to hurt or offend the other. "Yes, I was only six years old when Mom disappeared, and just seven when Dad remarried Evelyn. It was quick—*calculated*, if you will. My poor dad was too sad and tired to put up much of a fight."

As careful as Hazel was with her words, Cora found her description of events odd. She was clearly protective of her father, and the resentment she felt for a woman who had taken advantage of his state of mind all those years ago was still sharp and biting in its intensity. Cora couldn't help but think it had only magnified with time; a seven-year-old doesn't understand the details of an event, but a grown woman with hindsight sees things clearer as the years go on.

Eager to change the subject, Hazel watched the teenagers move garage sale ads around on the shop's bulletin board to position the homecoming poster front and center, only to realize that there were no more tacks left. They laughed the way that giddy girls do over the smallest of problems. "Dad mentioning Jack Manchester out loud really threw me for a loop," Hazel said. "I haven't seen him like that in years. He was so intense and angry again about Mom's disappearance. He's kept so much inside all these years, but I think Evelyn's death gave him the freedom to voice his anger without appearing disloyal. Seeing him like that made me angry again too, and I decided to renew our search for an answer. The topic that I tried to avoid for years has suddenly become one of my top priorities. I even went to the Historic Society to read up on town gossip from years ago to see if Jack or my mother was ever mentioned."

Cora hadn't realized how tense she was until she felt a sigh of relief leave her body. The mysterious patron who had combed through issues of *The Whispers* right before she did had now been identified and was sitting across from her. She wondered if she should mention the passages about Jack Manchester meeting the dark-haired woman, but decided against it. If Hazel hadn't already seen it, she didn't need to know the insensitive and callous way her mother had been described by gossip hounds years ago.

"I wanted to buy you a coffee to say thank you," Hazel said. "It's a small gesture, but I appreciate how dedicated you were to return the rings to their rightful owner. After all of these years, the rings are home." Hazel fidgeted with the long gold chain around her neck, revealing the two rings secured carefully on the necklace. Cora couldn't help but feel a bit of déjà vu from when Beverly had done the same thing, both Evelyn and Clarity's wedding rings hanging next to the hearts of those who loved them.

"No thank-you is necessary," Cora said. "I couldn't have imagined keeping them under the circumstances. Wedding rings are different—they're special—and they need to stay within a family." Cora's thoughts began dancing around again, some telling her to share her own investigation efforts with Hazel while others warned her that she'd sound like a lunatic for doing so. This wasn't her family. These weren't her rings. This wasn't her mystery to solve. These thoughts were still battling one another in her head when Hazel dropped a bombshell that Cora hadn't seen coming.

"It was hard enough losing my mom," Hazel said, looking squarely into Cora's eyes. "Here was my dad, already the center of talk in the town for divorcing Evelyn, and then his second wife vanishes. Some people even thought he did it, a man suffocating from guilt and regretful of his decision, disposing of one wife so he could do the 'right thing' and go back to his first."

Cora's heart rate quickened. Had she allowed her mind to analyze the facts, or had she allowed her judgment to become hazy by the innocent look of an old man with bright blue eyes? If she studied the facts, would she have acknowledged that he had been a viable suspect all along? As every great mystery novel teaches you, never overlook what's right under your nose. No, she couldn't imagine the frail old man she'd met doing such a thing, but she also couldn't have imagined him having a torrid affair either, and there was a temper there, one that changed the color of his eyes when unleashed. She had been witness to that when he identified Jack Manchester as the man who had murdered his wife.

Cora felt dizzy and overheated despite the goose bumps on her arms and the cool draft from the front door. Their innocent coffee klatch was beginning to feel like it had a hidden agenda, and Cora couldn't shake a growing and uneasy feeling.

"Nobody could ever truly understand what my dad went through in silence all those years," Hazel said, covering one of Cora's hands and squeezing. "Even as a little girl, I knew. I knew my daddy was suffering. Evelyn tried desperately to pretend like her family was intact again, and she did a good job convincing everyone that we were okay, that we were happy. I knew he wasn't, though. Not really. How could she expect him to move on when his wife had disappeared? How could she expect me to smile for the camera?" Hazel shook her head as if still in disbelief.

"I don't know," Cora said. "You were so young. I'm sure you did what you thought would make your father happy at the time. That's what children do."

That's what children do. They cover for their parents. They protect them. Cora's thoughts were racing now.

"It wasn't until much, much later that he confessed something to me that nobody else knew." Hazel closed her eyes to prepare for the memory. "He didn't just lose my mom that day." She leaned in a bit closer, locking eyes with Cora. "He lost the *baby*."

Chapter
Twenty-Two

~

"Of *course* everyone knew."

Cora realized that Mimi had two moods—annoyed and very annoyed. No matter the topic, she seemed annoyed that she had to explain as much as she did in as much detail as was required, or *very* annoyed that the topic was even worthy of explanation at all.

This discussion fell into the latter category.

Mimi opened the back door a crack and blew smoke out into the alley, shooing as much of the billowy grayness with it as possible. Smoking in an art gallery seemed an absurd thing to do given the damage that smoke could have on the paintings, but Mimi owned the gallery and really didn't seem to care. She was now puffing on the cigarette as if she could inhale away what Cora had told her. "*Everyone* knew she was pregnant," Mimi repeated, shaking her head in disbelief that Cora would think otherwise. "That's what made the story all the more salacious. Beautiful woman breaks up family. Snags guy. Messes around with handsome town doctor. Gets pregnant. Disappears. You can't write this stuff." Cora shot Juliet a look, her friend only shrugging at the nonchalance with which Mimi approached such a sensitive topic. She was apparently used to it.

"Did people really suspect Lewis?" The thought still seemed absurd to Cora, but hadn't people thought the same thing about Ted Bundy with his college-boy good looks and charm?

"You're asking me to dig deep, here." Mimi said. "I've buried these memories away with the ones that I never saw need to give thought to again. Yes, at the time, there was no limit to the talk or speculation. People thought that if he could leave his wife and kid, Lewis was capable of a lot more than you might think he was."

The open door brought a chill to the air that Cora wasn't prepared for, her light sweater no match for weather that had smothered any sign of summer. Autumn had officially arrived, and Cora's wardrobe had better adjust.

Cora dodged a lingering smoke ring in the air and followed Mimi and Juliet back into the main gallery area, pulling up a barstool to continue their conversation by Mimi's desk. "Hazel seems to think that nobody else knew about the baby," Cora said. She looked at Juliet, but her friend was peeling off a strip of nail polish from her thumb.

"Honey, this is a small town," Mimi said. "And if you think it's small now, think how small it was back in the sixties, and I'm not talking about size alone. Small *minds*. Small *talk*. Small—well, you know. Small *everything*. There was no way Clarity Shaw's pregnancy was going to be kept a secret, not around here. I mean, there was only one doctor in town, and he was the rumored baby daddy."

"What?" Cora and Juliet both shrieked in unison, the peeling nail polish now forgotten. "Oh my God, it was the *doctor's*? Holy shit." Juliet stood wide-eyed, finally showing interest in a topic that Cora had been trying to engage her in since the beginning. "Hickory Falls could have its own reality show, or maybe be featured in one of those unsolved mystery shows. I can't believe she was pregnant with the doctor's baby. I mean, it's pretty clear *he* had motive."

"Hold on, hold on," Cora said. "There's no proof, right? I mean, people might have talked about that, but that was just a rumor." Cora felt like she was betraying Hazel by allowing them to even entertain the idea, and wanted to put an end to it immediately. "This is all insane. This poor family."

Juliet started to say something but stopped herself when Mimi raised a hand to signal for silence. She stared at Cora—*glared*, to be precise—studying her face for a hint of something that Cora felt the sudden need to protect.

"Now, why would you come here to talk about all of this if you don't want to hear about it?" Mimi asked. "I agree that Hazel is about as sweet as they come, but that doesn't mean her mother was an angel. None of us are. If she could break up one family, what makes you think that she would stop herself from destroying another?"

The words stung, even more so because of their pointed accuracy. The fact was, Cora didn't know the truth and had no way of finding out, but she wanted to believe the loving woman described by Hazel and Lewis would have never betrayed them in that way. Yet, here she was, dark thoughts creeping into view that she couldn't keep at bay. Before her coffee with Hazel, she never would have dreamed about Lewis being a suspect, but if Clarity had been pregnant with another man's baby, who knows what he could have been capable of.

That being said, wouldn't his anger have been directed toward Jack Manchester? Waters that had been muddy before were now worse. *Jack Manchester. His wife. Lewis.* Some unknown other man in a neighboring town. The list of suspects for Clarity's disappearance was only growing the deeper Cora dove into the mystery.

"Oh, I remember my mom and her friends talking about all of this. Oh yes, the talk. And when she disappeared, that talk only continued because it gave people closure to a mystery that made them uncomfortable. For the first time, people had started locking their doors at night, fearful of some shadow in the dark who might take them in their sleep, or their children on the way to school. When the discussion turned to Clarity Shaw and a baby that had to disappear, people felt like it was an end to the story, with a rational explanation. They could unlock their doors again."

"Yeah, but assuming the doctor did it, was he ever arrested or charged?" Juliet asked. "I'm all for closure, but what happened to the good doctor?"

"No body. No evidence. All speculation." Mimi waved to a passerby like she knew them. In this town, she undoubtedly did. "Even as haphazard as things were back then, they needed at least a shred of evidence to arrest him. And, nobody was eager to take away the town's only doctor without cause, especially when his family's name was plastered on buildings."

Cora considered telling Mimi and Juliet about the police file but quickly decided against it. Her head was already spilling with scenarios, a rotating door of thoughts and speculation that changed with the wind and time of day. The case of Clarity Shaw had essentially taken over her life. She could convince herself that Lewis was involved over morning coffee, and then by lunch, be prepared to tell Elliott that his grandfather might have murdered someone.

At times, she even bought into the scenario of Clarity running off, but usually only until she remembered the presumed droplets of blood by the garden and the description of a woman who, by all accounts, loved her daughter fiercely and would never have abandoned her.

Although Mimi reluctantly entertained her interest in the story and Juliet considered it town gossip, she didn't think either of them would understand her efforts to obtain the actual police file. It even seemed a bit obsessive and absurd to her.

Cora felt a warm wave of hindsight roll over her. On more than one occasion, Elliott had mentioned being part of a multi-generational doctor-dentist family in Hickory Falls. Because his father was also a dentist, Cora had assumed he was referring to that side of his family. She had no idea that his mother's side of the family—the Manchesters—were equally prominent and of long-standing Hickory Falls heritage. The *good doctor* was on her wedding guest list. His place card would be written in ornate gold calligraphy—*Jack Manchester, Grandfather of the Groom*—displayed proudly on one of the tables. And yet, here she was, discussing the possibility that the family she was about to marry into was at the heart of a mystery that she'd broken open like a scab that wasn't fully healed. How was she going to be able to live with this secret and not tell Elliott? How do you tell someone you love that there's a potential monster in his family and at a wedding table reserved for those who love him the most?

You simply can't tell the man you love something like this. You have to bury it deep and hope that it doesn't burn a hole large enough for the truth to shine through.

Hickory Falls

~

Two Weeks Before Clarity's Disappearance

It's a little hard to make apple pie without apples.

Clarity clutched little Hazel's hand as she navigated the grocery aisles toward the produce section tucked inconveniently in the far back corner of the store. This new store marketed itself as so much more convenient than the tiny mom-and-pop shop that it had gobbled up, but she found it anything but, the increase in inventory overwhelming when one simply needed to grab a few items and get back home for dinner.

Hazel loved the new store, however, it's shiny displays and addition of nonfood items like small plastic bottles for her dolls and colorful hair clips adding a level of excitement to the trips. For parents, the new items added nothing but headaches as they removed items from their shopping carts that had been secretly tucked in under a loaf of bread; or, worse yet, when a toy emerged at the checkout line and they had to decide whether removing it was worth the public tantrum that would come with taking it away.

Hazel never asked for any toys but wanted to visit them every time she was at the store, and stare at them with admiration. Her favorite was the tiny plastic doll bottles filled with some unidentifiable goo that made it look like there was actually milk inside. This time was no different. Although apples were all that were on their list that day, Clarity didn't resist when the little hand clasped in hers started tugging gently to steer her in the direction of the doll bottles. Clarity smiled; a package of the bottles was hidden at home already, in anticipation of a midweek surprise, but she allowed herself to be directed toward aisle three, where they were displayed next to tiny metal cars and hair bows that were designed to look like candy cane swirls.

"Oh, they look so real," Clarity said, faking excitement as she did at each visit to the doll bottles. "How lovely. I'm sure your dollies would love bottles like those." Hazel just smiled and nodded in agreement. Annie and Grace, her most beloved dolls at home, would indeed love them. She would never ask for such a thing, however, understanding that apples were the only item on their list and all they would be leaving with today.

What occurred next would be retold for years to come, each rendition traveling a bit farther from fact and further into fiction. Most in town liked to remember the event as a courageous confrontation by a woman done wrong. Like most events, however, the truth lay somewhere far from any torrid description. On that day, Clarity had turned in search of apples, leaning down to say something to her daughter, when she crashed into a cart being steered by Joan Manchester. The collision left a baseball-sized bruise on Clarity's hip, but would be recalled—by zero eyewitnesses to the event—as a forceful attack by Clarity against her not-so-secret lover's wife in the most public and humiliating way.

In a small town thirsty for salacious stories, a small crash in aisle three would turn into Joan Manchester's moment of truth; it would be remembered as her brave reaction to a woman who blocked her ability to simply stroll down the grocery aisle, mocking her control over Joan's life and her husband's bed. The reality was so very different.

Joan apologized for running into Clarity, both women growing quiet when they realized who the other was. Clarity was well aware that rumors had started to swirl as a result of Dr. Manchester's unwanted attention, and prayed that Joan would know they weren't true. She had actually just come from seeing Jack Manchester for a prenatal appointment, feeling oddly guilty about this, even though she had no other doctor option within a ten-mile radius. She had recently promised Lewis that she would change doctors, a longer drive worth a renewed sense of peace in her household. Things had gotten out of control. She and Lewis had been arguing more than ever, their latest disagreement within earshot of their nosy neighbor, who, Clarity was certain, slowed her pace in front of the Five and Dime to hear them better.

Dr. Manchester had crossed a line, and his oath to do no harm had already been broken. His unwanted attention and actions were hurting her family, and she was now face-to-face with another of the good doctor's victims, a woman cloaked in a look of hurt and shame at being in the center of rumors she couldn't control.

After apologizing, Joan took a breath and stared at Clarity, clearly not sure how to address someone responsible—truthfully or otherwise—for tearing at the seams of her marriage. Clarity couldn't have known—what with supposed patient confidentiality and all—that Dr. Manchester had told his wife about Clarity's pregnancy, a strange disclosure under any circumstance, but even stranger coupled with rumors that the people of Hickory Falls seemed quite willing to build into a bonfire.

The truth was, Joan didn't know what to believe about her husband anymore. The marriage that she had so desperately wanted, the one that involved being the dutiful doctor's wife, looked up to by society ladies who resisted looking up to anyone, was not turning out the way she had expected. She was now standing before Clarity Shaw, a beautiful woman with kind eyes, and was hoping she wouldn't notice the two bottles of white wine in her cart. Wine, it seemed, had become Joan Manchester's most trusted friend these days.

Although no words were exchanged except for the cursory cart-crash apology and token 'It's okay, I'm fine' in response, Clarity was a bit stunned by the run-in. She had seen a photo of Joan Manchester in the doctor's office and had heard stories about her philanthropic efforts in the community, but the entire encounter left her with a sour taste. Jack Manchester had refused Clarity's return of the bracelet, brushing the gift off as something innocent. His follow-up request for dinner confirmed there was nothing innocent about it, and her decline of his invitation was met with shock—and a flash of anger—although she had trouble believing her reaction was a surprise. Despite the fact that she never led Jack Manchester to believe his feelings were reciprocated, the look in his eyes upon her rejection suggested that he was not a man told no to often.

Clarity had been shaken by her encounter with Dr. Manchester, which had occurred on a busy sidewalk in the middle of an afternoon. She was well aware that such a public discussion could be misconstrued, by anyone listening, as a lover's quarrel. It was anything but; Clarity simply wanted the good doctor to leave her alone and, true to her word, was already researching doctors in neighboring towns for her prenatal needs. Even with only a portion of the details and knowing nothing about the bracelet, Lewis had insisted on distancing themselves from a doctor who pushed any conceivable boundary of healthy space between doctor and patient. Enough with the gifts. Enough with the chance encounters. Enough with Dr. Manchester.

Clarity loved her family. She would never do anything to jeopardize the happiness that it had taken her so long to find. No, it hadn't been discovered in the conventional way, and there had been other hearts broken in the process, but she chose to believe Lewis when he told her that his marriage to Evelyn had been doomed from its beginning and that her presence in his life was simply light illuminating a burrowing crack in a foundation built on quicksand.

Wondering if she should use this opportunity to talk to Joan and dispel any rumors, Clarity looked up and down each aisle to catch her, only to see her abandoned cart at the end of the baking goods aisle and a flash of her red coat as she left through the front doors of the store. Clarity was so preoccupied in looking for Joan that she didn't notice that Hazel had let go of her hand and started running down an aisle in the opposite direction.

"Beverly! Beverly!"

Hearing her daughter's voice echo through the store is what brought Clarity back to the present. She followed Hazel's voice until she spotted her daughter running toward her half sister. Beverly looked shocked to see them, but not nearly as surprised as Evelyn, who looked like she was close to dropping the jar of pickles she was grabbing from a nearby shelf.

Hazel threw her arms around Beverly, always happy to see the young woman, who never seemed comfortable returning the affection. Beverly put one arm awkwardly around the six-year-old and glanced at her mother as if to see whether the small gesture met with her approval. Clarity couldn't believe her bad luck that day: the two women in town carrying the most disdain for her somehow both in the grocery store at the same time. She walked toward the awkward group of three and did her best to make light of the situation.

"Now, Hazel, maybe Beverly doesn't want to be squeezed so hard," she said with a laugh. "Sorry, Beverly. You know how your little sister adores you." Evelyn visibly winced at the statement, and Clarity immediately regretted it. She didn't know how to navigate this family dynamic; with each turn, her attempts at kindness came off as insensitive, and her desire to give everyone space came off as even more so. Beverly was now sixteen years old. Although she had always been protective of her mother in this unhealthy family dynamic, as she got older, this feeling had increased, her teenage hormones escalating even the smallest of comments into a dramatic affront for which Lewis would have to serve as mediator. Clarity could do no right by her, and she completely understood why. She simply hoped she and her stepdaughter could have a truce someday, although her relationship with Evelyn was never going to grow beyond painful cordiality.

"Hey, Hazel," Beverly said, patting the child on the back and then prying her little arms from around her. "Did you visit your baby bottles again?" Clarity smiled at this, even the smallest glimmer of kindness from Beverly to her half sister a welcome reprieve from her usual aloofness toward the little girl.

"I did!" Hazel shouted, clearly excited at the show of interest. "They have pink ones and blue, but I like the pink."

"I know you do," Beverly said, again, looking to her mother for some sign that the small exchange was okay. Before she knew what was happening, Hazel had grabbed her hand and was dragging her down the aisle toward the little plastic toys that filled her dreams with thoughts of baby feedings. Beverly couldn't hide her smile as she allowed herself to be steered by an excited six-year-old, one last glance given to her mother to express that she had little choice in the matter. When Clarity lost sight of them as they turned the corner, she found herself alone with Evelyn, a situation that had never before occurred.

"I'm on my way to the apples," Clarity said, trying to sound casual. "I promised Hazel that we'd make apple pie this afternoon." Evelyn said nothing. She glared at Clarity in a way that made the second Mrs. Shaw physically tense, her body in wait for an impending assault.

"I know all about you and Dr. Manchester," Evelyn said coldly. "Moving on already?"

Clarity was stunned. Evelyn was looking at her with such hatred that she didn't know how to respond or if it was safe to do so. She simply couldn't let such an accusation go, however, her disgust for such a rumor written all over her face, if Evelyn cared enough to notice. "Evelyn, there is absolutely no truth—"

"Oh, please," Evelyn said. "Spare me the story. What are you going to say? That you're not that type of woman? We both know that's not true.

"Everyone in this town knows the type of woman you are, even Lewis. I knew it was only a matter of time before you got tired of him and moved on. Set your sights a bit higher, perhaps?

Looking for an upgrade?" Each word spoken was drowning in contempt, Evelyn's mouth drawn so tightly that her lips had lost their color. Glancing down the aisle to make sure nobody was near, Evelyn took one step closer to Clarity and then another until she could feel the warmth of Evelyn's breath on her cheek.

"I believe in the power of karma," Evelyn whispered, leaning in. "You'll understand what it's like to lose everything someday. Perhaps sooner than you think."

The sound of Hazel's laughter growing closer released the grip that Evelyn's words had on the moment, and Clarity was spared a further onslaught through the grace of their daughters' return.

Chapter Twenty-Three

～

Midwest weather is a scary thing. Cora should have known that by now.

She was learning how fickle the weather here could be the hard way, especially in this odd time of year where it felt like summer at the beginning of the week and fall two days later, only to return to warm weather by the weekend. She didn't know how many times people commented, "Welcome to the Midwest" when they noticed her freezing in short sleeves. She quickly learned that it was best to dress in layers and strip them off as needed. Just when she thought she was getting the hang of the temperature swings, she found herself on a gravel road with dark clouds moving in, and still a mile from her car.

Another hard lesson learned is that dark clouds have their own spectrum in these parts. There are dark clouds that simply smother the sun's rays for a while, those that offer a burst of refreshing rain in an otherwise sunny afternoon—and then there are the off-color clouds, the ones with tinges of green and purple, that bring a menacing calm to the air. Cora wasn't an expert quite yet, but on the cloud spectrum, these looked ominous.

She had really just wanted to get away from it all and take a walk to clear her head. Cora didn't know what to do about the whole Jack Manchester story and couldn't avoid the wedding invitation process much longer. She couldn't stomach having this information and not sharing it with Elliott, but she didn't want to raise it, especially when the stress of his job and wedding-planning texts from his mother were already putting a damper on most days. And truthfully, she really didn't know if there was even any story to tell. Speculation and rumors dated from long ago, but Jack Manchester hadn't been the only questionable character in Hickory Falls back then. In fact, Mimi's description of Clarity's disappearance raised questions about a lot of people who could have been involved.

Cora was torn—she wanted to protect Elliott but also felt disloyal having information about his family that he didn't know. Then again, maybe he did. That would be an entirely different discussion and one that would explain why he wasn't too keen on her jumping into a decades-old mystery involving his family. What if he knew all of this and was protecting *her*? The thought seemed unlikely, but Elliott *had* been quick to shut down any attempt she made to shed light on Clarity Shaw's disappearance, even becoming angry with her at her unwillingness to drop the topic. It typically took a lot to make Elliott angry, so Cora's interest in a random small-town mystery didn't seem to warrant such a reaction, especially when he was from Hickory Falls and should have been at least a little intrigued by what she'd found. Then there was Lydia's coffee meeting with the Shaw sisters; the trio's meeting had always bothered Cora, but not as much as Elliott's dismissive annoyance that she would even raise it as an issue.

The growing cluster of recent events is what brought Cora to a gravel road that day, her car parked a mile away and a storm looming overhead. She had simply wanted to clear her head, and had driven to a little park outside of town to take a walk, hoping the crisp fresh air would rid her of confusion and point her in the right mental direction. Ironically, Cora realized that somewhere alongside the fields of corn and horses she had lost her physical sense of direction.

The clouds were growing denser, and the sun was close to becoming blocked out completely, casting the entire scene in sepia tones. Cora started walking toward a house right ahead, the only one within sight, hoping to find someone kind enough to give her a ride back to her car. She wouldn't have even considered such a thing in California, but the thought of being the second girl gone missing from this area made her reconsider. The absurdity of the situation made her laugh. Of course, she would get caught in a storm. Of course, she would lose her way. Of course, the gravel roads outside of Hickory Falls wound round like a labyrinth to keep people in or visitors out. Nothing surprised Cora anymore. For anyone who'd said her move to the Midwest would be boring, she would have quite a story to tell.

Her sense of panic only grew when she finally made her way to the farmhouse drive and realized where she was. The white paint on the black mailbox had faded, but she didn't need it to tell her who lived there.

"You've got to be kidding me," Cora said. "Of all the farmhouses."

Glancing farther up the road to look for another option, Cora saw nothing but mini dust storms getting kicked up from the wind as it collided with gravel. She debated whether getting caught in the rain was a more attractive option at this point than knocking on Beverly's door.

When a bolt of lightning pierced the landscape uncomfortably close to where she stood, she opted to humor fate by revisiting the scene of the crime. Besides, the temperature had dipped suddenly, and the rain would be cold, making this option the best choice.

Cora made her way up the long drive, relieved at least that she wouldn't have to explain her predicament to total strangers. The sun was losing its battle with the clouds, the last of its rays consumed entirely by dark clouds that were moving at an alarming rate in her direction. Perhaps because of this loss of light, a jump in her adrenaline from the lightning strike, or a combination of both, Cora focused her attention on putting one foot in front of the other as she maneuvered large rocks and well-worn pits along the uneven drive, concerned that one misstep could land her with a twisted ankle or shredded knee. She was too hyperfocused to notice that she wasn't alone. Birds had disappeared to their nests, and cows who rarely seemed bothered by weather— or anything at all—had moved in unison to the barn. But even with the animals out of sight, had Cora looked up, glanced for even a moment in the direction of the shed, she would have realized that she was not alone. She was being watched.

Cora didn't see the figure emerge from the darkness of the shed and start to walk toward her. She was too lost in her own thoughts and what she was going to say when she reached the front door to sense a presence moving swiftly among the raindrops that had started to fall in giant drops. The rain hitting the rocks and shed's metal roof camouflaged the sound of footsteps approaching. A few steady claps of thunder quickened her heart rate and drowned out the thud of heavy boots on loose gravel.

Any street smarts that Cora had developed living in a big city had vanished among the rolling hills of the countryside, her intuition no competition for the complexities of a small town determined to hide its secrets. Cora didn't notice any movement, hear any footsteps, or sense any danger. She certainly didn't see the hand grab for her arm as she reached the edge of the house's sidewalk. Cora struggled to remain standing when she was pulled backward, the heat of genuine panic gagging her as her mind processed that, unlike ten seconds before, the storm was not the source of danger. She jerked her arm to the side to release the grip and gasped as she turned to run toward the house.

"No! No, it's okay. Oh, I didn't mean to scare you." It took a second for Cora to place him. She had only met Beverly's husband one time but now recognized the man in front of her. "Joseph," he said. "I'm Bev's husband."

His tone was calm yet firm. He didn't look pleased by her unexpected appearance, but didn't look upset either. Cora wasn't sure how to take the man standing in front of her, all six feet something of him draped in a black raincoat, and wearing tall leather boots and a black hat that was sending rain drops off in various directions as they hit. He looked sincere in his apology, hands held up as if in arrest, a quick step or two taken from her to prove he meant no harm. Cora was still frightened by the shock, but there was something in Joseph's eyes that reassured her, a pleading look, and he almost seemed relieved to see her.

"Of course," Cora responded, now a bit embarrassed that she was the one trespassing and wandering up to his house in the rain, without explanation. "You probably wonder what I'm doing here, especially on foot. I went for a walk and got a bit too far from my car when the storm started rolling in. Any chance you could give me a lift back to my car? It's at the little park on the edge of town." Cora realized that it was bizarre to go from fear to trust in someone so quickly; but she wanted nothing more, then, than the warmth of her car and going home to the leftover vegetable lo mein in her refrigerator. She was willing to take the risk if it meant avoiding a rainy afternoon stuck to the vinyl chairs in Beverly's kitchen, making uncomfortable small talk.

Joseph didn't say anything at first. He glanced toward the house and then back at Cora before gesturing for her to follow him to the dilapidated barn. He neither nodded his head in agreement nor shook it, leaving Cora to simply hope that they were headed toward a vehicle with car keys in the ignition, ready to roll. The rain was now coming down hard, but through the blur of the relentless downpour, Cora spotted two vehicles—a truck and an older sedan—parked in the driveway and in the opposite direction to where Joseph was leading her.

Cora stopped. She could feel one of her shoes begin to sink into a muddy tire track. There were two vehicles in the driveway. They didn't need to walk to the shed.

She glanced at the front door of the house, calculating how long it would take her to run and gain entrance before Joseph noticed. Her trust had slipped back to fear so rapidly that even her heart didn't know how to process the situation—a few quick beats and then a slow and steady skip before revving up again. Time, it seemed, didn't even know how to measure the moment. Cora weighed her options, unsure at this point if she could even pull her foot from the mud. She waited too long. Joseph, now fifteen feet or more ahead of her, looked back and realized she wasn't following. Even through the rain, she could tell that his eyes didn't look kind anymore.

"I need you to come with me," he shouted through the rain. It wasn't a request.

He motioned for Cora to follow him, glancing first at the house and then at the road. She hobbled his way, her shoes getting suctioned in the mud, and followed him toward the shed's opening, careful to leave a few feet between them. Once inside, Joseph glanced at the house again before pulling the heavy wooden door closed. The movement shook the rafters, sending a few birds upward to find safety elsewhere and a confused field mouse out into the open.

Joseph took off his hat and shook the rain from its brim before tossing it onto a metal stool. He looked tired, but not only because of his age or the struggles of a long day. There was tired from *living*, and then there was tired from *life*. "I need you to come with me," he said again. "I need to show you something."

Cora did what she'd cursed every horror movie actor for doing. She followed a virtual stranger into the darkness of a shed because he had asked—or rather, told—her to do so. Even as she heard the crunch of gravel under her shoes, she berated her stupidity and told herself that she deserved whatever awaited her. The heart of the storm was now rolling overhead, bits of hail falling so heavily that a few made their way through the shed's roof, falling like marbles onto the floor.

Joseph approached an interior door inside the shed and held it open so Cora would enter first. Filled with fear, Cora smiled weakly at Joseph, in search of reassurance that everything was okay, but he didn't smile back. He simply stared at her, looked out a dirty window toward the house and then at the sky, waiting for her to enter.

Cora walked into the small room. It was cramped and smelled of mildew, its cement floor worn through in some places by time, to show dirt holes. A small lantern was lit on a workbench along the far wall, and a shop light hung from an overhead beam, casting a shallow glow across the floor.

Cora saw the things that you would expect to see in such a place: a wheelbarrow, an air compressor, and a lawn mower that she could only assume was the one he had been working on the first time she met him. The lantern illuminated a wall full of tools, some of which were hung on small metal hooks; others were piled on the bench or spilling out from a metal box used to store the odds and ends one would find in a farm's utility building.

"What did you want to show—" The sound of the door slamming shut cut her off. Cora spun around to face Joseph, growing more frightened when she found him no longer looking at her, but now doing something in the shadows. "Joseph, I'm sure Elliott is looking for me at this point. I was supposed to be home a while ago." Such a predictable lie was the best she could do. Cora started making her way to the door, but Joseph was too quick and blocked her exit.

"I need to show you something."

Joseph walked into the light of the lamp and Cora could now see that he was holding a metal box, this one much smaller than the one used for tool storage, but designed similarly with a latch and lock. Joseph pulled a set of keys from his pocket and opened it. Cora moved closer now that she saw the box itself was nothing to fear. At first, she couldn't see anything, but then realized that the contents were wrapped in a black cloth that Joseph was carefully removing. He moved the box closer to her, but its contents were still difficult to ascertain.

"I'm not sure what I'm looking at," Cora said. It was too dark in the shed to focus, something small and white protected in its black cloth blanket. Joseph was cradling the contents as if they could break. "What is that? Are those . . ." She paused, examining the small, creamy items more closely. She knew what she was seeing but was too afraid to say it. He didn't take his eyes off the contents, his breathing becoming more labored as the seconds ticked by.

"Are those *bones*?"

Joseph didn't answer, but simply nodded.

"I don't understand—what is this?" Cora asked. She took a protective step back.

Joseph motioned for her to come closer to the light and then handed her the box, which she reluctantly took in her hands. It was only then that she realized what was inside. "This is a *hand*. This is a *human hand*." She thrust the box toward him and moved back toward the door, her hand over her mouth in shock and disgust. "What the hell!" Cora said. "Why would you have this? What's going on?" Even as the words came out of her mouth, she knew. She had found herself in the middle of a decades-old mystery surrounding a missing woman and had now been presented with human remains.

Even as the panicked part of her brain struggled to make sense of it, the rational part knew that she had just held the skeletal remains of Clarity Shaw. She didn't move her hand from her mouth, afraid she would scream or vomit.

"The rings," Joseph said, so quietly that it was barely audible. "The rings were still on the fingers when I found them." She had now lost the poor man. His face glistened with tears at a memory so painful that he couldn't even form the words needed to tell the story. Yes, this man was tired, but even more so he was broken, and Cora realized that the fear she had felt following him in here was nothing compared to the fear, sadness, and desperation that was etched into every fine line and wrinkle on his face.

"I wanted to surprise her with a flower garden," he began. "I remembered there was a garden in the back corner of the yard when I started dating Beverly all those years ago. She always seemed to love that garden, to be protective of it, so I wanted to give her that when we moved in here after her parents went to a home. I didn't dig very deep before I found something." His voice trailed off now, the vision too painful to continue, so he changed course to maintain the strength to tell Cora what he needed to say. "The rings in the dirt are what caught my attention at first. And then the rest." He closed the box and returned it to the top shelf, a metal box of bones sitting next to an old can of kerosene, spark plugs, and a tangled string of Christmas lights. "The rings, of course, fell off, and I just tossed them into a jar in here. I didn't know. I couldn't have known the jar would be sold. I didn't know."

Cora's heart ached for Joseph as he sat down on the wooden stool, a man defeated by things he had learned in life that he didn't want to know.

Cora couldn't keep up with the facts taking shape. She had found rings in a jar, and she'd held bones in a box. There were affairs and secrets, broken hearts and jilted lovers. Cora was too busy wrangling these thoughts to fully process or hear the words that Joseph said next. She could see his lips move with words she couldn't make out, but just then the skies unleashed a storm full of rage, the heavens sobbing heavy tears for a life lost. At last—*clarity*.

When the thunder subsided and Cora looked at Joseph in confusion, he mustered the strength to repeat the words that he'd sworn he would never say.

"She didn't mean to do it."

Hickory Falls

June 6, 1960

The hat had become a joke in her family, its wide floppy brim hanging so low over Clarity's face that she could barely see. She claimed that was fine because she only needed to look down when gardening, and the cucumbers didn't much care about her fashion choices.

She clutched the hat in one hand and her bucket full of tools with the other, the heat from the early afternoon sun already making her regret her decision to work inside that morning and put off weeding until the afternoon. It was a novice gardener's mistake, one that she'd have to learn the hard way as her bare feet recoiled from the heat of the gravel path that connected the small garden to the shed.

Clarity dropped the bucket of tools at the edge of the garden and plopped the hat on her head, pulling it tightly down to prevent it from flying off if there was any wind. She stretched her back and looked up at the top of the tree close by, its still leaves suggesting that any hope for a breeze was in vain. She needed to finish with the vegetables quickly so she could move on to her favorite part of the garden—the flowers. She would pick daisies and surprise Hazel with a vase full of them in her room, but she didn't have much time. School would be out in a few hours, and she had so much to do before then.

Clarity knelt down by the first row of beans and started pulling weeds out by the roots and tossing them over her shoulder into a pile. Lewis hated that she did that because she rarely picked them up, brown drying piles littering the backyard.

Clarity repositioned the hat so it protected her neck, the sun's rays already heavy on her shoulders. She loved having a garden, for the thrill of nurturing life and watching it grow, but she hated the work involved. And she didn't even like green beans.

*   *   *

It was the third time in a month that Beverly had ditched school. It wasn't hard to fake her mother's signature on an excuse note; the office didn't pay much attention to a swirly signature under a few sentences about a sore throat and "much-needed rest." She was actually having fun thinking of new excuses, but hoped she hadn't gone too far this time by calling in and pretending to be a distraught Evelyn worried about new little spots that had developed on Beverly's torso. There wasn't a school around that was going to question a loving mother keeping her child home because she was showing signs of the dreaded childhood disease, but she hoped they wouldn't check in with the school nurse, who would be quick to point out that Beverly Shaw had already had the chicken pox.

She didn't have her own car, but it wasn't hard to find a way to the farmhouse from town. She hitched a ride to the Shephard farm in the back of Arnold Kremer's truck and then jumped out and walked the rest of the way. If they realized that a sixteen-year-old should be in school on Monday, they didn't mention it; farmers around here were not much for asking questions that didn't involve their crops or the weather forecast.

Beverly had anticipated a sleepless night given the task she'd set herself that lay ahead, but she had actually fallen asleep quite quickly, waking to the smell of bacon and her mother's warning that another tardy wouldn't be acceptable and Beverly needed to get moving.

Beverly hadn't given any of this much thought, but she knew that her journey to the house with the intent of harming her stepmother would qualify as premeditation. She had a pseudo plan, but even if it didn't work out, she was just a kid. It wasn't like they were going to lock her away for the rest of her life. Perhaps someday she would even tell her dad what she had done was out of love for him and her mom. But that would have to be much later, of course, once he realized on his own that this was all a blessing in disguise. Little Hazel would be fine. She would be taken care of, and it was better for this to happen now than when she was older.

These were the thoughts that raced through Beverly's mind as she convinced herself that she wasn't a bad person. She was only a teenager desperate to have her family back. Nobody could really blame her; in fact, they would pity her if this were ever discovered. *"That poor girl,"* they would say. *"She doesn't have any evil in her. No, of course not. It's love. She simply had too much love."*

Beverly felt her heart rate quicken as she made her way up the driveway, convinced that she could hear each pulsating beat. Surely, others didn't feel this much intensity. Every nerve inside her was about to combust; the human body was not equipped to handle this much emotion. Her feet felt both light and heavy as she walked, carrying her as if unguided from free will. *"Beverly was special."* That's what everyone would say.

She tried not to make much noise when she walked around the front of the house and toward the backyard. Careful to avoid the gravel, she walked softly along the grass, ducking behind a corner when the dog—a lovable mutt equal parts friendly and obstinate—spotted her and darted from his place next to Clarity to say hello. Luckily, Clarity was focused on her work and didn't seem to notice, probably assuming that Huck had caught sight of a bird or some object that he would try to sneak inside and eventually consume. Beverly knew he wasn't going to settle down without a little attention, so she scratched behind his ears and told him repeatedly that he was a good dog before shooing him away.

Beverly watched Clarity toss the weeds over her shoulder and felt her cheeks begin to burn. This woman in the ridiculous hat had hurt her family in unimaginable ways. Beverly had watched her mother dissolve into a shell of who she had once been, any confidence that she'd had now replaced with a bitterness and devotion to the fake appearance that everything was okay. She had fallen asleep to the sound of her mother crying after a few glasses of wine, and then woken up to the smell of coffee and her mother complaining about her father to a friend on the phone.

This woman in the ridiculous hat had robbed her of a happy life and was now on another assault, this one directed at her father because of some fling she was having with the town doctor. Beverly had heard the rumors; she had listened to her mother relay the details of their open affair to her friends and convey her hope that when Clarity eventually left him, Lewis would experience some of the pain that she had gone through. And then there was the baby. Hazel was enough; Beverly couldn't allow another baby to enter this family, further deepening the divide between her parents. No, this woman baking in the afternoon sun was not going to hurt another person that Beverly loved. Beverly would not allow it.

* * *

The sweat stung her eyes and ran like rivers along her skin. Still on her knees, Clarity leaned back to stretch and stare up at the sky, not a single cloud in sight. The garden looked so much better, and she promised herself that she would come back in the early evening to gather the piles of weeds and toss them over the fence. She encouraged Lewis to consider the organic arrangement to be nature's art, but he wasn't having any of it, an exasperated sigh heard every time he had to mow the yard and deal with the tiny piles. Clarity stood up and made her way over to the end of the garden, where her flowers grew, and began selecting the most perfect ones for Hazel's room. One was particularly vibrant and fully in bloom. Clarity leaned over to smell the flower before plucking it. She was too busy appreciating the perfection around her to ever see the unthinkable coming.

* * *

Beverly crossed the path and ran into the shed, grabbing the hoe from where it was standing at attention in the corner. She wiped off the blade's edge with her shirt sleeve, removing the caked-on dirt and rubbing the hoe's blade until the sharp metal shone. She wasn't going to turn back now. It was too late. She had considered her options, and this was the only one that gave her family a chance to heal *together*. Beverly had told herself that she was actually doing everybody involved a favor. With Clarity out of the picture, her father would realize his mistake and come back to them. And, Hazel, as much as she adored her mom, would be fine. She was young enough that the memory of all of this would fade. She would be raised as one of them, with a new and better mother. Beverly would make sure there was nothing horrific for the little girl to see. There would be no scene, no trauma. There would be nothing except a new beginning for everyone. It was the only way. This was for the best. Everyone would see it eventually.

* * *

In the end, life's highlights spin like a colorful reel at warp speed before your eyes. If there was comfort to be found, it was that Clarity was never aware of what was happening.

In a two-second span, there had been a flower and then a flash, the feeling of numbness and then the memories of her wedding by the lake and Hazel's delivery. There were images of picnics and nights by the fire, cups of tea, and a glow that comes with feeling safe and protected.

As the numbness grew, Clarity felt herself float—hover—as if she were in a magic show, with her limbs suspended by an invisible force carrying her toward the clouds. In those last few minutes of her life, Clarity was enveloped in a warmth and beauty that was too strong for any fear to take hold. She succumbed, feeling nothing but love and peace, and allowed herself to float, higher and higher, until she disappeared.

* * *

On that day, in the corner of the garden, behind the beans, tomato plants, and rows of daisies, was planted the seed of a secret. Like so many secrets in Hickory Falls, it had stayed hidden within layers of speculation and innuendo, kept safe by the failing memories that passing years brought. Sometimes, however, a search for the truth is stronger than the binds holding a secret together, and the dirt that once served as its protector falls into the hands of those who have the courage to dig.

Chapter
Twenty-Four

～

There's never any cause for celebration when it comes to murder. Even when questions are answered about the who, how, and why, there is still someone gone and other lives destroyed in the process.

Ruth took the news the hardest. Not only was she the closest to Beverly, but she now had to come to terms with the fact that had Clarity not died, her parents wouldn't have reconciled, and she never would have been born. She was left to grieve a sister and a life she thought she'd known while being both sickened at Beverly's actions and guilt-ridden that her own life was at the cost of someone else's. How do you process the unthinkable?

Cora scanned the crowd that had formed outside the small police precinct and spotted Ruth across the street, in the shadow of a tailor shop's awning. Her colorful clothes and vibrant energy had been replaced by black sunglasses and a dark brown cardigan that she pulled tightly around herself to protect against the wind. Seeing her so broken made Cora wonder something for the hundredth time since Beverly's arrest: Was it worth it? Is it true that some secrets should stay hidden, especially if they only serve to hurt those left behind?

A car horn was heard in the distance, a driver gesturing with his hands for pedestrians to move out of the street to avoid being hit. Sensational murders like this didn't happen in Hickory Falls, so the crowd was now desperate for a glimpse of their own killer, a woman whom they'd sat next to in church and worked alongside in fundraising bake sales. Cora could imagine the conversations happening in living rooms across town these last few days when news had broken that one of their own had murdered Clarity Shaw in cold blood and buried her in Beverly's own backyard. Like the weather she had grown to distrust, Cora wondered how quickly the town's sentiment had changed toward the victim in this case or if there were some who would still be reluctant to admit they had been wrong in feeling that Clarity Shaw must have brought this upon herself by her life choices. Cora wondered but was glad she wouldn't ever know. She was learning the hard way that some questions really should stay unanswered.

The two coffees she was holding were getting cold, and Elliott was waiting for her at the florist. They had decided to make a few changes for the wedding and keep things as simple as possible. Cora jogged across the street, nodding to a car in appreciation for its stopping for her as she turned her focus away from the crowd and toward a side street. The static of the crowd's voices softened as she walked farther away, and she was thankful for the peace of a quiet street. She took a sip of coffee and let her thoughts linger on her options for a wildflower bouquet. As she made her way across a drive, she was startled by another car crossing her path, one that had no intention of slowing down. It pulled out of the underground parking lot, and Cora came face-to-face with the person in the back seat of the police cruiser.

Beverly sat very straight, her hands apparently cuffed behind her, and looked shocked when she spotted Cora. She didn't look angry or upset; if she showed any emotion at all, it was one of resignation or perhaps shock. The encounter was seconds in length, but time seemed to stop for Cora as the women locked eyes. Maybe Joseph would have turned Beverly in eventually on his own . . . maybe not. Cora would never know for sure what role she'd played in all of this. What she *had* learned, however, was to never judge someone too harshly based on reputation and never, ever to underestimate what someone is capable of.

The car turned left to avoid the crowd of spectators, Beverly's eyes fixed on Cora until her neck could no longer twist that far, and she lost sight of her, traveling toward her long-awaited judgment.

* * *

Cora found a bit of shade under a big oak tree and pulled one of the lawn chairs over. She sat with her glass of punch and watched the lawn fill with people of all ages, who had come to help Lewis celebrate his one-hundredth birthday. He sat under a small tent to stay out of the sun, birthday balloons dancing behind him in a tangle of blue and green; three giant gold foil balloons with the numbers one, zero, and zero rose proudly above them all.

Lewis sat in his wheelchair as adults knelt to talk to him, and children darted between a table of cookies and another that held a big bowl of red punch. Hazel stood to her father's left, a hand never leaving his shoulder; Ruth stood to his right in the same position. Beverly wasn't there.

There was no reason for Lewis to know what had happened these last few days. Cora had stayed with Joseph while he made the call to the police, reassuring him that he was doing the right thing while they both anxiously watched for the front door of the farmhouse to swing open and Beverly to emerge. Cora had comforted him through his tears, patting his arm while he placed calls to their adult children with an urgent request that they get in their cars and come. He would have to explain when they got there.

It had all been a bit of a blur. Cora had stood like a statue off to one side when the police arrived, the yellow crime scene tape turning a sordid story into reality. Cora had stayed with Joseph through it all, even when his children arrived and were too distraught to help him themselves.

She had stayed with him when he'd talked to the police and told them everything he knew, and when he reached the realization that his wife—even at the age of sixteen—had very much known what she was doing. Even if the adolescent misfirings of her brain had fooled her into believing it was justified, teenage Beverly had understood what happens when you hit someone over the head with the sharp end of a garden hoe.

Joseph had developed his suspicions over the years but had buried them deep inside. An extra glass of wine or two would sometimes get Beverly talking about past sins, but never with regret, always with the self-righteous indignation that sinners use to justify their actions. And she had never confirmed his suspicions, which he had put aside as long as he could, until the earth decided enough had been buried and extended a skeletal hand for help.

No, Lewis didn't need to know any of this.

Cora waved to Juliet and Mimi when she saw them walk through the trellised entrance of the nursing home and into its backyard. She stood and greeted each of them with a hug.

Mimi looked out of place anywhere other than in the art gallery. "How are you, dear?" she asked. "Our little Nancy Drew of Hickory Falls." She smiled and began to pull out her cigarettes, only to be scolded quietly by Juliet for even thinking about smoking in a nursing-home setting. "What do they all care?" Mimi asked. "These people are in their most golden of golden years. I doubt secondhand smoke is a concern." Regardless, she put the pack back in her bag and pulled out a pair of huge black sunglasses. "It's bright."

Juliet looked around the yard and shook her head in disbelief. "The poor guy," she said. "All he wants to do is celebrate a century on earth, and he's now embroiled in the biggest crime that Hickory Falls has ever known."

"He doesn't know anything," Cora said. "And they have no intention of telling him. As far as he knows, Beverly feels under the weather and couldn't make it today. They'll deal with everything tomorrow."

"That's for the best," Mimi said. "He's been through enough." Cora sensed a hint of sympathy in her words and was touched to see her tough exterior soften, even temporarily. "So, are they serving alcohol?"

"No, just a bright red punch," Cora said, nodding toward a table on the far end of the lawn. "Please don't spike it. There are children here."

"Let's go wish Lewis a happy birthday." Juliet pulled on Mimi's sleeve to direct her toward the tent. "Don't go anywhere," she called to Cora. "We'll be back."

Cora sat back down and returned her gaze to Hazel and Ruth, both of whom were struggling to keep up happy appearances. How horrible for them to realize what their sister had been capable of.

"Hey there."

Cora hadn't even noticed Elliott arrive. He was dragging a chair to sit closer to her in the shade, a sprinkle cookie in one hand. "How are things going here?" he asked. "Definitely doesn't feel like a typical birthday party. Poor Lewis. I hope he never finds out what his daughter did."

Cora looked at Elliott and reached for his hand. She had come so close to sharing terrible allegations about his grandfather. When she had reached Beverly's house that day, she had decided to come clean with him and share everything she had found out about Jack Manchester, including the rumors about his involvement in Clarity's disappearance. The universe had stepped in instead, and she was forever grateful. Elliott's grandfather was many things, but a murderer wasn't one of them. Now in his nineties, he would come to their wedding, and she would be pleasant, accepting his congratulations and welcome to their family.

An entire family cannot be judged by the acts of its members, and Elliott was proof that the good ran deep in his bloodline. She held his hand and realized that she sat in the presence of two men, neither of whom needed to know more than what was necessary, to protect them.

"Everything okay?" Elliott asked. "You look lost in thought."

Cora smiled and squeezed his hand a bit tighter. "Small towns are filled with secrets," she said. "And some should just stay hidden."

Epilogue

In the end, the wedding included only Cora and Elliott. True, there were other people physically present, but they were like the blurred background of a photograph, only the most important subjects coming crisply into view.

Cora stood with Elliott's hand in hers as they exchanged vows, just the two of them on the rugged walkway in the arboretum. They made their promises to each other in front of God, their friends, family members, and a gathering of squirrels who had stopped harvesting nuts long enough to watch from the sidelines.

Cora's grandmother had almost missed her plane from California but had arrived with a few minutes to spare, and readied herself from the front row. She had connected with Hazel at some point, the two women sitting next to each other and commenting on the day's events like old friends whom fate had brought together. Hazel looked stunning in the blue dress that was now decades old, its fibers imbued with the vows of happiness from another wedding day so long ago. The dress was as beautiful now as it had been then. Hazel folded her hands on her lap, feeling the contentment of a life that had traveled so many winding roads, eventually coming full circle in a green park that was preparing to close down for the winter ahead.

Cora's dress was new. It was a simple satin ivory sheath. Cora wore it effortlessly.

The handkerchief tucked away in her purse was old. Her grandmother had hurriedly handed it to her before the ceremony. Stitched along the edge of the dainty white fabric was a design of orange and brown leaves, and it had been carried by both her grandmother and mom on their wedding days.

Cora's toenails were blue. She had painted them the shade of sapphire the night before, taking turns propping each foot up on her coffee table to polish her nails in a color that only she would know about—and eventually, Elliott when she later slipped off her heels and bid adieu to the formality of the day.

Tucked into Cora's bouquet was something borrowed, hanging securely on a satin ribbon tied around the flowers. She held onto Elliott with one hand, and in the other she grasped a bouquet of sunflowers guarded, protected, and made all the more beautiful by the presence of two rings.

One thing had always puzzled her: the engraving of *Y & M* along the inside of the band. Concerned about causing Lewis more distress, she had waited a while before asking Hazel about the mysterious letters etched inside. Hazel had asked Lewis about it during their next visit, and his answer carried a weight, meaning, and significance that only true love brings.

Y & M
You & Me
Always

Acknowledgments

It all started with a ring. Well, two actually, and my mom, who brought them to me with her hand extended one day, saying, "Look what I found." If it weren't for her natural curiosity and excitement over a mysterious find, this story never would have happened, so thank you to my mom, my biggest cheerleader. And thanks too to my dad, forever my rock and a perfect combination of wanderlust soul and practicality, pushing me every time to explore life through inquisitive eyes and challenge myself to live a life with no regrets. As always, thank you to my family—Alan, Max, and Finn—a houseful of energy, love, and support. You are my heart, my passion, my everything, and you make life brighter in ways you will never know. Thank you to my agent, Stephanie, for agreeing to meet for coffee all those years ago and believing in me ever since. You are a dream maker. A huge thank you to the talented team at Crooked Lane who took a trip to Hickory Falls and wanted to introduce the sleepy little town to the world. Finally, a girl is only as strong as her friends, so thank you to the group of amazing women who cheer me on, pull me up, and make sure that I never stop believing. And yes, you will all have roles in the coffee shop scene if this is ever turned into a movie.